Emmy & Oliver

ROBIN BENWAY

Emmy
&
Oliver

SIMON & SCHUSTER

First published in Great Britain by Simon & Schuster UK Ltd, 2015
A CBS COMPANY

Originally published in the USA in 2015 by HarperTeen,
an imprint of HarperCollins Publishers

Text copyright © Robin Benway 2015

1 3 5 7 9 10 8 6 4 2

Simon & Schuster UK Ltd
1st Floor
Gray's Inn Road
London WC1X 8HB

www.simonandschuster.co.uk

Simon & Schuster Australia, Sydney
Simon & Schuster India, New Delhi

A CIP catalogue record for this book
is available from the British Library

PB ISBN: 978-1-47114-413-4
eBook ISBN: 978-1-47114-414-1

Printed and bound by CPI Group (UK) Ltd, Croydon, CR0 4YY

Simon & Schuster UK Ltd are committed to sourcing paper
that is made from wood grown in sustainable forests and supports the Forest
Stewardship Council, the leading international forest certification organisation.
Our books displaying the FSC logo are printed on FSC certified paper.

For whatever we lose(like a you or a me)
it's always ourselves we find in the sea

—E. E. Cummings, "maggie and milly and molly and may"

The Note

The last time Emmy sees Oliver is on their forty-third day of second grade.

Oliver is her next-door neighbor and her friend. They were born in the same hospital on the same day: July 7—7/7. She thinks she's pretty lucky to have a friend who lives next door and shares a birthday with her. She can just visit him any old time she wants, but not all the time because sometimes Oliver goes to his dad's house on the weekends. They do fun things, Oliver says, pizza and ice cream and things like that. Sometimes movies. Emmy thinks that maybe having divorced parents isn't so bad, not if it means you get extra ice cream, but then at night, when it's dark in her room and she hears weird noises in the closet that may or may not be monsters, she's glad her mom and dad are still together in their bedroom down the hall.

On that forty-third afternoon of second grade, her friend Caroline passes Oliver a note when their teacher's back is turned. Emmy watches as the paper slips past her and onto the desk of their friend Drew, who gives Caro a sneaky smile and then passes the note to Oliver. Emmy looks over at Caroline, who's grinning wildly. They are seven years old and this is the first of many, many notes that Caro will pass in class, but this is the first and most special note Caro will ever give to someone.

Oliver is in front of Emmy now, his head down while he carefully does the addition problems in his math workbook. She can see the tag sticking up out of the back of his shirt, and what she doesn't know now is that she'll remember that tag for years, that she will dream about going up to him and smoothing the tag back into his shirt before she wakes up, her hand poised in midair, a gossamer dream melting between her fingers.

Instead, Emmy just glares at Caro and watches as Oliver unfolds the note and reads it. They could get in so much trouble for passing notes! Emmy glares at Caro, who just frowns and sticks her tongue out at Emmy, but Emmy knows she's not really mad. If Caro's really mad, she ignores you. That's way worse.

Oliver writes something down on the note and passes it back to Caro while their teacher is explaining how to borrow from the tens, and Emmy feels her skin start to prickle, like the time she got sunburned at the beach. Caro just grins at her, and Emmy puts her head back down and carries the one.

After school, Caro runs up to Emmy and hands her the note. "Look!" she cries. The paper's been folded so many times that it feels as soft as cotton, and Emmy opens it up. It says, DO YOU LIKE EMMY, YES NO??? And the word yes has been circled three times.

Emmy holds the paper and looks around for Oliver, but their moms and dads are waiting to pick them up; Oliver is already running toward his dad. His dad drives a sports car now. It's sooo cool. That's what Oliver says.

"Oliver!" Emmy yells. "I have to ask you something!"

He's already ahead of her, though, running toward the cool sports car and his dad.

"Oliver!" she cries. "Oliver, wait!"

But it's too late. Oliver is already in his dad's car.

And he's gone.

CHAPTER ONE

Oliver disappeared after school on a Friday afternoon, way back when we were in second grade, and small things seemed really important and important things seemed too small. That afternoon, it wasn't weird to see him get in his dad's car, a red convertible whose screeching tires rang out in my mind for years afterward.

Oliver and I had been best friends since the day we were born up until the day his dad picked him up from school and never brought him home. We even lived next door, our bedroom windows reflecting each other.

His window's been empty for ten years, but sometimes I can still see into his room and it's exactly how it was when he disappeared. Oliver's mom, Maureen, she never moved anything. In the past ten years, she remarried and even had two little girls, but Oliver's bedroom never changed. It's become a makeshift shrine, dusty and childish, but I get it. If you clean it out, it means he might never come back.

Sometimes I think that all superstitions—crossing your fingers, not stepping on cracks, shrines like the one in Oliver's room—come from wanting something too much.

Oliver's dad was pretty smart about the way he took him. It was a three-day weekend and he was supposed to bring Oliver to school on Tuesday morning. By ten a.m., they hadn't shown up. By eleven, Oliver's mother was in the school office. By three o'clock that afternoon, there were news cameras scattered across the school parking lot and on Oliver's lawn at home. They bore down on us like electronic versions of Cyclops, wanting to know how we were holding up, what we children were doing now that our friend was missing.

Caro cried and my mom made us sit at the table and eat a snack—Double Stuf Oreos. That's how I knew it was really bad.

We all thought Oliver and his dad would come back that night. And then the next day. And then surely by that weekend. But they never did. Oliver and his dad were gone, drifted into nothingness, like clouds in the sky and even more difficult to chase.

They could be *anywhere* and it was that thought that made the world seem so large, so vast. How could people just disappear? Oliver's mom, in her more lucid moments when she wasn't crying or taking tiny white pills that just made her look sad, said that she would go to the ends of the earth to find him, but it seemed like Oliver had already reached the end of the world and had fallen off into the abyss. At seven years old, that was the only explanation that made sense to me. The world was round and spun too fast and Oliver was gone, spinning away from us forever.

Before Oliver was kidnapped, my dad used to say, "Absence makes the heart grow fonder!" and give me smacking kisses on both cheeks when I ran to greet him after work. After, he stopped saying it (even though his hugs were tighter than ever before) and I realized that it wasn't true. It wasn't true at all. Oliver's absence split us wide open, dividing our neighborhood along a fault line strong enough to cause an earthquake.

An earthquake would have been better. At least during an earthquake, you understand why you're shaking.

The neighbors formed search parties, holding hands as they walked through wooded areas behind the school. They took up collections, bought officers cups of coffee, and told Caro and Drew and me to go play. Even our playtime had been altered. We didn't play house anymore. We played "Kidnapping."

"Okay, I'll be Oliver's mom and you be Oliver and, Drew, you be Oliver's dad," Caro would instruct us, but we weren't sure what to do after Drew dragged me away. Caro would pretend to cry and say, "My baby!" which was what Maureen had been screaming that first day before the tranquilizers kicked in, but Drew and I just stood there, holding hands. We didn't know how to end the game. No one had shown us how and, anyway, my mom told us to stop playing that, that we would upset Oliver's mom. "But she's always upset," I said, and neither of my parents said anything after that.

Sometimes I think that if we had been older, it would have been easier. A lot of conversations stopped when I came near and I learned how to creep down the stairs so I could hear the grown-ups talking. I discovered that if I sat on the ninth step I could see past the kitchen and into the living room, where Maureen spent nights sobbing into her hands, my mom sitting next to her and holding her, rocking her the way she rocked me whenever I woke up dreaming about Oliver, dreaming about the tag on the back of his shirt, my pajamas damp with nightmare sweat. There were always wineglasses on the table, lined with dark resin that looked more like blood than Cabernet. And Maureen's crying made my skin feel weird, like someone had turned it inside out. I couldn't always hear what they were saying, but it didn't matter. I already knew. Maureen was sad because she wanted to hold Oliver the way my mom was holding her.

"I can never leave," Maureen wept one night as I sat on the stairs, holding my breath in case anyone saw me. "I can never leave here, you know? What would we do if Oliver came back and no one was . . . ? Oh God, oh God."

"I know," my mother kept saying to her. "We'll stay with you. We won't leave, either."

It was a promise that she kept, too. We didn't leave. We stayed in the same house next door. Other neighbors left and new ones moved in, and all of them seemed to know about Oliver. He had become a local celebrity in absentia, famous for not being found, a ghost.

As time went on, it became hard to imagine what he looked like, even as the police age-progressed his second-grade school photo. We all watched an artist's rendering of Oliver grow up over the years. His nose got bigger, his eyes wider, his forehead higher. His smile wasn't as pronounced and his baby teeth morphed into adult ones. His eyes never changed, though. That was the strange part. The hopeful part.

We stayed and looked and waited for him to come back, as if our love was a beacon that he could use to light his way home, to crawl up the sides of the earth and back through his front door, his tag still sticking up in the back.

After a while, though, after years passed and pictures changed and false tips fell through, it started to feel like the beacon wasn't for him anymore. It was for those of us left behind, something to cling to when you realized that scary things could happen, that villains didn't only exist in books, that Oliver might never come home.

Until one day, he did.

CHAPTER TWO

I remember it was a Thursday because I had gone surfing that afternoon. I always go out on Thursdays because both my parents work late those days, which makes it easier to sneak a surfboard in and out of my car. It had been soft that afternoon, the sky hazy and the waves no bigger than three feet or so, and I was rinsing off in the shower at the edge of the sand when I heard someone screaming my name. "Emmy! Emmy! Where is she? Is she here?!" I looked up from the end of the path and saw my best friend, Caroline, tearing toward me.

Her hair was tangled, as tangled as mine after dousing it in salt water and sea air for a few hours, and she was dashing barefoot toward me, her shoes dangling from her hand. The whole beach stopped and watched as she hurtled down the hill, and I heard one surfer say to his friend, "Dude, she's *fast*."

I stepped away from the water, my heart racing. Was it my

parents? An accident? Where was our friend Drew? Oh God, it was Drew. Something had happened to Drew! "Em," she said, and there was something scary in her eyes, wild and hopeful and terrified all at the same time.

I had never seen her look like that before and I probably never will again.

"Emmy," she said. "They found Oliver."

It's funny. You think about hearing certain phrases and you plan how you'll react to them. *They found Oliver.* And yet when you do finally hear the three words you've been too frightened to even think about, for fear of jinxing them, for fear that you might never actually hear them, it's like they aren't real at all.

"Emmy!" Caroline grabbed me by the shoulders and bent down so she could look me in the eyes, her grip so hard I could feel her fingertips through my wet suit. "*They found Oliver.* He's okay."

"Caroline," I said slowly. "You're hurting me."

"Oh, sorry! Sorry!" She let go of my shoulders but stayed close. "Are you in shock? Are you okay? Do you need something with electrolytes?"

I shook my head. "They found him? How——?"

Caroline grinned. "Your mom just called me. You weren't answering your phone so she sent me to find you." My mom knew what she was doing. Caroline is definitely the sort of person that you want to deliver news. Good or bad, she will rip that Band-Aid clean off.

"He's in New York," she continued. "He's coming home."

My knees were shaking. Maybe I needed something with electrolytes after all. "Who's in New York?"

"Oliver, Emmy! God, focus!"

"Can I—? Where's my phone? I need my phone!"

Caro was still jumping up and down as I ran up to my towel, digging around underneath it for my bag and finding my phone at the bottom. Seven missed calls and three texts from my mom: CALL HOME NOW, they all said.

"Did you tell my mom where I was?" I asked Caro, shoving my phone back into my bag and trying to get my wet suit off as fast as possible without taking my bathing suit along with it.

"No, of course not," she said, then added "Here," and offered me her shoulder for balance as I peeled off the lower half of the suit. "I said I thought you might be at the library and that's why your phone was off."

"Good." My parents would never approve of me surfing, which is why they could never know. I love them, but if they had their way, they would have constructed a suit for me made entirely of Bubble Wrap and cotton balls. I didn't want to be the kind of kid that snuck around and did things behind her parents' back, but I loved surfing too much to stop. So I just lied to them instead, which, yeah. Not exactly the best solution to the problem, but it was all I had.

"They might wonder why your hair's wet, though," Caro said, interrupting my thoughts.

"We'll think up a reason in the car," I said, finally yanking a dress over my bathing suit. Caroline grabbed my towel and my hand and we took off up the hill toward the car. It sounded like there were jets flying overhead, but when I looked up and saw nothing but a few low clouds, I realized that the sound was just the blood rushing in my head, pulsing to keep me upright and alive.

"They *found* him," Caro whispered, and when she squeezed my hand, I squeezed back harder and came down from the clouds once again.

I quickly dumped my surfboard into the back of Drew's van before throwing myself in the backseat. Drew was waiting behind the steering wheel, frantically texting someone. His cheeks were flushed and he was wearing his soccer uniform. Drew used to be my best surfing buddy until soccer began taking up more of his time. Now he's on track to get a full scholarship to Berkeley, just like his older brother, Kane.

"Oh my God," he said without looking up. "Can you even believe it?"

"Not really," I said. "Can you?"

"Nope," he said, his thumbs flying over the mini keyboard. "How are you going to explain your hair to your mom?"

"Think something up for me," I said, realizing too late that my feet were covered in sand and silt and gravel. Now all that mess was smeared over Drew's floor mats.

Drew loves his van. It's actually not a van, but a restored 1971 tomato-red VW camper bus. People actually take pictures with it, it's so beautiful, and it has lots of room for surfboards in the back. The van used to be his brother's, but after Kane went to college three years ago, he gifted it to Drew, like he knew that Drew was going to need it as a means of escape.

"Oh no!" I said once I saw the sand. "I'm sorry, Drew, I should've—"

"Who cares?" Caro screeched. "It's sand, not acid. Just drive, okay?"

"Wait," I said. "*My* car. My backpack's in there, my homework. I have a quiz tomorrow!"

"Are you kidding me?" Drew backed the car up and the force of his acceleration smashed me into the seat. "Buckle up," he said. "No one's doing any homework tonight." When we were finally cruising down the road, he glanced at me in the rearview mirror. "Em, seriously, are you sure you're not going into shock? You look pale."

"I already offered her electrolytes," Caroline said.

"I'm fine," I told them. Only it came out sort of high and squeaky and any moron with average vision could probably tell that I was not fine.

Caro reached over the backseat and grabbed my seat belt. "Here," she said. "Drew's driving. It's a requirement." She snapped it into place and then squeezed my shoulders. "Is this really happening?"

Caro and I have known Drew since kindergarten. Actually,

half our school has known one another since kindergarten. It's one of those Southern California suburbs where few people move away from their pink stucco houses.

Here's something you must know about Drew before becoming his friend: he drives as if he's being chased by a carful of depraved, evil clowns. I took driver's ed with him in sophomore year, so I can tell you that he's always been like this. (I can also tell you that our driver's ed instructor had to renew his Xanax prescription after Drew's first on-the-road lesson.)

But when Drew's upset or nervous or excited, that's when he really lets it fly, and the day Oliver was found was probably the craziest driving I've ever seen from him. Caro kept one hand on her seat belt as he flew through a yellow light and when he hit a pothole, she yelped. "Drew, this van isn't exactly built to break the sound barrier!"

"Oh, relax, Caroline," he said, and I knew he was using her full name just to annoy her. No one ever calls her Caroline. It's just too many syllables.

"I'd like to *see* Oliver before suffering from debilitating whiplash," I told him, trying to loosen my iron grip on my seat belt.

"So how real do we think this is?" Drew asked.

He had a point. This wasn't the first time that Oliver had been "found." The sightings had been intense at first, hundreds of calls pouring in to the hotline saying that they had seen a sandy-haired, freckle-faced seven-year-old in Omaha, Atlanta, Los Angeles, even Puerto Rico. The calls died down over the years, but every year or so, there was a ray of hope. A short-lived ray, but hope nonetheless, enough to live on for another year.

"Maybe real?" I said. "I don't know, I . . ." I trailed off, not really sure what to say.

Caro took over.

"Emmy's mom called me because Em wasn't answering her phone," she said. "Something about a fingerprint. He was in a police station for a school field trip? I'm not sure. Anyway, it matched the one in his file and they went to arrest Oliver's dad at home. He wasn't there, but Oliver was."

"New York?" Drew asked. "Really?"

"New York *City*," Caro emphasized. "But here's the part that's bonkers: they still haven't found his dad. Apparently, he's on the lam." Caro always liked the police lingo. I don't think she's ever missed an episode of *Law & Order: SVU*.

"Wow," Drew murmured. "New York." I didn't have to look at Drew's face to know what he was thinking. He would pretty much like to be anywhere else but our town. New York must've sounded like a dream.

We live in a tolerant community, so long as there's nothing to tolerate. So when Drew came out and announced he was gay last year, it caused a bit of what he called the "muffled kerfuffle." Caro and I already knew, of course, but Drew's parents were a little . . . different. They were accepting at first, lots of "we love you just the way you ares" and all that, but to hear Drew tell it, the mood was heavier at his house. The silences longer, the words shorter. "They look at me sometimes," he said one night when we were sleeping over at Caro's, his voice quiet in the dark. "And I can't tell if they like what they see."

I could understand why Drew sounded wistful about New York.

I glanced out the window as Drew turned right, all of us quiet for a moment. In our second-grade class picture, we were lined up by height in the middle row: Caro on the end, then Drew, then Oliver, then me. And then Oliver went away and there were just three of us, with no idea of how to make sense of our loss. And to make it worse, every adult was super nice in the months after Oliver disappeared: *"Ran your bike into my car? It's just a tiny scratch." "Threw a ball through my window? Be more careful next time."* It was unsettling. When the adults are full of indulgence, you know things are really bad.

Drew swung a left and pulled onto our street. His normal routine is to careen until the last possible second and then spin a U-turn in our cul-de-sac before zooming into my driveway. You can imagine how exciting that is in a top-heavy VW bus. The first time my mom saw Drew zipping toward us, she said, "He *does* know that the street dead-ends, right?"

It was a fair question.

I have to admit, though, Drew knows what he's doing, and ten seconds later, he was pulling the parking brake as we eyed a caravan of news trucks and cameras. "Hello, hello, old friends,"

Drew drawled when we saw them. "How long has it been?"

"Two years," I replied, glaring out my window. After Oliver didn't show up to school that Tuesday ten years ago, the news cameras became a noisy cavalry for a few months. At first, everyone thought it was great. They were bringing attention to the case! Surely, someone would see Oliver and call the police and he'd come home in time for Drew's eighth birthday party. Caro and Drew and I used to draw pictures of Oliver and try to get the newscasters to film them, but mostly they just stood in front of Oliver's home and said things like *This tragic disappearance has left a community shaken* . . . [dramatic pause] . . . *to its core."*

The ironic thing is that even though Oliver's disappearance was a huge deal in our town, it didn't really get that much attention outside of the city. He was a young kid taken by a non-abusive parent who had no citizenship in a foreign country. It was terrible, yes, but when it came to criminal investigations, finding Oliver wasn't at the top of most people's lists. That's when I first learned about true frustration, that wrenching ache when the thing that matters most to you barely makes a ripple in other people's lives.

One afternoon, after the story had faded slightly in the local headlines, the reporters decided to talk to *me*. My parents were inside and didn't know that I had snuck out to see if Oliver was secretly in his backyard, and the cameras descended on me. Even now, when I think about it, it makes me want to throw up.

"How does it feel to know that your friend Oliver might never come home?"

"What can you tell us about Oliver, sweetheart? Do you think he wanted to be with his dad more than his mom?"

"Did Oliver say anything to you? Did you know that his father was going to take him?"

I'm not sure when I started to cry, but when my dad came storming out of the house, I was in full-blown hysterics. He grabbed me up and told all the newscasters to go fuck themselves (which definitely did not make it into the seven o'clock broadcast), then carried me back inside. Soon after, he taught Caro and Drew and me some Beatles songs and told us that whenever we saw people with cameras, we should just sing those songs.

At the time, I thought it was just fun to sing really loud, but then I realized what an evil genius my dad is. To broadcast Beatles lyrics, you have to have the rights to the songs, which costs somewhere around a billion dollars. So whenever we popped up singing about yellow submarines or Lucy in the sky with diamonds, they couldn't use the footage.

We've done that ever since. Works like a charm.

"Which song?" Drew asked, unbuckling his seat belt like he hadn't just commandeered his car like a rocket. "I vote for 'Hello, Goodbye.' It's appropriate."

Neither Caro nor I disagreed, so we hurried out of the car and up my driveway as the anchorpeople dashed toward us. I recognized some of them—the ones that hadn't been promoted to better jobs in San Francisco or Houston or New York—and they were already eyeing the three of us, painfully wise to our wacky sing-alongs.

"'You say goodbye and I say hello!'" we sang. What we lack in talent, we make up for with enthusiasm and nefarious glee.

We were barely done with the first chorus before we made it through the front door of my house, where my mom was waiting.

"Oh, honey!" she wailed, grabbing me up and then hugging Drew and Caro as an afterthought. "They found him! He's alive!"

I hadn't seen either of my parents cry in years. When Oliver was taken, there were whispered conversations and stressful quiet moments, but they never cried. I think they thought they had to be brave for me and strong for Maureen, Oliver's mom. But now my mother was weeping against my shoulder and I hugged her tight, not sure what to say.

Drew was better in these situations than I was.

"Don't worry, Mrs. Trenton," he said. "Oliver's in New York. If he can make it there, he can make it anywhere."

She started to laugh through her tears and she let go of the three of us. "Drew," my mother scolded, "this isn't a time for jokes." But she was still laughing and Drew just winked at me.

"Mom," I said, "is it true? Really, this time?"

My mother nodded and used a ragged tissue to wipe at her eyes. "Maureen called us an hour ago. She's already on her way to the airport to go to New York. She said . . ." My mother stopped to stifle a sob. "She said he's six feet tall and has dark hair."

I just nodded, but I knew what my mom meant. When Oliver left, he was barely as high as my shoulder and had blond highlights from spending summers outside in our backyards.

"What about his dad? Is he——?"

"They don't know," my mother said. "Apparently, he wasn't home and he hasn't come back since. They're looking for him now, though. I'm sure they'll find him." (I wasn't so sure. My mom had been saying that for ten years about Oliver: *"I'm sure they'll find him."*)

"Your dad's on his way home from work now, Em." She dabbed at her eyes again. "Are you kids hungry?"

"Yes," Drew and Caro chimed together. My mom runs a catering business so there's always food around. They like to take blatant advantage.

"Come on, come on," my mom said, ushering us into the kitchen. "There's leftover crêpes."

Crêpes! Caro mouthed at me, grinning. I stumbled along behind them, discreetly wiping sand off my ankles while my mom's back was turned.

My mom had the kitchen redone several years ago and it looks like a Martha Stewart showcase combined with an operating room. There are shiny gadgets that completely befuddle my dad and me, and yet it's somehow warm and inviting. I like to hang out in there, just so long as I don't touch anything and accidentally get puréed.

"Do you think Oliver's dad will follow him here?" I sank down into a chair next to Drew, who looked as worried as I felt. "I mean, Oliver's been with him all this time. To be separated now, that has to be hard."

"His *dad*?" Caro said. "That's who you feel bad for right now? Seriously?"

"No, I feel bad for Oliver," I told her. But I felt kind of bad for everyone and I didn't know why.

"Is there Nutella in this crêpe?" Drew asked.

"Here, mine's Nutella. Switch with me." I swapped the plates around before Drew could say anything. Caro muttered something under her breath that sounded suspiciously like "people pleaser," but gave me an innocent look when I glanced at her.

"Does he know that Maureen's remarried?" I asked. "Or about the twins?"

"Oh, man, that's going to be a shock," Caro said, digging into her snack.

"I'm sure Maureen will tell him all about Rick and Molly and Nora," my mom reassured us. "That's not exactly news that she can hide."

"Do you think he even remembers us?" Drew asked. "It's been ten years."

"Don't say that," I snapped before I could stop myself. Drew's fork froze in the air as he stared at me. My mom was watching me across the kitchen, too. I had seen that look too many times over the years, the "oh my God, is our child damaged beyond repair?" look, and I was in no hurry to see it again.

"Of course he remembers us," I said. "Why wouldn't he? We remember *him*. How could he forget *us*?"

Both Caro and Drew blinked at me, but I glanced away and

tried to calm down. For years I had imagined Oliver coming home, what it would look like, and it never involved crêpes or him not remembering us. I crossed my fingers and knocked my hand softly against our wooden kitchen table, Oliver's and my secret way to undo a jinx. We had made it up two weeks before he disappeared and I wasn't about to let it go now.

"I'm sure he remembers," my mom said in that soothing way that made me want to scream. "Oliver's coming home and he's safe. That's what matters right now."

I looked at Caro. She crossed her eyes back at me.

My mom suddenly stopped. "Hey," she said. "Why is your hair wet?"

All three of us froze, Caro almost choking on her crêpe.

"We dared her to try out for the swim team," Drew said, not missing a beat.

"That's why I didn't get your messages," I added, tapping Drew's ankle under the table in a silent thank-you. He kicked back his own version of you're welcome.

My mom just laughed. "Crazy kids," she said, then turned around to get more food. "You know Emmy can't swim very well."

Caro, Drew, and I looked at one another, then Caroline leaned over and brushed some sand off my elbow, wiping away my secret.

CHAPTER THREE

The day dragged on as we waited for more news about Oliver. Not that there was anything to hear, of course. He was on a plane in the sky, hurtling back to us with the same instantaneous force that had caused him to disappear in the first place. His dad was still missing, but my parents kept Caro and Drew and me away from the news and computers. (They don't know that Caro and I figured out how to disable the internet parental controls years ago. Plus, hello? iPhones.)

Drew and Caro immediately got permission to sleep over. Caro's parents hadn't even heard that Oliver was found and I could hear her enthusiasm diminish with every sentence between them. "They found him! . . . No, they don't know where he is. . . . No, I already cleaned my half of the room. . . . That's Heather's mess, not mine. . . . Okay, yeah. No, I don't know. Thanks, bye."

Sometimes, I suspect that Caro's parents lose track of their kids. There's six in all, and Caro's the youngest. "I'm shuffled to the bottom of the deck," she says whenever it comes up. I think the biggest problem is that she's had to share a bedroom her entire life with Heather, her older sister, and Heather is basically a tornado with legs. Caro, on the other hand, is a very organized, neat person, and watching them share a room is like watching two movies on one screen. Caro is desperate for Heather to move out.

Drew's parents were beside themselves with joy that he wanted to spend the night with us girls. "Just Caro and Emmy," he said into the phone, wiggling his eyebrows at us lasciviously. "We just want to hang out and talk . . . no, Mom, it's Friday. No school tomorrow . . . okay, fine. Fine. Bye."

"You lucky guy," I said as soon as he hung up. "Spending the night with two lovely ladies such as ourselves."

Drew just grinned and pushed his hair out of his eyes. It was getting long and I suspected that it was a metaphorical middle finger to his straitlaced parents. Who could blame him? "Water, water everywhere, and not a drop to drink," he said mournfully, then plopped himself on my bed next to Caro and sighed.

The nervous energy started to creep in once the sun set. It had been setting later now that Christmas was over, and by seven o'clock, the sky was dark. No one really ate dinner, and finally my dad pushed his chair back from the table and said, "Well, I'm done," and the rest of us followed suit.

There had been so much food when Oliver first disappeared. So much, in fact, that Maureen's kitchen couldn't hold it all and much of it made its way to our house. Not that anyone was eating then, either. Casseroles don't look appetizing even in the best of times, and there were just so many of them. Even at seven years old, I knew there was a limit to the magical healing powers of baked ziti. Neighbors kept bringing them by, trying to look past us and into our house and Maureen's house, like we had shoved Oliver into a cupboard under the stairs. We gave some of it to the nicer reporters. Caro and I spent an afternoon eating an entire bowl of ambrosia salad with teaspoons and then an entire night in total abdominal agony. We weren't in trouble, though—that creepy indulgence was in full effect—and for the first time in my life, I had wished we had been. At least that would have been normal.

From the moment they discovered Oliver was found through the next day, a few neighbors came knocking on our door. "I didn't want to disturb Maureen," they said, then offered their brisket/creamed-corn casserole/Jell-O mold with mandarin orange slices jiggling in the middle. Drew looked at all of it and shook his head. "Why don't people just bring alcohol?" Drew wondered aloud.

"Hear, hear." My dad sighed as he tried to make room for the Jell-O in the refrigerator. He had spent the entire Saturday with Drew, Caro, and me hanging out in our backyard, not eager to leave the house in case something happened and we missed it. I didn't know what "it" would be, but it felt better to be at home than anywhere else. (Well, besides surfing, but I had no idea how to sneak out to the ocean and back with news crews parked all the way up the street.)

"Ugh, ambrosia," Caro muttered when she saw the salad in the refrigerator. "I can't even use coconut body lotion without feeling ill."

"Pretty much," I said, then helped myself to some tomatoes off the veggie tray that our neighbors across the street had delivered an hour ago.

I knew we'd eventually toss most of the food, like we had ten years ago. Seeing the dishes lined up on the countertop made my stomach flip and I gripped the tile in my hand just as I heard some shouts from the cameramen.

"Mom!" I yelled, since that seemed like the right person to call for, and suddenly my parents, Drew, Caro, and I were tumbling out the front door and onto the porch. The camera lights shone like high beams as a police car made an eerily silent path toward Oliver's house. There were two figures in the backseat, one much taller than the other. I saw the outline of Maureen's hair and realized with a sickening feeling that I didn't recognize the other person at all.

And right then, I wanted it to stop. I wanted to go back to surfing yesterday afternoon and have Caro announce nothing more exciting than a pop quiz in calculus that she totally failed. I wanted the neighbors to mind their own business and to my complete horror, I realized I wanted Oliver to go back to New York. His disappearance had created such a huge chasm that it still hadn't fully repaired itself, and I didn't know if I was ready to have it ripped open all over again. As terrible as the past ten years had been, they were familiar. I wasn't sure if I was ready to trade them in for a brand-new set of issues and worries.

The police car's passenger-side door opened and Maureen climbed out, along with the officer in the front seat. Cameras descended like electronic locusts and next to me, I saw my mom grab my dad's arm. There were tears in both of their eyes. The police did their best to clear a safe path up to Oliver's front door, but they couldn't stop the barrage of questions that the reporters began to yell.

"Are you angry with your father?"

"What was it like seeing your mother again?"

"Do you know where your father might be?"

"What's the first thing you're going to do now that you're home?"

Oliver's door opened and he stepped out.

He was a stranger.

Taller, broader, dark hair, just like my mom had said. He was glaring at the cameras as Maureen put her arm around him. Maureen had seemed smaller and frailer ever since that day Oliver hadn't come home from school, but next to her son, she looked tiny. I tasted blood and realized I was biting my lip too hard. Caro was crying next to me and Drew put an arm around each of us, hugging us tight. He was shaking. I think we all were.

When Oliver looked up and over at us, I made a noise in the back of my throat. I hadn't seen him in ten years, but I had seen his face every night in my dreams, his little seven-year-old face that seemed way too young, and when his eyes met mine, I knew that it was him. He had the same frown, the same eyes, the same posture.

"I wonder if anyone checked his shirt tag," I wondered out loud, and before anyone could ask what I was talking about, Oliver disappeared into his house, the door shutting behind him.

And that was it. He was home.

CHAPTER FOUR

"**G**ive Oliver *space*."

That was the mantra for the next week, at least as far as my parents went. On the advice of several psychologists and therapists, Maureen, Rick, the twins, and Oliver all went on virtual lockdown. "It's time for us to be a family once again." My mom read one of Maureen's group emails out loud one night as my dad and I were cleaning up after dinner. We had gotten a lot of these emails over the years—various "thank you so much for your thoughts and prayers" emails that Maureen had sent to friends and family members—but this was the first one that had an ending to it.

"Maybe Oliver doesn't need space," I said, drying a wineglass and trying not to get fingerprints all over it. "Maybe he wants to just be alone and not hang out with his old and new family. No one wants to be locked up with Molly and Nora." They were

Oliver's half sisters. I babysat them every so often for money that my parents thought I was saving for college and I was actually saving for a new wet suit and board.

"According to the therapists, they need some intense bonding time," my mom replied, delicately swiping her finger across the phone to turn it off.

"I've spent plenty of time alone with the twins," I replied. "Oliver will be crawling out through the chimney in a day if they put him through that."

"*We* need intense bonding time!" my dad said. "Pizza night on Friday!"

"I have a work thing," my mom said.

"I have a 'don't want to hang out with my parents' thing," I added.

"You love hanging out with us!" my dad chided me. "We're cool. Your friends love us."

It was, unfortunately, true. Caro and Drew thought my parents were great. And they were. Most of the time. But when it came to curfews or personal freedom, my parents were dictators.

"Anyway," my mom said, ignoring my comment, "we just have to be patient. I'm sure we'll all have a chance to see Oliver again soon. He just needs some *space*."

"Space?" Caro frowned when I told her that. We were in my bedroom the next night, doing our English homework. It was a

group project and luckily we could pick our own partners. Of course I chose Caro. She organizes her Post-it notes by color and size. You can't go wrong in a group project with someone like her.

"Space," I replied, raising an eyebrow at her.

"It's not really space if you're on lockdown with your own family." Caro seemed dubious and I saw her glance out my window toward Oliver's, where the blinds had been permanently shut. "That sounds like the opposite of space."

"Not all of us have five siblings like you," I told her. "And it's not lockdown. He's not in prison."

Caro raised her eyebrow right back at me. "Would you want to be holed up with *Maureen*, day and night?"

Caro had a point. Maureen was not an easygoing person. It seemed mean to make fun of her for it, though. "She went through a horrible trauma ten years ago," I chided Caro. "No one would be mellow after that."

"I know, I know," Caro said. "She just makes me nervous."

"This from someone whose pencils are all sharpened to equal lengths."

Caro paused, then threw a Post-it pad at me, giggling when I ducked. "You're lucky," she said. "It could have been a pencil."

"Space," Drew said thoughtfully when I told him what my parents had said. "Didn't he have enough space for ten years?"

"Not if he was in New York," I said. "They tend to pack 'em in there."

"I heard that he lived all over," Drew said. "I read it online."

"Yeah, I saw that," I grumbled.

Apparently, some cousin of Maureen's who lived one town over had leaked Maureen's email to the press. Oliver's news story wasn't as exciting as it had been the week before, but new information was new information.

"They called him *Colin*." Drew went on like I hadn't said anything. We were sitting on the sand after surfing together, perched on our boards. The sun was an hour or so away from dropping into the ocean, which meant I had thirty minutes before we had to leave and get back before my parents became suspicious.

"Colin?" I repeated, and Drew nodded sagely. "Wow. Okay. Why Colin?"

"No clue. I read it online. But I don't know what staying inside with Maureen and her husband, Ray—"

"Rick."

"Whatever. I don't see how that's going to help Oliver. They can't keep him hidden the same way his dad did and call it progress." Drew brushed his hair out of his eyes. The wind always picked up at sunset and we were both suffering for it.

"He needs to reassimilate," Drew continued. "Jump into the deep end of high school and get it over with."

"Maybe," I said. "Do you think he wants to see us, though?"

Drew glanced at me. "Why? Don't *you* want to see him?"

"Well, of *course* I want to see him!" I scoffed. "He was gone for ten years, it'd be nice to get to know him again."

But the truth was that I *had* seen Oliver. The night before, after Caro left and my parents went to bed (*"Lights out soon!"* my mom had said, which meant I had an hour or so before she checked on me again), I snuck into my closet, stood on a rickety old step stool, and felt around on the shelf for an old shoe box. It was shoved so far back that I could barely touch it, but as soon as my fingers grazed the top, I managed to pull it down.

I have things hidden all around my room. I don't think I would describe myself as a sneaky person, but if I count off all of the secret hiding spaces I have, well, *you* might describe me that way. The more something needs to be hidden, the sneakier I become. My babysitting cash lives in the back of the closet, in the pocket of a winter coat that I have worn exactly once. My old surfing magazines that I got at the used-book store are stashed in my third desk-drawer down, covered up by piles of printer paper and used-up ballpoint pens.

The shoe box is my oldest hiding spot and it holds just two things, things that no one knows about, not even Drew or Caro, not even my parents.

The first is a copy of my application to UC San Diego.

I had been thinking about applying for a while, ever since junior year when someone mentioned that they had one of the best surfing teams in the nation. San Diego was only about ninety minutes south from where we lived, so it wasn't like I would be leaving my parents for the other side of the country. It was just far away enough, where I could have some *space*.

The same space, in fact, that I was giving to Oliver.

I pulled out the application once more, feeling the paper's crispness in my hands. I had printed it out at the public library just so it would feel real, a reminder that I had actually applied to college. It felt more real that way, more possible. Caro and I had talked about going to community college together, then transferring to a university after two years, but I wanted out now. I didn't want to wait anymore.

The second secret was at the bottom of the shoe box, a piece of paper folded and refolded so many times that it was starting to tear a little at the creases. Unlike the application, the paper was as soft as bedsheets, and I ran my thumb over the edge before carefully opening it up.

DO YOU LIKE EMMY, YES NO??? it said. Caro's handwriting was precise and exact, just like it is now, and the word *yes* was circled. It was the only thing I had left of Oliver after the kidnapping, the only thing that was truly mine, and I had kept it that way for ten years. I used to look at it for hours at a time, holding it in my pocket and pulling it out when I was alone in my room. I had thought that if I kept it close, it would bring Oliver back home, and now was the first time in ten years that I held it while knowing where Oliver was in the world.

The idea took my breath away.

After I put the shoe box back up on the shelf and went to get ready for bed, I realized that I could see into Oliver's room. The blinds had been blown askew by the wind, leaving a part of the window bare, and I could see him sitting in his desk chair, his profile illuminated by a light coming from across the room. He was holding his lip between his fingers, toying with it absently, and I suddenly remembered him doing that in second grade whenever he was nervous, usually while we were dividing up for kickball teams. (He hadn't been the best athlete.)

His hair was dark and longer than it had been when we were kids, and he looked sort of like some of the surfers that Drew and his brother, Kane, hung out with on weekends, strands of hair tucked behind his ear. His face was the same, just bigger, and his gaze was intense.

Creeping across the floor (and feeling like a stalker), I managed to turn off the light switch before tiptoeing back over to the window. My room was totally dark so there was no way Oliver could see me, but I hunched down below the windowsill, anyway. I felt like a hippopotamus in one of those nature documentaries, when they're submerged in water and you can only see their eyes.

Oliver was watching a movie. That's what had his attention. It was projected from his laptop onto a white sheet that he had taped up over his bookshelf, the same bookshelf that Maureen had dusted for ten years. It was something older, maybe from the sixties, with dramatic music that floated out even through his closed window. Whatever it was, Oliver was entranced. I probably could have been standing inside his room and he wouldn't have noticed me, but I stayed hidden, anyway.

Suddenly, the space that had always been between us felt too big. For the first time in ten years, I could see Oliver right in front of me, but he was still much too far away.

CHAPTER FIVE

Oliver's first day of school didn't go well.

My day didn't start off great, either. First thing, my mom cornered me in the kitchen. I was shoveling Frosted Flakes into my face while reading the back of the cereal box. (Those mazes are getting more and more difficult, I swear.)

"So," my mom said in a way that made me look up from the box with my eyebrows already raised. "Oliver's going to start school today."

"Today?" I repeated. "But it's raining out."

What does that have to do with anything? I immediately thought, just as my mom said, "What does that have to do with anything?"

"I don't know, shouldn't it be sunny? Rain on your first day is not a good omen. These are not good omen skies."

My mom eyed me. "Have you been drinking coffee again?"

I had. She wasn't supposed to know about that.

"So it's Oliver's first day," I prompted her, ignoring the question. "And?"

"And it would be nice if you were nice to him."

"I thought we were giving him space. And if we're not, why wouldn't I be nice?" Then I added, "I'm very nice. I'm nice to everyone who deserves my niceness."

"I just mean that I'm sure it won't be an easy transition for him."

"So be nice, but don't tell him that I'm being nice?"

"Emmy. He's probably nervous."

"He should be," I muttered. Oliver was pretty much starting off his first day of public high school as a quasi celebrity. And to attract that kind of attention in high school often meant disaster.

"What?" my mom asked.

"Nothing," I muttered.

"Well, I know that Maureen is just a wreck. She's convinced that Keith is just going to show up on campus and spirit him away again. I've told her that's not going to happen and Oliver needs to go to school, get back into the routine of things, but you know Maureen."

I wondered if my mom even realized I was still in the room.

"Anyway," she suddenly said. "You'll be nice to Oliver." It wasn't a question.

"Yes, I'll be very nice to Oliver. Do you want me to carry his books for him? Open his juice at snack time?"

My mom tried to swat me with the dish towel, but I was

already dumping my bowl in the sink and dodging away from her. "Oh, you missed!" I cried. "Too bad, so sad! And *you* should be nice to *me*. Take your own advice!"

"Drive safely!" she called after me. I could tell she was trying not to laugh. "Have a glorious day at school! There, are you happy?"

"Elated," I yelled back. "Bye!"

Outside, I fired up my car and let it run for a minute while I got situated and threw my bag into the backseat. It was actually a minivan, a bright-blue used one that my parents had gotten me for my seventeenth birthday, sort of the sad twin to Drew's spectacular VW. "For being such a perfect daughter!" my mom had said, which made me feel a little guilty about the fact that I was using the thing to sneak around, surfing. "Don't you want something a bit . . . sportier?" my dad had asked when we were at the lot. But I had done my homework. I knew that my surfboard would fit perfectly in that car. And I had been right.

The rain was falling harder now, smearing dirt and sand and salt into rivulets that blocked my view. I turned on the windshield wipers a few times, then rolled down my front windows so I could at least see out of them.

In the next driveway over, Oliver was doing the same thing from the passenger seat of his mom's car.

Our eyes met as his mom started the engine. She was talking to Oliver while putting on lipstick in the rearview mirror, her eyes steady even as her hand shook a little bit. I couldn't hear everything that she was saying, but a few words stuck out: *positive attitude, give it a chance, have to try.*

My mom probably helped her write that motivational speech.

Oliver was still looking back at me, both of us not moving to roll the windows back up. He looked bleary-eyed and tired, like me. I wondered if he needed coffee. *Does he even drink coffee?*

Maureen rolled her lipstick back down, tucking it into her purse before frowning into the mirror and fluffing her hair. (The rain wasn't doing anyone any favors, hair-wise.) Oliver hadn't looked away yet. He was inscrutable, just like those age-progression pictures of him on the missing children databases. I couldn't read his face at all and it was . . . weird.

So I crossed my eyes and stuck my tongue out at him.

The minute I did that, I realized that I was an idiot. A first-class idiot that clearly had no idea how to interact with people—or how to roll her window back up and avoid getting rain all over the car's interior, for that matter. Who just crosses their eyes at someone? Four-year-olds, that's who. Four-year-olds and people who need corrective lens wear.

But Oliver's face suddenly split open into a confused smile, like he wasn't sure what he was seeing, but liked it, anyway. His eyebrow arched as he started to roll the window back up and I quickly did the same, my cheeks on fire.

The second I ran into Caro in the hallway, I grabbed her arm. "Ow and hi," she said, taking her arm back.

"You won't believe what I just did," I said to her.

"I probably will, but try me."

"So I saw Oliver in the driveway this morning—"

"Why was he in the driveway?"

"He's starting school today. Anyway—"

"He is?" Caro gasped, now grabbing my arm. (She was right, it hurt.) "Oh my God, is that even a smart idea? Everyone knows who he is!"

"I know, right?" I said. "I tried to tell my mom the same thing, but she didn't get it."

"Moms never do," Caro said in sympathy. "Okay, so you saw him in the driveway, heading straight toward this torture chamber, and . . ."

"And both of our windows were rolled down."

"Yeah?"

"And he wouldn't stop looking at me."

Caro widened her eyes a little. "He wouldn't stop looking at you? Or you wouldn't stop looking at him?"

"Caro, that's not important. We were both looking at each other, and it was really weird, so I crossed my eyes and stuck out my tongue at him."

Caro just shrugged. "It sounds cute. You're adorable when you cross your eyes. What'd he do?"

"He smiled," I admitted. "And then we rolled up the windows because it was raining."

"Well, you were wrong, I totally believe this story," she said as we arrived at her locker. "Why does it always smell like old sandwiches around here?" she muttered as she spun the lock.

"Someone's hoarding food and it's disgusting. Anyway, I'm pretty sure that your reputation with the most famous person in our school is still intact. He smiled and that's a good sign." Caro gave me a meaningful glance. "You should cross your eyes more often. You'll have a date to prom like that!"

I socked her in the shoulder even as I started to laugh. "You're the worst best friend ever."

"I take pride in that," she said, and was about to say more when Oliver walked out of the school office and started to head toward his locker.

It wasn't too difficult to find. It was the one that had milk cartons stuck all over it.

"Oh my God," I whispered.

"What?" Caro said, then looked up from her phone to follow my gaze to Oliver's locker. A few other people were already looking at it, taking pictures that would probably end up on the internet in the next thirty seconds, even before Oliver had a chance to see it for himself.

"Milk?" she whispered. "Why milk?"

"Milk *cartons*," I whispered back. "You know, missing kids. Oh God, this is awful."

"How did they even know that was his locker?" Caro asked, running her hand through her hair the way she always did when she was pissed off about something.

"One of the suck-ups who work in the office must've tipped someone off," I said.

"What is that, fishing wire?" Caro said, squinting to see what held the cartons to the locker.

"Assholes," I muttered. I was about to storm over there and start yanking them down when Oliver walked past Caro and me. His gaze was the same as it had been in the car, sort of expressionless and cautious at the same time, and it didn't change when he saw his locker.

"Oh no," I whispered to Caro, who was clutching at my arm again. It still hurt, but I didn't say anything. "This is so bad."

"It's milk, Emmy," Caro whispered back. "Not arsenic. Unless he has a lactose thing, he'll live." She paused. "Hey, remember when Kaitlyn Cooper was in the library and someone opened a package of peanut M&M's? Oh my God, she blew up like a balloon. People were practically throwing EpiPens at her like she was a dartboard."

"Yeah," I said, half listening.

"It was nuts. No pun intended."

I shook Caro off and went over to where Oliver was spinning his locker combination, consulting the tiny sheet of paper from the office that had his schedule and info. The milk cartons were literally knocking into his knuckles as he worked, but he didn't acknowledge it, just like he wasn't acknowledging the people that were staring at him or giggling nearby.

"So mean," I heard a few girls whisper into their cupped hands, but they were standing together in a tiny gaggle, hiding smiles behind their fingers. Probably freshmen. They loved drama at school because it was just like all the movies they had grown up watching. A delivery on a promise: *high school will be so exciting!* When in fact, it was normally just boring as hell.

I glared at the girls as I went over to Oliver. My cheeks felt like someone had packed hot coals into them, but his were still East Coast pale. "I'm really sorry about this," I said, blurting out words before I could put any actual thought behind them. "Everyone here is an asshole. You should know that."

Oliver glanced down at me, blinking a few times in slow motion and reminding me of Mr. Snuffleupagus on *Sesame Street*. "Why are *you* apologizing?" he asked. "Did you do this?"

"What? No! No, of course not." I shook my head and crossed my arms. "No, I just . . . I'm sorry this is your first day and people are treating you like this."

He pulled a brown-bag lunch out of his backpack (so new that I could see where either he or his mom had forgotten to remove the sales tag) and shoved it into his locker. The milk cartons were still thudding against the door, drawing even more attention to the spectacle. Behind me, I heard someone's camera phone click. "Like what?" he asked.

"Like . . ." I gestured toward the locker. *Like what, Emmy? Like a kid who was missing and then came home? Like the new kid who has to be hazed? Like Caro said, it's milk, not arsenic.*

And then Oliver blinked again and it was like a shutter went off in his own eyes so I could see the picture of the anger, the hurt, the embarrassment. It was a private viewing just for me, gone a second later when he blinked once more and his face smoothed back into its normal, passive shape.

"Emily, right?" he said.

It took me a few seconds to realize he meant me. No one ever called me Emily, not unless they were my parents and they were furious. "Um, yeah," I said. "Emmy, actually." It felt odd to introduce myself to him all over again.

"Want some milk?" he asked. He snapped a carton from its wire and handed it to me before I could even answer. "In case you're vitamin D deficient. Courtesy of our classmates."

"But I—I'm not—okay, thanks." The carton was cold, which meant someone had done it right before school started.

Small mercies. The milk could have been spoiled.

Oliver slammed his locker shut, then took his own carton, opened the top, and drank the whole thing in one gulp as he walked down the hallway. Just before he rounded the corner, he sank it into a trash can.

"What did he say?" Caro said, suddenly at my elbow again.

"He gave this to me," I said, showing her the carton.

"Yeah, I know, genius, but what did he say? Is he pissed?"

I couldn't help but smile as I shook my head. "He said I could have this in case I had a vitamin deficiency." I handed it to her as she frowned at me. "And he called me Emily."

Caro wrinkled her nose. "Do you think he's . . . you know . . . ?" Caro tapped her index finger against her temple. "Addled?"

"No," I laughed. "No, I think he's really smart."

"Well, I hope so, for your sake."

"Yeah? Why's that?"

"Because it's Wednesday."

Wednesday.

"Oh my God," I said, whirling to face her. "It's Wednesday."

"That's right." She smiled and handed the milk carton back to me. "Babysitting night."

CHAPTER SIX

I've been babysitting for Nora and Molly off and on for the past six months. It was originally my idea. I needed cash to buy a new surfboard and wet suit because my old ones no longer fit me, and Maureen had asked me to watch the girls that night so she and Rick could have a date night. Which, judging from the tension that always seems to be between them whenever I go there, they desperately need.

"Oh, hi, Emmy. Hi!" Maureen said when I let myself in through the back door. She was fluttering through the kitchen, stacking magazines and newspapers on top of the counter before going to fluff the couch cushions. Their house has always looked impeccable, even after the twins were born. My dad says that Maureen has control issues.

"Well, wouldn't *you* if your child was kidnapped?" my mom always says in her defense. "You have to do *something*, you might as well dust."

"Is that what you would do if I went missing?" I had asked her, incredulous. *"Dust?"*

"It's a metaphor, sweetie."

I do not think my mom understands the meaning of *metaphor.*

"Hi, Emmy!"

"Hi, Emmy!"

I glanced up to see the twins looking at me through the banister. "Hey, ladies!" I said to them. "What are you doing up there?"

"Playing spies!" Nora whispered in a way that, not to be critical, was not very spy-like at all. Next to her, Molly nodded.

Molly definitely had the better chance of making it into the CIA.

"I left money for pizza—" Maureen said.

"Pizza!" Molly cried, pumping her fist in the air.

"Pizza!" Nora echoed.

"—and Oliver's upstairs if you need anything. Rick's still at work so I'm going to meet him and . . ." Maureen trailed off as she wiped crumbs off the crumb-less table. "Oh, I don't know. I don't even think I should be going out tonight."

The pizza celebration stopped midcry.

"You should go," I told her. "We'll be fine. We're going to do awesome, fun things. Right, you guys?"

"Yeah!" Nora said.

"I'm not a *guy*, I'm a *girl*," Molly announced as she trooped down the stairs. "And I want pizza."

Maureen took a deep breath. "I'm just not sure that it isn't too soon. The therapist said it's important to stick to a routine but——"

Nora came over so she could hang on to my leg. Her hands were probably sticky and I tried to peel her off without wincing. "The therapist said that *I'm* a good colorer," she said, head tilting back so she could look up at me. "I can see up your nose!"

I disentangled her. "Wonderful," I said. "Go play spies with Molly. Pretend it's the 1980s, during the Cold War.

"And Maureen, it's fine. We'll have pizza, watch TV or something, they'll go to bed. Easy times all around."

"The therapist said that I'm a good jumper!" Molly announced as she started jumping around us.

"The therapist said that I'm also good at playing video games!" Nora cried. "And coping!"

Maureen looked horrified. "She must have overheard us," she whispered. "Oh God, I——"

"They're *fine*," I said to her. "I have your cell; obviously, I'll call you if anything goes wrong, and Oliver's upstairs, right?" I didn't mean for that last part to sound so much like a question.

Maureen glanced toward the upstairs part of the house, and the two little girls followed her gaze. "Okay," she finally said. "But if you need anything—*anything*—just call or text me. Or Rick. Or your mom."

"Got it," I said, half shoving, half escorting her out the door as she blew kisses to the twins. "I'll call the SWAT team if anyone gets a paper cut."

She gave me the kind of Look that all mothers are capable of giving, then blew one last kiss in the general direction of the kitchen. "Bye, girls, love you!" she called out behind her.

"Bye!" Neither of them looked up from their game.

"Okay!" I said, clapping my hands together as I went back into the kitchen. "What do we want?"

"Pizza!" the kids yelled.

"And when do we want it?"

"Now!"

"Well, we have to order it and wait for it to be delivered, but I see where you were going with that."

The kids just blinked at me. Sometimes they're not the most appreciative audience for my sense of humor.

"Find the menu," I told Nora. "Let's get this party started."

An hour later, the twins were fed and sprawled on the couch, watching a movie that was very loud and very animated. I was doing my calculus homework in the chair farthest away from the TV, with Molly's head resting on my ankles. Nora was wearing a paper crown that had been colored blue and pink, curled up on the corner of the couch, her thumb in her mouth and her finger hooked around her nose. (It's the easiest way to tell the twins apart.)

I heard the footsteps before I saw Oliver's feet on the stairs. He had on white athletic socks, gray sweatpants, and a white T-shirt, his hair rumpled like he had been sleeping. "Um, hey," he said, waving a little. "Is there pizza still?"

The movie was immediately abandoned just as my heart started to pick up speed.

"Yes!" Molly said. "We have three kinds!" She held up three fingers as she leaned across my legs. "'Cause there's three of us."

"Why do you guys—"

"I'm a girl, not a *guy*!"

"Oh. Sorry. Why do you *girls* need three kinds?"

I pointed at Nora. "Hit it, Nora."

"I can't eat gluten," Nora announced, beaming at her older brother. "It makes me barf."

Oliver winced. "Good to know."

Molly shoved her way in front of her sister before I could even point at her. They adored Oliver, it was obvious. I felt like I was watching a bunch of peasant girls compete for the prince's affections. "Let me guess," Oliver said. "You . . . can't eat tomatoes."

"No!" she giggled. "I'm a veggietarian!"

Oliver started making his way to the kitchen, both girls trailing along behind him. I was just the boring next-door neighbor/babysitter, so of course I was abandoned. "Do you eat pizza?" Nora asked Oliver. "Do you like pizza? Or do you like sushi? I like sushi, too."

"I thought you were a vegetarian."

"That's me!" Molly said.

"Well, I like pizza and sushi," Oliver said, picking up a slice and folding an end expertly in half and biting off the pointed part. "This must be the gluten-free pizza," he said after a few chews. "Who knew gluten was so important?"

Nora just smiled at him.

"Why do you eat it like that?" Molly asked. "It's all folded up."

"That's how you eat it in New York," Oliver told her. He was already halfway through his slice, talking with his mouth full. I tried not to be grossed out.

"Really?" Nora said.

"Yep. There, you can go into stores and just buy a slice of pizza and then you eat it standing up, like this."

The twins immediately dove for the pizza boxes again. That was my cue.

"Hey, hey, we'll try it some other time," I said, reaching them before they ate more pizza and caused an unpleasant end to the evening. "You both had enough tonight."

"You're no fun." Nora pouted.

"I think I can live with that," I told her, then shut the boxes just as Oliver was going for another slice. "Oh! Oh, sorry, I mean . . . *you* can have more. Sure."

He raised an eyebrow at me. "You sure, babysitter?"

It took a few seconds to find my voice again. "Um, yeah. The rules only apply to anyone under four feet tall."

"I'm taller than Molly," Nora immediately told Oliver.

"I'm older!"

"I can count to three hundred!"

"I can count to a bazillion!"

"A bazillion plus one!"

"Got it," Oliver said, then smiled at them before taking his slice and heading back upstairs. "Enjoy your movie!" he called behind him, and I realized that the girls and I were watching the stairs even after he disappeared.

Nora turned to look at me. "Mommy says he spends too much time in his room."

"Oh yeah?" I said. "What do you think?"

"I think that he has the biggest room so he should spend the most time there."

"That's very sound logic." I smiled down at her, then used the back of my hand to wipe some stray sauce off her cheek. "C'mon, let's do what Oliver said and enjoy the movie."

The kids enjoyed the rest of the movie.

I don't remember anything that happened in it, though. I was too busy thinking about what Oliver was doing upstairs. Homework? Watching his own movies, ones that didn't involve zany music and bright color explosions? *I should have invited him to watch with us,* I thought, then wondered what I would've done if he said yes.

CHAPTER SEVEN

Drew and I stayed on campus the next day at lunch while Caro disappeared to Del Taco with three senior girls from the cheer squad. "Bring me a bean burrito!" Drew called after her as she ran down the hill toward the parking lot. "With red sauce!"

"Okay!" Caro yelled back, her voice disappearing into the breeze.

"She's not going to remember," I said to Drew as she disappeared. "She never remembers."

"I'm forever hopeful," he said. "That's what friends do. They hope. They have faith in each other."

"Well, I have faith that she'll forget," I said, hiking my backpack up onto my shoulders. "You have to be a realist with Caro."

"I'm a hopeful realist," Drew said. "I'm a healist! Like those guys on TV late at night that cure people of cancer." He grinned down at me. Even when we were kids, Drew was always the tallest

kid in our class and when he hit his growth spurt in eighth grade,
he became the Beanstalk to our classroom of Jacks.

"Yeah, speaking of that, I saw Oliver last night," I said.

Drew paused midstep. "What does being a healist—don't steal
that, by the way, I'm having it copyrighted even as we speak—
have to do with Oliver?"

"Nothing, I was just trying to change the subject." I tugged at
his elbow to keep him moving. There are conversations you have to
have face-to-face, but others that require perpetual motion. Shoes
scuffing, the crunch of fallen leaves, blades of grass whispering
together keeping the other person from looking into your eyes
and realizing that you don't believe a word of what you're saying.

"So Oliver. Mr. Mystery," Drew said. "Did you hear about the
milk cartons the other day?"

"Dude, I was there with Caro. I saw the whole thing."

"Sucks," Drew said, scuffing the toe of his Vans along the
cement walkway. "People are assholes. Milk-wasting assholes."

"Yeah." It was always a little easier to talk to Drew than it was
to Caro. He gave people more space in between their words, let
them figure out how to make their thoughts sound the same on
the outside as they did on the inside. He was patient where Caro
was urgent. Drew would remember to not only bring back the
bean burrito, but extra packets of red sauce, too.

"I saw him yesterday morning, too," I said. "He was in the car
with his mom."

Drew shuddered. "That's my biggest nightmare right now,

having my mom drive me to school."

I glanced up. "Really?"

Drew tucked his thumbs into his backpack straps, now scuffing his shoes in rhythm with my steps. "She's being super nicey-nice, handling me with extra care. Like I'm a live grenade or something."

I didn't say anything at first. I let him find the right words, the same as he does for me.

"I think they're waiting for me to freak out or, I don't know, have this crazy breakdown or something. My mom's even reading this book right now, *How to Talk to Your Teenager*."

We both rolled our eyes at the same time.

"Gross," I said.

"*Right?* Like, if you want to talk to me, don't read a book about it. Just *talk* to me. I'm a person." Drew sighed and gave his shoe a final scuff. "Anyway, yeah, parents are weird. But *Oliver*." He glanced down and waited for me to look up at him before wiggling an eyebrow.

"Stop it," I said, laughing a little. "You know it creeps me out when you do that."

Drew, of course, did it even more, and I shoved him away and tried to cover my eyes. "Stop!" I said. "Or I won't share my sandwich with you and you'll starve for the rest of the day!"

Drew stopped and flicked his hair out of his eyes. He always looks cool when he does that, even though I know he doesn't mean to. "Why would I want your sandwich? Caro's bringing me a delicious burrito from Del Taco."

"Hope springs eternal," I said as we wandered into the quad. There were scattered freshmen (most of them hung out near the cafeteria's exit, like it was difficult for them to move too far away from the food) and a few juniors whose names I didn't know, and then a figure sitting on a long cement-block wall under a tree, wearing headphones and eating something out of a brown paper bag, gazing off into the distance like he was at a museum and the rest of us were moving sculptures.

"Oh," I said.

"*Oh,*" Drew replied.

I elbowed him. Hard. "Shut up."

"What? All I said was oh!" He elbowed me back, but I moved away. "Are you blushing?"

"No," I said. (I totally was.)

"He's sitting by himself," Drew said.

"Yes, thank you, I can see that."

But Drew was on a roll. "Here we see the typical teenager during an average high school lunch period," he said, doing his best PBS documentary narrator voice. "This creature is normally sedate, but can be provoked with milk cartons and conversation."

"I'm going over there," I said.

"What? No." Drew grabbed my arm before I could even take a step. "You're not talking to him."

"He's sitting by himself!" I hissed. "Look at him, it's sad. And, like, we grew up together and now he's back and he lives next door to me. I can't just *ignore* him."

"We're supposed to give him space, Emmy."

"He's not a rabid animal at the zoo!" I cried, shrugging off Drew's arm. "How much space are we supposed to give him? He goes to our school now. It's not like we can pretend that we don't know him. Or, I mean, *used* to know him."

"You're not good at making conversation. In fact, you're pretty much the worst at it."

I thought of how I crossed my eyes and stuck out my tongue at Oliver the day before, then said nothing. Drew didn't need to know any of that.

"No, I'm not," I said instead. "I took public speaking in freshman year, remember?"

"Remember?" Drew repeated. "I'm trying to *forget*."

"I was good!"

"Yeah, you were good, but every time you gave a speech, you'd kick the podium and your microphone would screech!" Drew swung his foot a few times, mimicking me. "And you're terrible without a plan. Oliver would probably be in physical danger. You'd take out his kneecap or something."

"Drew. I am going over there. So you can help me or watch me make a total fool of myself."

Drew sighed. "Fine."

"So, what do I talk to him about?"

"Just go over and say hi—"

"Got it."

"—and then ask him if he needs your notes for any classes—"

"Easy."

"—and then offer to make out with him."

"Okay, I—*DREW*!"

He giggled and ducked away from me as I swung my notebook at him.

Drew didn't know what he was talking about, I told myself as I stalked away. I could make *great* conversation.

"Hey," I said when I was close enough, before realizing that Oliver probably couldn't hear me with his earbuds in. I waved my hand a little, trying to get his attention, and I didn't even have to turn around to know that Drew was smacking himself in the forehead.

Doing great so far, genius, I scolded myself.

"Oh," Oliver said after a few seconds. "Hey."

"Hi," I said. "Sorry, am I . . . ? I mean, I don't want to . . ."

So, Drew *may* have had a point.

"No, it's cool." He slipped his earbuds out of his ears and let them dangle over his shoulders. "What's up?"

"Hi," I said again. "I just wanted to say that. I mean, I wanted to say hi and, um, see how you were doing."

"I'm good," he said. "Getting a lot of calcium, as you know."

He was so deadpan that it took me a few seconds to realize he was kidding. "Oh!" I laughed. "Yeah, sorry about that. Drew and I"—I gestured to Drew behind me—"were just saying that people can be assholes."

Oliver just shrugged. "Law of averages. Some are, some aren't."

"Yeah. Speaking of, do you need any notes or anything?"

Oliver frowned a little at my segue (which was, to be fair, nonexistent). "Notes?" he repeated.

"For class," I added, patting my backpack. "Like, if you're not caught up."

"I don't think we share any classes," Oliver said. He was squinting up at me now, like the sun was in his face even though it was behind a cloud. "I'm a junior."

And I wanted to die. Right there, right then, I wanted that cloud above us to throw a lightning bolt down and strike me dead. I had forgotten that they had put Oliver back a grade from the rest of us. Apparently, his dad had homeschooled him, so his math and science skills were off the charts, but his history and English were behind. He was easily the oldest-looking junior in our school, yet another thing that made him stand out when he needed more than ever to blend in.

"Oh, *riiiiight*," I said, knocking myself in the head and grinning like an idiot. "I'm sorry, I totally forgot."

"That's okay," he replied. "Just adds to my rebel image. New guy in school, mysterious past, being held back a grade." He smiled up at me. "Girls like it."

"Really?"

"Oh yeah." He smiled wider. "That's why I'm eating lunch with all these people."

I laughed despite myself and then he laughed, too, a familiar sound that I hadn't heard in years. His laugh was deeper now, but still Oliver's, as unique as a double helix. Or a fingerprint.

"You have fun with my sisters last night?" he asked, tearing off a piece of sandwich and eating it, rather than biting into the bread.

"You do that," I said, pointing at him, and Oliver stopped midchew and looked down at the sandwich.

"What?" he asked, then swallowed. "Eat?"

"No, you do this"——I mimed him tearing the sandwich——"and then eat it. That's how you used to eat sandwiches when we were little."

"You remember that?"

"I do now."

Oliver smiled, almost to himself, then tore off another piece. "My mom keeps saying things like that," he said. "You do this or you do that."

"Preserved in amber," I said before I could stop myself, and he laughed again.

"Yeah, something like that," he said. "A fossil in a brave new world."

"Hey," Drew said, coming up behind my left shoulder. "We should, uh, go get to that thing."

I had no idea what thing he meant, but I knew a friendly rescue attempt when I saw one. "Yeah, that thing," I said. "Oliver and I were just talking about sandwiches."

"Hey, man," Oliver said, and he and Drew did the fist-bump

thing. (I will never understand how so many guys always know how to do that. Is it genetic? Is it a talent carried on the Y chromosome?)

"Hey," Drew said. "Sandwiches? Uh, they're cool, I guess." He shot a quick smile at me. "Did you maim him yet?"

"Oh my God, please shut up," I said, then started shoving Drew away and following close behind. "See you later, Oliver," I said, and he waved before putting his earbuds back in and popping the last crust into his mouth.

"Sandwiches?" Drew hissed at me. "You're terrible. Is there a dating elective at this school, because you need to sign up for it immediately."

"Hey, who doesn't like sandwiches?" I shot back. "People who hate life, that's who. And I was just saying that I remembered the weird way he ate them."

"You talked about sandwiches . . . and called him weird." Drew closed his eyes and took a deep breath in through his nose. "Caro's going to die when she hears this. Secondhand embarrassment will claim yet another young life."

"I didn't say the word *weird* to him!" I protested. "Tell Caro whatever you want."

"Tell me what?"

Caro was just coming in through the glass doors, carrying a huge soda from Del Taco and pushing her sunglasses up onto her head. "I'll totally believe whatever you say." She put her arm around my shoulder. "Even if you're lying, I'll believe you. That's what friendship is."

"Don't become a lawyer," Drew muttered.

"It's a long story," I told her, stealing a sip from her soda.

"A long story about *Oliver*," Drew added. "Where's my burrito?"

Caro looked at him. "What burrito?"

"Caro!" he screamed. "You were supposed to bring me a burrito! I'm starving!"

"I'm sorry! You know I never remember these things!"

I pulled my sandwich out of my backpack and silently handed half to Drew.

"Thank you," he sighed.

"*That's* what friendship is," I told him. "Just don't eat it *weird*."

THE LIGHT

Emmy devises the lamp system when they're in kindergarten. Oliver perfects it.

"So I'll flick the light three times," she starts to explain, but he interrupts her.

"No, just once. Just turn it on once 'cause our moms might see if we turn it on three times. Just once."

"Okay, just once. Okay. And then . . . and then you turn it on once."

"Yeah!" Oliver's totally excited. He loves secret things. "Then what?"

Emmy hadn't thought this far. She's only five years old, after all, just like Oliver. "Ummm . . ." She bites her lip. "Then you look out the window to make sure it's me. 'Cause what if I'm not there and there's a witch instead, Ollie?" Emmy is the only person allowed to call him "Ollie" so she likes to say it a lot.

Oliver lights up and hops onto the swing next to her. They swing when they have supersecret conversations because that way, no one can overhear. (That was Emmy's idea, too.) "What if the witch is wearing a disguise?" he asks her. "How will I know it's really you?"

Emmy pumps her legs and thinks for a minute. "Well, that's dumb," she finally says. "You're always gonna know it's me. And I'm always gonna know it's you." She pushes her hair out of her face and swings harder. "You're Oliver. Who else would you be?"

"Yeah," he agrees, and they fly higher toward the sky.

CHAPTER EIGHT

"**S**o we were thinking," my dad said on Saturday. "Maybe you could take Oliver out this afternoon."

I glanced up at him from an old issue of *Real Simple* that my mom hadn't recycled yet, no longer interested in the best way to iron a linen tablecloth. "What?"

My mom came over to stand next to my dad. Ah, the parental sneak attack. I should have seen this coming. Seventeen years of living in the same house with them and yet they still surprise me.

"We were talking earlier with Maureen," my mom said. "It seems that Oliver is having a hard time making friends at school."

I snorted a little, but my stomach was flipping around just like it did whenever I saw a wave that seemed a little too big to ride and a little too strong to avoid. "Get in line, Oliver," I said to my parents, trying to keep my voice light.

"You know what I mean," my mom said. "Maureen says that he

spends all of his time in his room watching movies."

I already knew this, of course. "So don't give him any more space, is what you're saying? Basically, just do the opposite of everything that you said two weeks ago."

My mom rolled her eyes as my dad patted my arm. "Maureen's worried, kiddo. Maybe you could just hang out with him for a few hours, show him around town or something."

I bit the inside of my cheek as I thought about it. On one hand, I would finally get to really talk with Oliver. On the other hand, I would finally have to really talk with Oliver. It was different on campus last week, back when I had Drew right behind me. What was I supposed to say if it was just the two of us? "Sorry your dad kidnapped you ten years ago and ruined your life"? Yeah, that probably wouldn't do much to stir up conversation.

"You're not worried about his dad being out there somewhere?" I asked.

"We've discussed that with Maureen," my dad said carefully. "And we've all agreed that Keith is probably not going to try anything." My mom looked slightly less sure of that, but she nodded, anyway. "It's best if we all just move forward. Including Oliver."

"What if I say the wrong thing?" I asked my parents, pointedly not looking at them. "What if I ask him something and end up traumatizing him and he goes completely mute?"

My parents glanced at each other before looking back at me. "You," my dad said, "give yourself entirely too much credit."

"Thanks a *lot*."

"Maybe you could go out for ice cream——" my mom suggested.

"You mean coffee?"

"——or the movies?" My dad dug his wallet out of his pocket and fished out a few twenties. "On the house, of course. You could discuss——*the movie*! See, no trauma there. Make sure it's a comedy, though. And be back by seven."

I looked at my dad, who was doing his best "I'm kidding, but no, seriously" face. "You mean right now?" I asked him.

"You had plans?" my mom asked.

I had actually planned to say I was going to hang out with Caro, then secretly sneak down to the beach to surf for a few hours, but I was still a little suspicious of my parents' motives. "You're not trying to set me up with Oliver," I asked them. "Because that would be creepy and invasive, right?"

I waited for them to agree. *"Right?"*

"Of course not!" my mom said. "We just thought that maybe Oliver would like to make a few friends and since you *were* friends . . ." Her voice trailed off, her eyes hopeful.

I sighed as I took my dad's still-offered money, and he kissed my forehead just before I ducked away and went to find my shoes.

My mom watched as I trudged through the back door a few minutes later, her eyes on me as I slipped through the broken slat in our backyard fence. "Drive safe!" she called. "And check in after the movie, okay?" I pretended I didn't hear her, even though I always heard her. In the years since Oliver had disappeared, my parents had reacted by making sure *I* wouldn't disappear, too: early curfews (in the summer, the last dregs of sunset still streaked the sky when I had to come home), homework first, and a slew of extracurricular activities up until this year, when I put my foot down and insisted that I needed more time to study. It was kind of true, but I had really wanted—no, I *needed*—more time to surf. And breathe. And get some space from them and all their nervous reminders of the ways things could go so wrong, so fast.

Oliver's backyard had gotten weedier and more overgrown in the past two weeks, which was understandable. Who has time to mow the lawn when your son comes home after ten years? I knocked on the back door, three fast knocks that echoed my rapidly beating heart. I squinted a little against the sun, and when Oliver opened it, I sort of took a step back. "Oh," I said. "Um, hi. Hi."

"Hi," he said. "My mom's not here, she took the twins to get new shoes." His hair was rumpled, like he had been lying on his bed for too long, and his shirt was a little wrinkled.

"Oh, cool." *Why would that be cool, Emmy? Shoe shopping with four-year-olds is not cool.* "No, actually I'm here to see, um, you? My mom and dad thought that maybe we could hang out?" Once the words were out of my mouth I wanted to cram them back in. I sounded ridiculous, like some made-up character in a health class textbook. *No, thanks, I don't want any drugs. Hey, how about we play a board game instead?*

"Hang out?" Oliver repeated, but he didn't sound entirely disinterested. "Yeah, sure. Okay."

"Okay!" I said, entirely too cheerful. "Cool, yeah! Okay. Cool. I have my car, or you could drive or—"

"I don't have a license," he said. "I didn't really need one in New York."

"Oh yeah. Right. Okay. Well, then, I guess I'll drive. Don't want to do anything illegal, right?" I tried to smile as I realized, *I just made a joke about illegal activity to someone who had been kidnapped for ten years.* Oh God. Let the trauma begin.

But Oliver just turned around. "Give me a few minutes. Gotta find my keys." He patted his pockets, like they were hiding somewhere in his jeans.

"Sure!" I said, then went to fire up my car, my jaw tight with embarrassment.

This was all my parents' fault.

"So," I said once Oliver was settled in the front seat of my car, "what do you want to do?"

"I don't know." He shrugged. "What do you do here?"

"Not a lot," I admitted. "The movies, coffee, ice cream. Just hang out at the Spectrum, usually." I paused for a few seconds before adding, "It's a new shopping center. Well, not *new* new, but it went up right after . . ."

Right after you were kidnapped.

I needed a subject change, fast. "What did you do in New York?"

"Oh, you know, movies, coffee, ice cream," he said, then looked over and smiled. That motion made something in my heart seize up for a few seconds. "No, seriously, whatever you want to do," he said, not realizing what he had done. "It's cool. I have one question, though."

"Yeah?" I asked as I backed down the driveway. I could see my parents peeking through the blinds and I ignored them.

He glanced down at the floor. "Why the hell is there so much *sand* in your minivan?"

I glanced over at Oliver, then back at the blinds, which had quickly snapped back into place. "You really want to know what I do around here?" I asked him. "Because if you do, you *cannot* tell my parents. They'll murder me."

Oliver raised an eyebrow. "Literally?"

"Metaphorically," I amended. "Which would probably be worse."

"Deal," he agreed.

"Cool," I said. "Do you have swim trunks?"

Oliver hesitated for a few seconds. "Yes?"

"Go get them and then we'll find Drew."

Drew lived five minutes away and when we pulled into his massive driveway, he was standing in the garage, surrounded by boxes and a broom. "I'm helping my dad," he said before I could even ask. "We're"—he made finger quotes around the word—

"*bonding*. Oh, hey, Oliver. Hey."

Oliver startled a little but just nodded at Drew. "Hey, man."

"Drew," he introduced himself. "I'm Drew."

"Oh, right," Oliver said. "Right. Sorry."

Drew gave me a look that clearly begged to know more, but I ignored him. "Can we borrow your board and wet suit?" I asked him. "I'm going to teach Oliver how to surf."

"You're what?" Oliver and Drew both said.

I grinned at them. "You asked me what we did around here," I said to Oliver. "This is what I do. Just don't tell my parents, remember?"

"Because they'll metaphorically kill you," Oliver repeated dutifully. "Got it."

"They will," Drew agreed. "Or send her to Bible camp."

"My parents don't even go to church!" I said.

"Bible camp is the last refuge of every desperate parent, regardless of religious affiliation," Drew said, his eyes cutting over to Oliver as he realized what he said. Luckily, Oliver just seemed amused. "C'mon, dude, let's get you suited up."

We left a few minutes later, Drew's old wet suit and board shoved next to mine in the back of the minivan. "So when did you learn to surf?" Oliver asked as we waited at a light, the ocean shimmering down the hill below us.

"A few years ago," I admitted. "Drew's older brother, Kane, taught me when I was fourteen. It was the summer before he went to college and he had already taught Drew and it was just . . ." I searched for a word that didn't exist. "It just felt like I discovered something that made me feel different than I had felt before. It made *me* different. I didn't think I'd like it at first, but I loved it. I still love it." I adjusted my sunglasses as the sun came pouring in through the windshield, the afternoon bright and warm. "Drew goes out a lot with me, but Caro doesn't like it too much. She hates the seaweed."

Look at me, conversing with Oliver! I thought to myself. *And no one's been traumatized yet!*

"Got it." Oliver had his elbow resting against the open window, the air blowing his hair back and forth across his forehead. "So how long has Drew been gay?"

I bristled immediately, my voice sharp. "Um, since he was conceived?"

"No, I meant—sorry, that's not what I meant at all. I meant, when did he come out? Or—has he yet?"

Stand down, tiger. I told myself. *Just some innocent questions.*

"He came out to his parents last year," I said, my spine relaxing. "But we've known for, like, ever. It wasn't exactly a secret, but I think Drew's parents were a little surprised. They were cool with it but . . ."

"But not really?" Oliver offered.

"They say they love him all the time," I told him, remembering how Drew's voice had shaken when he told Caro and me about that. "But I think they have to learn to love a different version of him than the one they were expecting. Which is silly, because

Drew is just Drew. He's not different, you know? It's just the way they're looking at him that's changed."

Oliver nodded, his lips pursed as he thought about that. "Sometimes love isn't something you say, it's something you do," he finally said. "Or, I don't know, at least that's what it seems like."

I glanced at Oliver and wondered whose parents we were discussing now.

"Agreed," I said, then decided to take a risk. "I'm sorry people are being such creeps at school. It sucks. And that milk carton shit was stupid."

"Yeah, well, what are you gonna do?" Oliver shrugged. "I'm the star of the month, I guess. My mom and the principal had a meeting about it, which was *totally* helpful." The sarcasm practically dripped off his teeth. "Don't tell anyone about that, okay? It won't help."

"No worries," I said. "What'd they say, though?"

"That I should see the guidance counselor in addition to a therapist." Oliver sighed a little, his breath disappearing into the wind as I turned a corner. "Don't tell anyone about that, either."

"Well, lucky for you, you are in the perfect car for keeping secrets." I gestured to the surfboards in the back. "And therapists are the worst," I added. "If you wanted to talk about things, you'd talk about them, right?"

"You've been?"

I realized my mistake too late. "Yeah, well, after you . . . you know."

"After my dad kidnapped me. You can say it."

"After your dad kidnapped you," I echoed, but the words sounded a lot sadder coming out of his mouth than they did coming out of mine. "Me and Caro and Drew, we all went, but then one of them made Drew cry—I don't remember what he said, exactly, but he said something—and so Caro kicked the therapist and then I kicked him and we didn't have to go anymore."

"Why'd you kick him?"

"Because I," I said, placing my hand over my heart, "am a very loyal friend, Oliver."

He startled a little again, even as he laughed. "Good to know. So you're saying I should kick my therapist?"

"You have a real gift for reading between the lines," I said, then pulled the car into a parking space and clapped my hands down on top of the steering wheel. "Now then. Are you ready for the best surfing lesson of your life?"

"You mean first and maybe only surfing lesson?"

"Possibly."

"Absolutely," he said, and we climbed out of the car.

CHAPTER NINE

Oliver was terrible. I mean, I thought Caro was bad when Kane first taught us that day on the beach, but Oliver made her look like Laird Hamilton.

"Okay," I said when we carried our boards down to the beach, trying not to trip on the steep wooden steps. "First, suit up." I pointed at Drew's wet suit. "Zipper goes in the back. You want it to be tight but not so tight that you can't move your arms or legs. You don't want to look like a penguin."

"I didn't think the first rule in a surfing lesson would be 'don't look like a penguin,'" Oliver said, trying not to fall as he stepped into the legs of the suit.

"Hey." I shrugged. "You get what you pay for." I had never taught anyone how to surf, but I remembered my first lesson with Kane like it had just happened a few hours earlier, rather than three years ago. What could go wrong?

Oliver stumbled a little and I moved so he could hold on to my shoulder. I still hadn't taken off my dress and I realized that I was about to be standing in front of my childhood friend in a bathing suit for the first time in ten years.

Real smart, Emmy. You're a genius. Definitely apply for that Fulbright scholarship as soon as you get a chance.

I waited until Oliver was busy trying to pull up the zipper on the back of his suit, then turned around and quickly slipped my dress over my head before stepping into the wet suit. I always felt better when I had my wet suit on, like all the feelings and thoughts I had could be contained, like they had a safe place to be. "It's your second skin," Caro had once laughed, but she was right. It was. I just wished it fit better. It was secondhand from Craigslist. It sagged in the legs and arms, and I fantasized about buying a brand-new one that fit perfectly, but babysitting money only went so far.

"Okay, lie flat on the board," I said once we were outfitted and I checked to make sure that the neck closure on Oliver's suit was Velcroed into place. "Palms on the front of the board. You want to be right in the middle so you don't lose your balance on the water."

"Got it," he said, grunting a little as he got into position. He was squinting against the afternoon sun's rays reflecting on the water, tiny little diamond glints of light. "Am I surfing now?"

"Not quite." I laughed and then moved his hands a little bit. They were warmer than mine. "Did you ever see the movie *Point Break*?"

"About a million times. It was on cable a lot when I was home alone."

"Well, I'm Patrick Swayze and you're Keanu Reeves."

"Righteous," Oliver said, and we grinned at each other. "When do we rob the banks?"

We practiced popping up for a few minutes. He was pretty good at this part, but everyone is. Surfing is a lot easier when you're not in the water.

After I thought he was ready (which, it turned out, was a *slight* miscalculation on my part), we walked down to the water, dragging our boards behind us in the sand, the leashes attached to our ankles. "You ready?" I asked him, wishing I had remembered to wear sunscreen. The sun was hot and it always feels warmer when you're encased in a rubber suit.

"Quick question," Oliver said as he scanned the horizon. "What is the shark population like around here?"

I blinked at him. "Are you being serious right now?"

"I don't know." He laughed nervously. "No. Yes. Maybe? Sharks?"

I sighed. "There are no sharks here."

"Do you mean 'here' as in the 'Pacific Ocean' or . . . ?"

"Okay, yes, there are sharks in the Pacific Ocean *somewhere* but I don't think—"

"Could you be a little more specific about the word *somewhere*?"

"Oliver," I said. There was the flinch again. "If Patrick Swayze saw a shark, what do you think he would have done?"

"I also didn't see this surf lesson involving that question."

"Patrick Swayze would punch that shark in the nose," I answered for him. "And that's what I will do for you, okay?"

"For me?" He put his hand to his chest and pretended to be flattered.

"I told you, I'm a loyal friend. Kicking therapists, punching sharks, whatever it takes."

"Okay," he finally said. "Let's do this."

"Great," I said. "Now let's see what you're made of."

"I bet that's what the sharks are saying right now," Oliver muttered, but he paddled out behind me.

He had strong arms, it turned out, and the waves were flat enough that it wasn't too hard to get past them and out to a few bigger swells. "What do you do if the waves are big when you're paddling out?" he asked when I pointed that out.

"You turtle," I replied, then held on to the sides of my board and flipped it over just as a slightly bigger wave crashed over me. The board protected me from the wave and I waited until I felt the whoosh of the water recede before I turned over and came back up. "See?" I sputtered, wiping my hair out of my eyes. "Like a turtle. Your board becomes a shell to protect you."

"Pretty cool," Oliver said. He looked impressed.

"Lucky for you, these are baby waves." We continued to paddle out and when we were far enough, I hopped off my board and went to swim next to him. "Do you remember what we practiced on the shore?"

"Yeah, it happened, like, three minutes ago."

I just smiled. "It's amazing what you can forget when a giant force of nature is rushing toward you."

"That's . . . really reassuring, thanks."

"I like to provide a dose of realism," I said, then watched as a wave started to build about fifty feet away from us. "You see this wave?"

Oliver craned his neck to look over his shoulder. "What wave? Is that even a wave?"

"It will be. And it's going to be your wave."

Oliver just looked at me. "You're serious."

"Like a heart attack. I'll give you a shove. Now, just before the wave hits you, start paddling. Paddle like"—I had a burst of genius—"like a shark is after you, all right? Just go until you feel the wave pick up the board, then use your arms to pop up. Easy peasy."

Oliver's eyes widened. "Tell me again why you do this for fun?"

"Because it's awesome!" I told him as the wave came closer. "Are you ready?"

"No! Yes!"

"Go go go go go GO!" I gave the tail of his board a shove just as the wave started to crest, and Oliver began to paddle furiously, his hands going in and out of the water at an impressive speed. "Faster!" I yelled as he started to cruise away from me. "You can do it! Stand up, stand up!"

"What?" I heard him yell, but then he let out a shout, like a battle cry or a victory sound, and I watched as Oliver . . . did nothing.

"Stand up!" I yelled. "You can do it!"

I heard him yell something but I couldn't hear him this time, and I climbed back up on my board just so I could see a little better. He was laughing at least, his hair wet across his forehead as he literally lay on top of his board until it ground into the shore and got stuck in the sand. I caught the next wave, taking advantage of the white water so I wouldn't have to paddle too much and wear myself out, and rode it in to meet up with Oliver.

"That was so cool!" he yelled when he saw me.

"You didn't even try!" I laughed, falling off my board and righting myself before I was completely submerged. "You just stayed there!"

"No, what you just did. You made it look easy!"

I wiped the salt water out of my eyes (Visine was my friend, lest my parents think that my red eyes were a part of a raging pot-smoking habit) and looked at him. "What happened? There was no actual surfing!" I teased.

"I decided to take it easy my first time," he said. "Also, that shit is hard."

I grinned at him. "Round two?"

"Race you."

We paddled back out.

✳ ✳ ✳

Three tries later, Oliver managed to get to his knees, but wouldn't let go of the edges of the board. By the fifth time, he was standing. "YEAAAHH!!!" I screamed as I rode in just behind him. "You did it!"

"I fell, like, two seconds later," he said, but I could tell he was proud. His cheeks were flushed, and whether it was from pride, embarrassment, the cold water, or the hot sun, I couldn't tell.

"But it counts!" I said. "You surfed!"

Oliver was hanging on to the edge of his board, his legs dangling in the water, and I circled back to meet him. "What's wrong?" I said. "Need a break?"

He shook his head. "No, I'm fine. It was just . . . I haven't had fun since I've been back. And that was really fun."

Now I was the one whose cheeks were flushed.

"Oh. Oh, well, yeah. Of course. I like surfing and I don't really have anyone else to go out with besides Drew, so . . ." I shrugged. "Anytime you need a buddy."

A buddy, Emmy? Good Lord. What is this, AA or something?

"Go again?" Oliver said. "I think I've gotten my second wind."

I glanced at the sun. Judging from its position, it was almost five, and I had to be home (with passable dry hair) by seven. "Two more rides," I said. "I'm on this ridiculous curfew. I'm basically only allowed outside during daytime hours. Do you have a curfew or anything?"

Oliver shrugged. "I have no idea. I don't really go anywhere. I could call my mom. . . ." he added, but the look on his face told me that that wasn't his favorite option.

"Two more rides," I said again. "C'mon, let's go. Sunset and surfing. What more do you need?"

Oliver needed a lot, I knew that. He needed more than anything I could provide on that afternoon. But right then, sunsets and surfing, just maybe, were enough.

CHAPTER TEN

By the time we got out of the water, I was shivering a little and Oliver's lips were blue. "I thought this was California," he said, his teeth chattering as he spoke. The sun was setting, a glorious firework of reds and pinks and oranges as it sank behind Catalina Island, leaving us until tomorrow. With the sun gone, now it was just cold. "I thought it was supposed to be warm in winter."

"It's all relative," I said, wrapping my towel around my shoulders and bringing the corners up to my mouth, warming my face a little. Next to me, Oliver was doing the same thing, both of us watching the waves.

"Thanks," he said after a minute. "Sorry I sucked."

I shrugged. "I was terrible the first time, too. You just have to keep practicing, right?"

"If you say so."

I shivered again as a breeze blew up behind us. "Are you hungry?"

"Yeah. Yeah, definitely." Oliver opened his towel so that it fanned out behind him like a cape, the ends clenched in his fists. He looked so much different like this, not the skulking guy I saw in the hallway at school, not the little boy I used to go on the swings with back in kindergarten. He looked like a stranger, and then he met my glance, and it was like I had never stopped seeing him.

I shivered again. This time, there was no breeze.

Oliver came to stand next to me as the sun continued to set. The sand was peppered with tourists taking pictures, and locals out for walks with their dogs, and everyone looked so soft and pretty, bathed in the pink-and-golden light that only ever seemed to exist at the edge of a continent. "What island is that?" Oliver asked.

"Hawaii," I replied.

"Shut up, it is not."

I smiled. "It's Catalina. There's a ferry that goes back and forth a few times a day, but I've never been. I'd rather go to Hawaii, to be honest."

Oliver nodded and I wondered if that's where'd he rather be, as well.

And then the last sliver of sun disappeared and the spell was broken and we were still standing in the same place, whether we liked it or not.

"You said something about food . . . ?" Oliver nudged.

"Yes! Food. Starving. Must eat. Do you like burritos?"

"I like all food," he replied.

"Follow me."

We used the shower at the base of the stairs to rinse off the sand and salt. I peeled off the top half of my wet suit and tried to rinse it as best I could. The spray from the shower was cold and stinging, yet it never really managed to get all the sand off. "Ow!" I said as some salt got into my eyes. "I hate this shower, I really do."

At the nozzle next to mine, Oliver was wincing as the water hit his shoulders. After much hoopla that saw him hopping up and down on one foot and me laughing hysterically, he had managed to get out of the wet suit and now held it up under the shower. "That was more of a workout than surfing was," he said, trying to keep getting hit by the wonky spray. "Is this supposed to hurt this much?"

"They're not the best," I admitted, quickly pulling my dress over my wet bathing suit. "You get used to it."

Oliver just muttered something I couldn't hear and winced again as the spray knocked him right in the chest.

We managed to get the boards back up the stairs, where we threw them into the trunk of my car, and I reached into the back of my van and pulled out a pair of jeans for myself and some hoodies for both of us. "Here," I said, tossing one at him. "Thank me later."

Oliver, to his immense credit, didn't say anything about it being a "girl" hoodie and just tugged it over his head. It was enormous on me, so much so that it was still big on him, and the hood settled on the top of his head, making him look like an overgrown garden gnome. "What?" he said as I started to giggle. "What, does it not match my jeans? Is it last season?"

"You look like a Disney cartoon reject," I said as I tugged my jeans up under my dress. (I was definitely warmer, but wearing wet bathing suit bottoms under jeans can be filed under the category "NO FUN EVER.")

Oliver looked at his reflection in the passenger window, then grinned. "I'm the eighth dwarf," he said. "Surfy."

"Ha! If anything, I'm Surfy. You're . . ."

"Newbie?"

"Perfect." I shucked the dress and threw it into the van before pulling my own hoodie over my head. It smelled like it had been in the van a little too long, which was definitely not pleasant, but it was warm enough that I didn't care. "Okay," I said, slamming the door shut. "Let's eat."

"After you," Oliver said.

We crossed PCH and went to the Stand, a tiny outdoor restaurant that was aptly named. The menu was written underneath the ordering window, but I didn't have to look. "You already know?" Oliver said, not taking his eyes off the menu.

"Yep. Same thing every time. Potato and guacamole burrito, green juice. It balances out the guacamole," I added when Oliver side-eyed me.

"I'm not sure that's how nutrition works, Emmy."

I pretended not to notice that it was the first time that he had said my name since he had come home.

"Are you a nutritionist?" I asked, then continued before he could answer. "No, I don't think you are, so be quiet."

He smirked like someone who knew that science was on his side.

I gave them my order while Oliver stood next to me, then slid the twenty-dollar bill my dad had given me under the window. "It's for both of us," I told the cashier, jerking my thumb at Oliver.

"Hey, wait, no—"

"It's on my dad," I said. "He thinks we went to the movies."

"Oh. Okay. Well, now that you've brought me into your web of lies . . ." He looked at the menu for another second, then said, "I'll have the same as her."

"You've chosen wisely," I said. "The web of lies will totally be worth it."

We grabbed a tiny table on the side of the restaurant, two stools and a rickety wooden table that looked like it wouldn't survive the next rainstorm. We were looking directly at the parking lot, but if we sat up straight, we could see across the street and out to the ocean where we had just surfed a few moments earlier. "Just think, Oliver," I said, pretending not to notice the way he winced. "You conquered that today."

"I think YOU conquered that," he countered, playing with the paper-napkin dispenser. "I just sort of . . . floated."

"No, you did really well!" I insisted. "You stood up on your board, that's a big deal."

He shrugged. "Maybe. You're the expert, you would know."

His gaze was a little further away than it had been when we were in the ocean, though, and his voice was flat. "Can I ask you a question?" I said.

"Only if I can ask you one."

"That's fair." It also wasn't the response I had been expecting, but I rolled with it. "Do you want me to call you Colin?"

Oliver set down the napkin dispenser with a small *clang!* then turned to look at me. His eyes were bright—some thought or emotion burning behind them. "Why?"

"Because you flinch every time someone calls you Oliver," I said. I wondered if I had just waded into a conversation that was over my head. My dad was right. We should have just gone to the movies.

The food arrived then, nestled in red plastic baskets lined with wax paper. I'm always happy to see a burrito, of course, but I don't think I've ever been so happy for a distraction as I was right then. "Thanks!" I said to the server with *waaaay* more enthusiasm than the situation required, but he just nodded and left us alone again.

"Sorry," Oliver said. "I didn't mean to sound, like, mad or anything. No one's called me that name since I've been back, is all. It kind of startled me. Sorry."

I was still looking at him. His hair was falling over his forehead again and I had a sudden urge to push it back, run my fingers across his skin and ease the worry away. "You don't have to apologize," I said quietly. "I get it. I mean, I don't really *get* it, but I just wondered if you would feel better if I called you something else, that's all."

Oliver sighed a little, picking up a chip and shaking it between his fingers before popping it into his mouth. "You're right, these are good," he said, then grabbed a few more. I ate some, too, then took a sip of my juice. I think we were both waiting for someone to say something, anything.

"When we first moved," Oliver said, his eyes watching as pelicans flew over our heads in a wavy line that swooped up and down over the rooftops, "my dad said that he had always wanted to call me Colin, but my mom was the one who insisted on Oliver. So he asked if it would be okay if I started using that name instead. And I just wanted to make him happy, because y'know, he was my dad and he seemed so upset that my mom was gone, so I said yeah. And it stuck." Oliver shrugged as he balled up a napkin in his fist. "I guess I'm just not used to hearing Oliver. I thought Oliver disappeared with my mom, only it turns out that both of those things were never really gone, soooo . . ." He looked at me and smiled. "I'm really fucked up, in case that wasn't clear."

I took a page from Drew's playbook and gave Oliver some space to think. Then he took a sip of his green smoothie. "Oh my God," he spat, wincing. "I'm fucked up, but not as much as this smoothie. You drink these things on purpose?"

I giggled and bit my straw. "It's good for you!" I insisted. "It's *green*!"

He pushed it toward me, wiping his mouth on the back of his hand. "Here, have some extra health. My treat."

I couldn't tell if he actually hated it or if he was just lightening the mood, but I didn't protest.

Oliver laughed a little, then reached for his burrito. "You're *sure* this is good?" he asked before taking a bite. "Because that smoothie ruined your credibility."

"See for yourself," I told him, then took a huge bite out of mine. Lettuce and cheese spilled out and I arched an eyebrow at Oliver, who laughed and took a bite of his own.

"Okay," he said after a minute of chewing. "Credibility restored. And now I get to ask you a question."

"Hit it," I said.

"How come you don't want your parents to know that you surf?"

"Because they're crazy overprotective," I said, reaching for a napkin. "They don't want me to do anything dangerous or something where I might get hurt."

"Why?"

That was the question I didn't want him to ask. But he had been honest with me, so I decided to be honest with him.

"After you went missing," I said carefully, wiping my mouth and trying to look anywhere but at Oliver, "everyone was so scared. All the parents went on lockdown mode, especially mine and, I don't know, they haven't really stopped. I think it was hard on them, you know? The kid next door, one day he's there and the next day he's gone. And I'm their only kid and they just wanted to protect me."

"Do you ever think about telling them you come here?"

"Sometimes," I admitted. "But at the same time, it's nice having it just for myself. Like, no one tells me when to surf or how to do it or whether or not it's good enough. I can just . . . do it." I blushed a tiny bit at the phrase. "No one's grading me or making me take the AP Surfing test, you know?"

Oliver laughed at that. He had a tiny bit of guacamole in the corner of his mouth, which looked endearing instead of gross. A second later, though, he wiped it away. "AP Surfing," he repeated. "That would be cool."

"There's a surf team at school," I said. "But I need parental permission and there's lots of fees and I'd have be at the beach by five forty-five every morning and I haven't really figured out how to explain that to my parents, so yeah." I shrugged and ate another chip. Surfing always left me starving afterward. "On my island."

"Excuse me?"

"It's something Caro and I say. Like, if you don't like the way something is, you just say 'on my island!' As if things would be different on your own private island where you could make up all the rules."

"Well, on my island, no one would have ever created that smoothie-juice thing," Oliver said, moving the cup even closer to me. "Because that's not right."

"It's all natural!" I protested even as I laughed. "Made from nature!"

"Nature is cruel," Oliver replied.

"Well, we'll just see who's stronger and fitter when we go surfing next time," I said without thinking, then realized that I just invited Oliver to hang out again.

He looked at me a second longer than he had before. "Again?" he repeated before chowing down on another chip. "Yeah, that'd be cool. It's not like I have plans or anything."

I twisted the napkin between my fingers. "Not to sound like I was stalking you or anything, but I saw you watching movies in your room."

Oliver just nodded. "Yeah, my dad and I, we used to watch movies together. He was a big film buff and he got me into it." Now Oliver was shredding his napkin. Between the two of us, the napkins didn't stand a chance.

"That's cool," I said. "You know, there's a film-appreciation club at school, you could . . ." But I trailed off as Oliver just looked at me, skepticism in his eyes.

"Not joining any clubs," he said. "That's not my thing."

"Not everyone is an asshole at our school," I pointed out, "but I'm sorry you're getting harassed. It's just because you're new. They'll get over it."

"What makes you think I'd want to be friends with them in the first place?"

I didn't have an answer.

He looked at the skyline, which had turned blue and purple to match the ocean. "Thanks for asking me to hang out today," he finally said. "It was fun. I'm glad I didn't die."

"I'm glad you didn't die, either," I said. "It'd be bad if you disappeared for ten years, then you died on my watch two weeks after you got back."

"Yes, it would," Oliver said, smiling at me. He looked like his second-grade photograph, the one that had been plastered on MISSING signs everywhere. "I was starting to go nuts just hanging out with my mom and Rick the whole time."

"Well, they said we should give you some sp—*time* to adjust," I said. The word *space* sounded mean all of a sudden, like Oliver was a shrapnel bomb set to explode.

He just laughed. "Not enough time for that." Before I could respond, he looked at me. "Hey, you cold? You're shivering."

"A little," I admitted. I hadn't even noticed until he said it. "What, are you going to do something chivalrous like give me your coat?"

"What coat? All I've got is your hoodie and it smells like the back of your car," he replied. "C'mon, finish so we can crank the heat and get back so you can lie to your parents."

"Sounds like a plan," I agreed, and we finished our burritos and went back across the street to the car. My hair was almost dry, but hopefully I could sneak into the shower before my parents noticed all the salt that would inevitably crust up around my hairline.

In the car, Oliver looked at me as we sat at a light, his face highlighted in red. "Hey," he said. "What movie did we see?"

"Oh yeah, right. Let's get our story straight. Um, the new one with that Australian actor guy."

"Okay, good. Don't screw up under pressure, Emmy. We've come this far, we can't go back!"

"I won't!" I laughed. "I've been lying to my parents way longer than you have, don't forget."

"True. Hey."

"Hmm?"

"I'm sorry there's a gap in our friendship."

"Yeah," I said, glancing at him. "Me too. But it's not our fault."

He was about to say something, but the light changed to green and he sat back as I hit the gas, the light telling us it was time to go.

CHAPTER ELEVEN

When we got back, I pulled the car into the driveway and cut the engine. "I'm covered in sand," Oliver said, brushing at the leg of his jeans. "How are we supposed to keep this a secret, again?"

"We went to the Stand for dinner after the movie because we were starving, and then we walked on the beach." I turned in my seat to look at him. "Please do not blow this for me."

"I won't, I won't," he said. "And, wow, you're good at lying."

"We aren't *lying*, per se," I said as I unbuckled my seat belt. "We're just protecting my parents from the truth that would kill them."

"We weren't anywhere near a movie theater," Oliver protested, but stopped talking once he saw the look on my face. "Sorry, okay. Zipping it now."

I narrowed my eyes at him, then got out of the car. "Lying is relative," I whispered after he slammed his door shut. "And what people don't know won't hurt them."

"I have ten years' worth of experience that says otherwise," he replied.

"Shit, sorry, that's not what I meant—"

Oliver winked at me. "Partners in crime, I got it." He held his fist out and I bumped our knuckles together. "Get home safe."

"I'm literally ten feet away from my door," I said, glancing toward the front window to see if my parents were still peeking out between the blinds. (I wouldn't have been surprised if they had set up camp with comfortable chairs and some snacks.)

"Well, you never know." Oliver shrugged. "Accidents happen closest to home. You could trip over a sprinkler head, a loose brick, anything's possible."

"Thanks for the vote of confidence," I told him. "I appreciate it."

"Later, gator," he said, jogging off toward his front steps, and I watched as he clicked the lock open and then disappeared into the light.

My own house was quiet, deceptively so. My dad was sprawled on the couch watching an infomercial for a vacuum that cleans up pet hair, but my mom was nowhere to be found. "Hey," I said to him.

"Hey," he said without looking up from the TV. "You hungry? Your mom left dinner."

"No, we ate," I said. "What are you watching?"

"It gets rid of pet hair."

"We don't even have a goldfish."

"You've got to think toward the future." My dad smiled at me. "Maybe one day you'll move out and your mom and I will get a golden retriever to replace you."

"We can only dream," I said. "It'll probably be more loyal than me. Where's Mom?"

"At a thing with some friends, I'm not sure. A fund-raiser thing with Oliver's mom, maybe."

"Good thing you're not an investigative reporter," I replied, then went into the kitchen for a drink.

"Hey, how was the movie?" my dad yelled.

"Dumb!" I called back. I didn't actually know, but I had seen a few previews online and they didn't hold much hope.

"How's Oliver?"

"Fine!"

"Are you eating?"

"Maybe!"

"Bring me something."

I tossed my dad a package of Goldfish crackers as I went up the stairs.

An hour later, I had showered and washed my hair, which kept dripping all over my history work sheet. I was listening to music, so loud that I didn't hear the knock on my bedroom door.

"Come in," I said, half hoping it was my dad with more Goldfish crackers.

"Have fun?" my mom asked, poking her head in.

I nodded and shut my laptop before she came any closer. Not that there's even anything interesting on there, but I didn't want her to get any ideas about violating my privacy. Best to keep the parents guessing. "Yeah, it was cool." The silence was suddenly very loud in the absence of the music.

"Care to offer up any details for your old mom?"

I shrugged. "I don't know. We went to the movies, it was dumb, and then we went to dinner and hung out."

She sat down on the edge of the bed. "Did you talk?"

"About what?"

"About anything. Maureen said that Oliver doesn't really talk to her."

"We . . . talked," I said, trying to figure out how much to tell my mom before she would tell Maureen. Oliver hadn't said that I should keep any secrets, but I felt like it wasn't my information to share. "Sometimes it's just weird to talk to your parents, y'know? Maureen's overreacting."

My mom nodded slowly, the way she always does whenever she disagrees with me but doesn't want to say so for fear that I'll stop speaking to her altogether. "Well, I'm glad Oliver has you for a friend."

"Oliver's always had me for a friend," I replied.

"Did you have fun?"

"Yeah, sure. He's funny. He's really smart, too."

"Funny?" my mom repeated. "How so?"

"Spanish Inquisition," I said to her, which made her smile. "I'm sorry, you've exceeded your maximum amount of questions today. Please try again tomorrow."

She stood up and kissed my forehead. "Don't stay up too late, okay? You need your rest."

The jury was still out on that last statement, but I let it go. Sometimes it was just easier to pretend to agree. "'Kay," I said.

After she left, I turned the music back on and reached to turn off my lamp, trying not to think about anything for a few minutes. That's always impossible, though. It's easier to stop breathing than it is to stop thinking. After Oliver vanished, I used to try to not think about him, but he just bobbed to the surface of my thoughts again and again, the boy who disappeared but never went away.

My hand was still on the lamp.

I was almost too scared to do it, to turn the light on and off. When we were kids, we used to flick our lights to signal each other after we had to go to bed. We tried working out a system but I usually got impatient and just opened the window and yelled across the air to him instead.

The first few nights after Oliver left, I used to sit in bed and turn the lamp's plastic switch on and off again and again, my silent, desperate Morse code. At first, I thought that maybe he was just hiding in his room in a really expert game of hide-and-seek, but a few weeks later, my parents found me at three in the morning, my nightgown soaked in tears, my fingers red and raw from turning the switch so hard and so often.

After that, I usually left the light on at night. If Oliver came home, I wanted him to know that I was there.

Now I was sitting in the dark, looking out the window. The light was off in his room, just like before, but I could see movement in the hallway outside his door. Was Oliver there? I thought about the tall guy that had sheepishly climbed out of the cop car, had stood up on that surfboard, his brow furrowed both times. It was and it wasn't him, and I wondered if he was thinking the same thing about me.

The plastic knob hurt my fingers when I clicked it on and off.

Sunspots lit up my vision for a minute. My heart was pounding so hard that I was pretty sure I could see it moving my shirt. *It's okay if he doesn't remember this,* I thought. *It's okay if he doesn't remember. It doesn't mean anything.*

Across our yards, Oliver's light flicked on, then off a few seconds later, and I smiled into the darkness.

CHAPTER TWELVE

A week later, the news crews came to interview Oliver. It was just for the local station, nothing national, Oprah wasn't knocking down the door or anything. But the cameras are always the same size, hulking and unblinking, and they took over Oliver's living room for the afternoon while Maureen hustled the little girls over to our house.

"I've been cleaning all morning," she said, breathless as she practically shoved Molly through the front door. "Oops, sorry, sweetie. Mommy's sorry." She blew the hair out of her eyes, her bangs fluttering before landing in the exact same spot on her forehead. "They wanted to do it at home, you know, just make it look really . . . homey. Like, where he belongs."

My mom and I, neither of us sure who she was talking to, both nodded. Molly frowned up at her mom, then leaned against my legs while Nora took hold of my hand. "Let's *plaaaaaay*," she whined. "Let's play Interview."

"Oliver wouldn't play," Molly murmured.

"He didn't have time, sweetie," Maureen said, then smoothed some stray hairs down. "Thank you so much for watching them. I didn't want them around all the . . ." She waved her hands and mouthed the word *media* at my mom and me before wrinkling her nose.

"We've just had so many calls," she continued, and I wondered if she had even taken a breath in between her words. "They all want to talk to me, to Oliver, find out how he's doing. They keep calling the house and it's just . . . you want the phone to ring for ten years and then one day it does and it doesn't stop."

Her voice was starting to sound dangerously wobbly, her eyes began to well up, and I quickly steered the girls toward the TV room. "Cartoons!" I said. "Don't fight over the remote!"

They scampered off.

"I'm sorry," Maureen said as soon as they were gone, fanning her fingers in front of her eyes again. "He's not talking to me and I don't know if he's happy and I got him this shirt but it's patterned and I remembered this morning that I read once that you shouldn't wear patterns on TV and—"

I knew about that shirt, but only because Oliver had dangled it out the window that morning and made the thumbs-up/thumbs-down sign at me. "Yeah?" he had called. It was a blue-checked shirt, not too dressy, collared with long sleeves. It would look good on him. Neither of us considered how it would look on a forty-six-inch flat screen in someone's living room. We didn't even know that was a thing that someone could worry about.

"Did your mom buy it?" I called back.

"Yeah!"

"Looks good!"

"You sure?"

I gave him the thumbs-up sign.

Now my mom was moving in, grasping Maureen by the upper arms. I recognized this as the Get a (Literal) Grip. A classic Mom move.

"Look, Mo," my mom said to her. "Oliver is *home* now. That's what's important. He's not *going* to talk to you, all right? He's seventeen. Emmy's seventeen and she *never* talks to me."

"It's true," I said. "I'm actually legally obligated to ignore her. The other teenagers and I made a pact. There were lawyers involved, it's a whole *thing* now."

"See?" My mom shot a grateful glance in my direction as Maureen laughed a little. "Just go do the interview, let people know that Oliver is home, that you and your family will be okay, and take it from there. Don't worry about his *shirt*, of all things." She squeezed Maureen's arms again, then let her go. "And your hair looks wonderful," she added. "I love the new highlights."

Maureen rolled her eyes but still patted her hair. "Oh, this. I just needed to do something for myself, you know?"

"Absolutely," my mom agreed. "We don't take enough time

for ourselves. Now go back. The girls are fine here and Emmy will keep an eye on them."

I was already edging away. "Good luck," I said, not sure if it was bad luck to wish someone good luck or vice versa, then scurried into the den before I had to hear any more mom conversations. They always made me uncomfortable, like they were the Ghost of Christmas Future, a life laid out for me that I wasn't even sure I wanted but felt destined to live, anyway.

The girls were toppled over each other on the couch, watching something loud and animated whose theme song would be stuck in my head for the rest of the day. The girls were both singing along with it under their breath, like the TV was compelling them to do its bidding.

I slipped in behind Nora on the couch. She stayed where she was, forcing her to sit on my legs. "Oliver got a new shirt," Molly said without looking away from the television. "It has blue squares on it."

"I heard," I said.

"I want a new shirt, too."

Nora was about to add something, probably about if Molly wanted a new shirt, then she wanted one, too, but then the show started and they were distracted again.

When the interview aired that night, the shirt looked good, not as bad as what Maureen was worried about. Oliver looked like, well, Oliver, his head oddly huge on the flat screen in Caro's living room. "Maureen looks like a long-tailed cat in a roomful of rocking chairs," Caro said, waving her hands over her just-painted toenails.

I smiled. "You got that saying from my dad."

"True and true. It's a good saying." She held her hand out to me. "Can you pass me the slutty one, please?"

I handed her the bottle of bright-red nail polish. "I think it's actually called Crimson Cabaret," I said. "Don't be a slut-shamer."

She unscrewed the bottle just as the screen shifted to a shot of Oliver's backyard, the twins' swing set front and center, a newer, safer version of the one he and I used to play on after school. "It's just such a relief to see him here again," Maureen was saying off camera as Oliver walked through the grass, flanked by both his mom and stepdad. "He was gone for so long and now that he's here, I just want to get to know him again."

"And how does it feel to be home?" the interviewer asked. Colleen Whitcomb had been the main news anchor since I could remember, her hair color and facial structure never changing once in fifteen years.

"Colleen's had work done," I said, carefully painting tiny blue dots in the center of each of my fingernails.

"Oh, *totally*," Caro agreed. "She probably makes so much money that she could hire a team of tiny elves to hide in her hairline and hold her face up."

"Creepy. They'd probably sing all these songs and be annoying."

"Good point. Wait, back it up, I missed what he said."

I reached for the remote and rewound it a few seconds, back to the original question of how it felt for Oliver to be home.

"It feels good," he said, smiling a little and tugging self-consciously at the button on his wrist cuff. I could see Maureen's fingers twitch, restraining herself from reaching out and stopping his fidgeting. "I just missed my mom and so it's good to see her again."

"Simple words," the newscaster's concluding voice-over said as Maureen smiled at Oliver, "that say . . ."

"Aaaand, dramatic pause . . ." Caro muttered, her eyes on the screen.

". . . so much more. Colleen Whitcomb for Channel Seven news."

I reached for the remote and muted the sound, trying not to disturb the blue dots. "Well, he looked happy, at least."

"Simple words that say? So much more," Caro repeated, mimicking Colleen's tone. "Who actually talks like that? That doesn't even *mean* anything. If I wrote that down on the AP English exam, I'd get a one. Maybe a two if the grader was hungover."

I nodded in agreement, eager to not talk about AP tests anymore. "Do *you* think he looked happy, though?"

Caro glanced back at the TV, even though the story was over. "I guess," she said. "I don't really know what Oliver's happy face looks like. Maybe he's just one of those people who looks perpetually underwhelmed."

"He doesn't always look underwhelmed!" I protested. "When we went surfing, he—"

"When you *what the what?*" Caroline all but chucked the bottle of Crimson Cabaret over her shoulder. "You went *surfing* with *Oliver?*"

"I didn't tell you? My parents made me, they practically shoved me out the door." I avoided Caro's eyes as I turned back to my nails.

"And you didn't *tell* me? Where's my phone?"

"Why do you need your phone? Are you going to tweet Colleen Whitcomb and give her the scoop?"

"No, I'm texting *Drew*. I don't care if he's out with Kevin right now, he needs to know about this."

"Wait, who's Kevin?" I ran through my mental Rolodex of the guys that Drew liked. "I don't know a Kevin."

"He's the homeschooled one. They played soccer last week and Drew's team beat his and then I guess they did that whole 'line up and shake hands' thing afterward and love blossomed." Caro fluttered her eyelashes dramatically. "You haven't met him yet."

"Why didn't Drew tell me?"

Caro was typing like her fingers were on fire, wet nail polish be damned. "Drew already knew about you and Oliver?" she cried, reading off her phone screen.

"There's no me and Oliver!" I said. "And of course he knew! Where do you think we got Oliver's board and wet suit from?"

"You're both dead to me," Caro muttered, still texting.

"Wait, though. Is Kevin cute?"

"He's cute in that tall, chiseled, soccer-playing way," Caro said. "So yeah, pretty much. Although, let's be honest, water polo is where it's at." She paused to read the screen. "Drew says he needs a ride to school on Monday because his van's getting detailed."

"Tell him I'll pick him up at seven."

"She'll . . . pick . . . you . . . up . . . at . . . seven." Caro narrated her text as she typed.

"Does Kevin look like David Beckham?"

Caro just raised an eyebrow. "How many high school seniors do you know that look like David Beckham?"

"Zero?"

"Exactly. And I don't even care about Kevin anymore. I care about you and Oliver surfing together." She sat on her knees next to me, like an eager puppy who had been promised a treat.

"What?" I laughed and turned back to my nails. "We surfed, we had dinner—"

"Oh my God, you went on a date with him."

"It was not a date!" I protested.

"If you eat food with a guy, it's a date. Proven fact. Don't argue with me, I don't make the rules. This is just how it is." Caro flapped her hands at me. "So? What else?"

"I don't know, I just taught him how to surf—"

"Was he good?"

"No, he was terrible. Almost as bad as you." I waited for Caro to respond, but she just nodded in agreement. "And then we went to the Stand and had food and then we came home."

"Do your parents know you guys went surfing?"

I bopped her on the head with one of the couch throw pillows. "No, are you crazy? I can't tell them that!"

"But they know you went out? What happened to giving him space?"

"Well, apparently, *now* we're easing back into suburban life."

Caro shook her head. "Sometimes you've got to cannonball into the pool," she said. "Just get it over with."

"Yeah, well, that works for *pools*, Caro." I waved my hands to dry my nails faster. "Not always actual real-life experiences."

Caro just looked thoughtful. "So you went with Oliver to the beach, ate dinner—"

"I paid, though."

"—I like your style, Emmy, very modern—and then lied about it to your parents. Sounds like a date to me."

"You know nothing," I told her. "I babysit for his sisters, he lives next door, we were friends a long time ago. We're just picking up where we left off."

Caro took the pillow from me and hugged it to her. "You can't pick up where you left off," she said, her voice softer, "because he's not the same person he was back then. You're on an entirely different road now."

This time, I didn't have an answer.

"Oh God," Caro finally said, and sat back on her heels. "You are in *so* much trouble."

CHAPTER THIRTEEN

I drove home from Caro's later that night, after texting my parents to reassure them that I was on my way home. It was a five-minute drive, three if I made all the lights, and I rolled down the window as I drove, letting the eucalyptus-soaked air blow my hair back. It was cold, but after the conversation I had had with Caro, it felt good, normal, a steady constant of the past ten years when things now felt like Dorothy's Kansas farmhouse, picked up and dropped aimlessly into a land that I couldn't recognize anymore, a light so bright it made me squint and wish for familiar black-and-white dimness instead.

I parked and was halfway up the steps when I heard the *screech-screech* sound of the twins' swing set next door, cutting into the night's silence. I paused and waited for it to stop, but it didn't. There was no way anyone inside could hear it, but to me, it was all I heard.

I pushed through the back gate, my front-door key still clutched in my fist in case the swing set was being used by a serial killer or something, but it was only Oliver. He was way too big for the swing, of course, his shoes dragging in the grass underneath the seat as he moved back and forth. His shirt was undone at the neck, the sleeves rolled up, looking more blue than checked in the muted backyard light.

"Hey," I whispered.

"Hey," he said back, using his feet to stop himself. "What are you doing here?"

I pointed up to where the swing's chains met the bar. "I heard you," I said. "I just got home from Caro's." I sat down in the swing next to his, setting my keys in the sand. "We had a super important TV interview to watch, you know."

Oliver huffed out a breath before he started to sway back and forth again. The movement was so small that his feet barely moved, looking like he was balanced on his toes. "Oh," he said. "That."

"And we did our nails, too," I added, holding up my hand. "Don't be jealous."

Oliver smiled and examined the blue dots. "You look diseased."

"You're really good with compliments."

"Don't let the secret get out."

I smiled and rested my head against the plastic chain of the swings. "What, should I tell Colleen Whitcomb? Give her the exclusive?" I held up an imaginary microphone, still giggling to myself even as I tried to do my best faux-newscaster voice. "So,

Oliver, how does it feel to *finally* . . . be home?"

He smiled, but I realized later that it wasn't turned up as much at the corners, that it didn't reach his eyes the way it should. "Well, Colleen," he said, playing along and speaking into my fist, "I'll tell you the truth. Can you handle an exclusive?"

"Yes," I said. "Our viewers"—I winked into an imaginary camera—"want to know."

Oliver looked up at me, his face solemn and pained, and I realized with a terrible rush that we weren't playing anymore. "Colleen," he said, "coming home feels like being kidnapped all over again."

I looked at him, waiting for the laugh or the "Just kidding!" something that wouldn't make my heart feel like it was free-falling. "What?" I said. My hand dropped to my side, the imaginary microphone plummeting into the grass.

"I'm sorry, I shouldn't—" Oliver blew out a slow breath and leaned back in the swing, still holding on tight to the chains. "I shouldn't have said that."

"Did you mean it?" I asked. Both of our houses were dark, the closed blinds letting out no cracks of light.

He bit his lip and looked away, then right back at me. "Yes," he said. "I meant it."

"Then you should say it," I whispered. "I don't want you to lie to me. You never lied to me before. Don't start now."

"It's just, it just feels the same." He shrugged, tipping his head to the sky like the stars had advice to offer him. "I got taken away from everything I knew, my friends, my dad, our apartment, homeschooling, and now I'm in a new house with sisters—I have *sisters*, Emmy, I don't even know what to say about that—and a mom I don't know and a stepdad I've *never* known, new friends, new school. And this house just feels so small, like the walls are touching sometimes when I sleep, and this town . . ." He trailed off, glancing toward the street like he could see a way out. "I don't know how you do it. I don't know how Drew does it."

I didn't know what to say. I had never thought of my town as small before, but Oliver had been all over the country. He had been living in New York. Suburbia must have felt like an itch he couldn't scratch.

"And I can't talk to my dad because I don't know where he is," he continued. "I can't ask him where he went, why he did this, just like I couldn't ask my mom where she went, why she left us."

"But she didn't leave you, Oliver, she—"

"I *know* that!" he said, sharper than usual, but his voice still sounded sad. "Sorry. I know that. But knowing something and feeling something are two totally different things. I barely even remember you, Emmy. Sorry, but it's true. I don't."

I didn't realize my eyes were filling with tears until he reached out to blot them with his thumb. "Shit," he sighed. "See? This is why I didn't want to tell you. I knew it would hurt you. This is why I don't tell anyone."

I pushed his hand away, though, shaking my head and wiping my own eyes. "You don't have to protect me," I said. "I told you, I don't want you to lie to me."

"But it's hurting you."

"It's hurting you, too." I dragged my wrist cuff across my eyes. "That's not fair."

"Nothing about this is fair," he said. We were both resting our heads against the swing chains now, swinging opposite each other in tiny arcs. More like rocking than swinging, really. "If this was fair, I wouldn't have left."

"Did you tell your therapist?" I asked. "Could she help?"

"Maybe. But, you know, I don't know her, either. She's a stranger."

"And I'm not?"

He looked up and smiled at me as we passed each other again. "Apparently not," he said, making us both laugh. "I wish I remembered more about you."

"Me too," I murmured. "I wanted you to come home so bad that I never thought about what would happen after. I just wanted my friend back."

Oliver beckoned his fingers toward me and I reached out, clasping on to his chain. He wrapped his hand around mine, his fingers cold, and I realized he had been outside for a long time. "I guess we both have a new friend now," he said. "I didn't really have a lot of those growing up."

"Because you moved a lot?"

"Well, yeah, kind of," Oliver said, then gestured to me. "My dad homeschooled me, too. It's just disappointing because

I thought maybe I would finally get to do that, y'know? Just be normal, with friends."

"Well, you're friends with *me*, right?" I asked.

"Yeah," he said, then was silent for a few extra seconds. "Caro and Drew, though. We were friends, too, before I . . . left. Are they . . . are they, like, mad at me or something?"

"*Mad* at you?" I repeated before I could stop myself.

"Yeah. They don't really talk to me or that day when you came over to say hi at lunch, Drew didn't say anything and then he came over and sort of pulled you away."

"Oh, Oliver," I sighed. I felt so horrible. Picturing Oliver alone was one thing. Picturing him lonely was another issue entirely. "When you first came back, everyone said that you needed some space. They told us to let you ease in on your own, so Caro and Drew gave you space. That's all it is, I swear. No one's mad at you. Why would they be? What'd *you* do?"

Oliver swung a little more, his feet making an empty pit in the sand. "I don't know. Nothing. Maybe that's part of the problem."

I dropped my head into my hands. "Ugh, this is the last time I listen to my parents," I muttered, then sat back up. "Look, no one's mad. We were just trying to give you space to adjust to a new school, a new neighborhood"—I thought of his earlier confession—"a new life. That's all. But we totally want to hang out with you."

"You do?" Oliver looked at me and even in the darkness, I could tell that the question wasn't casual.

"I do," I said, then corrected myself. "*We* do. We're still friends. That hasn't changed. It never did."

Oliver laughed through his nose. "Weirdest friendship ever," he said.

"Definitely," I agreed. "But it's ours." I retwined our grasp so that my hand was on top of his. "Hey."

"Yeah?"

"Thanks for the exclusive."

He just nodded, resting his forehead against my knuckles, and we hung there together, not moving, suspended in midair, as if we were waiting to fall.

CHAPTER FOURTEEN

We finally got up when it was too cold to stay still anymore and the shirt and sweater Oliver and I were wearing, respectively, did nothing to block out the coastal fog that always rolled down the street after dark. "See you tomorrow?" he said, just before opening the sliding-glass door. I could see the TV on in the den, one of the twins' Barbies lying sprawled on the floor, hair hacked off and her pink party dress gathered around her waist.

"Yeah, of course," I said, and then Rick was standing in the doorway. "Oh, *there* you are," he said. "Emmy, your parents are worried about you."

They were?

"I'm right here?" I said, looking at Oliver as if to say, *Isn't that right?* "We were just sitting back here."

"Your mom sounded a little frazzled on the phone," Rick said. It was always so odd to hear him speak; his voice was so different from Maureen's. She had always been fond of the verbal italics, especially during a crisis. I guess living in a nonstop nightmare for ten years could do that to a person. Rick, though, was always cool under pressure. Maybe that's why Maureen had married him, an anchor for her lost ship. "She said she tried calling your phone," Rick said, "but it just kept going to voice mail."

I pulled it out of my pocket and looked at the screen. Dead. *Wonderful.*

"Better go," I said. It was so quiet out that I could hear the wet grass crunching under my shoes, the kind of quiet that made your head hurt because you knew it was about to shatter into the loudest sounds.

I was right.

"Where have you been?!" My mom was standing in the kitchen and I saw her standing there, phone in hand, her eyes frantic. "We've been calling and calling you! We even called Caro!"

"I was next door!" I cried, gesturing to Oliver's house. "I just came home and I heard him in the yard and we started talking! I'm sorry, I just forgot."

"And you couldn't answer your phone?" my dad asked, but he didn't seem that worried. I wondered if he was keeping up the pretense for my mom, if it was easier to keep up with her than let her lead the charge alone.

"It died," I said, holding it up to prove my point. "I'm sorry, Oliver and I just started talking. My car was in the driveway the whole time," I added.

My mom rested her hands on the countertop and took a deep breath. It was one I had come to know well, the "give me strength to not throttle my child" deep breath. Every mom had one. "Next time," she said slowly as she exhaled, "when you text us that you're coming home, come home."

"Okay," I said, then debated whether or not I should ask my next question. "Am I grounded?" If they took my car away, I was screwed.

"Yes," my mom said.

"No," my dad said.

I looked between them as they looked at each other.

"She's late!" my mom said.

"She was next door with Oliver," my dad pointed out. "And her phone died."

"Standing right here," I muttered, waving a little. My dad's eyes cut to me and I dropped my hand back down. "I'm *really* sorry. Oliver was just stressed after the interview, that's all."

Now both of my parents turned to look at me.

"He was?" my mom asked.

I nodded. "We were just talking. I was trying to be a good friend." I made my eyes wide and blinked once, twice for good measure—just an innocent girl next door who was merely chatting with her long-lost childhood best friend.

"Nice try, Bambi eyes," my dad said, shaking his head at me, and I went back to my normal expression with a sigh.

My mom finally set down her phone on the counter, which she had had in a death grip since I walked through the door. "Next time," she said, "come home. Or call. Or do something so that we're not running around worried about you."

I bit back my comment about how, if they had really been running around, they would have seen my car in the driveway or heard Oliver and me talking in his yard. "Got it," I said. "Absolutely. Learn and grow, I always say."

I saw my mom's lips twitch, trying to repress a smile, and I took advantage to put my arms around her and give her a kiss on the cheek. "Does this mean I'm not grounded?" I asked in my nicest daughter voice. (You don't live with worrywart parents for ten years and not pick up a few tricks here and there.)

This time, she couldn't suppress the smile. "Get upstairs," she said. "It's late."

"It's nine—" I started to point out.

"Bed," my mom said, pointing at the staircase. "Or homework. Or something that keeps you upstairs for the rest of the night and doesn't have me worried to death."

"Consider it done," I said, then gave my dad a kiss on the cheek for good measure before dashing up the stairs. Once I was in my room, I plugged in my phone, watching as the battery sign flickered to life, then checked my computer. There was an email from Caro:

Your parents are making me be a Luddite and resort to email you to find out where you are. Do something pls.

I smiled and tapped out a fast message. "I'm fine, was talking to Oliver. Thanks for sacrificing your beliefs for the cause." Then I shut it before Caro could reply. She would have questions that I didn't want to answer, like *What were you talking about?* And questions I didn't know how to answer, questions that I was scared to ask myself. *Why were you talking to Oliver? Is he all right? Why does your heart beat faster when you think about him? Why can't you stop feeling his fingers on top of yours? You've thought about him every day for ten years, so why is it different now?*

"Everything's fine," I whispered to myself as I clicked out the light. Across the way, I saw Oliver's light flicker on, then off, our signal, and I repeated it with a smile. *"Coming home is like being kidnapped all over again,"* he had said, his words cushioned by darkness and privacy, and I lay down on my bed and tried not to think about what, or who, would go missing this time around.

THE TEAM

Emmy isn't having a lot of fun at Drew's fifth birthday party.

She went to it directly after her T-ball game, for starters, which means her uniform feels hot and scratchy and dirty in the afternoon sun. Worse, all the other little girls are wearing party dresses, not stirrups and cleats, and Emmy catches one of them—a little girl with a huge pink bow in her hair—eyeing her. Emmy glares right back.

This is all Oliver's fault, she decides. He's the one who wanted to play T-ball. She just joined because that's what friends do. They stick together. But the only good thing about T-ball, Emmy quickly learned, is the granola bar and juice box they get at the end of the game.

Emmy tries to cheer herself up by eating two pieces of cake (her mom is busy talking to Oliver's mom, so she doesn't notice), but all the frosting makes her feel sick and she finds herself sitting in Drew's brand-new gazebo in the backyard, watching the other kids jump around in the bounce house and wishing she could just go home and watch TV.

"Hey!" Oliver says, running up. "What are you doing out here in the zagebo?"

"This party is stupid," Emmy tells him. "And I'm not wearing a dress."

"Drew has an older brother named Kane," Oliver says, climbing up to sit next to her on the stairs. "Did you know that? I want a big brother. Or a little sister."

"You can have mine," another voice says, and Emmy sees Caro coming over to them. She's new in their kindergarten class, but Emmy likes her because she shares toys and doesn't tattle if you use too much paste. "I have five brothers and sisters." She looks as hot and annoyed as Emmy feels.

Drew comes running up to them. He's wearing two party hats on either side of his head, which make him look like a creature out of a storybook, and there's a smear of frosting on his cheek. "Why are you guys sitting out here?" he says. "Kane's gonna let us play with his remote-controlled car!"

"It's too hot," Emmy says.

"I want to play!" Caro says. "I want to go first!"

"First after me and Kane!" Drew corrects her and the two of them go off, leaving Emmy and Oliver behind.

"Don't you want to play with the car?" Emmy asks him. They're sitting next to each other.

"Not really," Oliver says. "I like the zagebo."

"Me too," Emmy replies. "It's our supersecret hideout!"

"Yeah!" Oliver agrees. "Just for us!"

"Yeah," Emmy says with a smile. "Just for us."

CHAPTER FIFTEEN

The next morning, Drew caught me in the hallway.

"Hi!" he said, landing in front of me as if he had been perched on top of the lockers like a puma.

"Your hair is wet," I said, and he shook it in front of me. "Did you go surfing without me this morning?"

"Maybe. Okay, yes. The swell was good and I thought I'd let you sleep in. You're welcome." He gave one last shake in my direction and then swept his bangs off his face.

"Jerk," I said, because I knew Drew would recognize it for the term of endearment that it was. "Next time take me with you. Hey! Wait!" I came to a halt in the middle of the hallway and turned around to glare at him. "I forgot. I'm not talking to you. *You*"—I poked him in the chest—"didn't tell me about Kevin."

"Ow. And *you*"—Drew poked back but not as hard—"probably forgot to tell me about something at some point in our friendship, so we're even." He smiled brighter. "Anyway."

"Why are you so . . ." I waved my hand around his face. "Shiny?"

"Guess who's parents are going out of town?" he said.

"Kevin's."

"Nope."

"Caro's."

"Nuh-uh."

"*Mine?* Oh please, say mine are going on a romantic spa vacation in Big Sur or something."

The happiness fell away from Drew's face. "Look, Em, I love your parents, but I *never* want to imagine them in a spa together ever. *Ever*. Now stop distracting me and just guess already!"

I paused and looked at him. "*Your* parents are going away?"

Drew nodded, his smile spreading so that it seemed to crack his face in two. (In a good way, I should add. That sounded creepier than I meant it to.)

"Your parents never go away!" I cried, clutching at his arm. "This is so great! Your house is so big!"

"I know!" He clutched me back and we jumped up and down together. "So you have to come over. A bunch of people are already coming over, but I want you to be there first."

"A party?" I asked. "An honest-to-God *party* at your house. This is, like, unbelievable."

"I know, right?" Drew paused and then stood up straight, a perfect imitation of his mom. "Something tasteful, though, not tacky. And no *themes*, of course."

"Simple, but elegant," I chimed in. "A chilled white-wine spritzer, perhaps, served only in the finest red plastic cups."

"We'll put the Flamin' Hot Cheetos in the good crystal, though," Drew added, giggling. He paused and then said, "Kane's coming home this weekend and he said he'd get us booze. And *Kevin* might be there." He wiggled his eyebrows at me.

I laughed even as I shoved him away. "Stop doing that, you know I hate that!"

Drew just shook his head. "Whatever. I really want you to meet him, Em. He's nice."

"Caro said he's hot."

"Caro is not a liar."

"How come Caro's met him and I haven't?"

"Because you"—Drew wrapped his arm around my neck and began to walk down the hall with me in tow—"have been busy with Neighbor Boy."

"Neighbor Boy, as a nickname, is a lot better than Milk Carton Boy. And we need to talk about him."

Drew just looked down at me. It's a real disadvantage when your friends are a) taller than you, and b) right. "You took him surfing," he said, "and you didn't tell Caro."

"Because Caro would make it *a thing*," I told him, emphasizing the last two words. "And it wasn't *a thing*."

"You had dinner after?"

"We ate food together!"

"And did that food consist of dinner-like items?"

"Okay, fine, yes. And I know, Caro says it's a date if you eat food together, but if that's true, then I've dated half the population at our school and do *not* make a snarky comment right now."

Drew widened his eyes and looked innocent, the way I had tried to do the night before with my parents.

"Cut it out, you look like a Kewpie doll."

"Look," Drew said, going back to his normal face and tugging me closer, "you can tell your old friend Drew anything. You know that, right?"

"Yes, but—"

"And you can tell me nothing," he continued. "I don't really care. As long as my best friend is happy, then I'm happy."

"Oh my God, stop talking! Oliver thinks that you and Caro hate him!"

That stopped Drew in his tracks. It was rare that he was serious, but when he was, it changed his whole face, made him look older. "Hate him?" he repeated. "How could I hate him? I barely know him!"

"Yeah, I know, but that whole 'giving him space' thing made Oliver feel like he was Patient Zero. So we've got to hang out with him more, okay? Go surfing or whatever."

"Or *whatever*." Drew wiggled his eyebrows at me.

"Stop that! And I said *we*!" I added. "Let's invite him to the party, okay? We were friends once, we can be friends again."

"Emmy, you are a saint among saints," Drew said, then hugged me to his side as we walked down the hall. "Let the healing bonds of friendship ease all of our wounds!"

"Oh, shut up."

"That's not very saintly language," he pointed out, then kissed the top of my head and then released me with a shove. "Now get off me before Kevin thinks I'm straight."

"He's homeschooled. He doesn't even go to school here."

"Rumors, Emmy. They respect no boundaries." Drew raised an eyebrow at me, then ducked into his history class.

I didn't see Oliver until lunchtime that day, and even then, I didn't see him until he was standing right in front of me in the library. I was making flash cards for French verbs and he stood over me just as I was writing *je ferais* on my lined card. (I can't have unlined note cards. It's just not natural.)

"Hey," Oliver said, his hair (still) in his eyes. "Let's go surfing again."

"Right now?" I whispered back, glancing around me.

He pulled out the chair next to me, sitting down and heaving his backpack onto the table with a loud *thwop!* that made the librarian look up and frown. Former kidnap victim or not, everyone had to be quiet in the library.

"Not now," he said. "I mean after school. Today. It's supposed to be a good swell."

I tried to hide a smile, failing miserably. "It's a one- to two-foot swell," I said. "But it's sweet that you think those are good waves. Adorable, really."

"Those are good waves for *me*," he clarified. "And I had fun last time. I want to go again."

I sat back in my chair and crossed my arms over my chest. "So you're not worried about sharks anymore?"

"Only slightly. I just want to do something!" he said, drawing another look from the librarian. He raised his hand in apology before leaning closer to me. He smelled like the same baby shampoo the twins used. It was an odd dichotomy.

"I'm tired of sitting in my house," he said. "I feel like everyone's always watching me in there. And the twins actually *are* watching me. I can see their little noses under the door."

"That's sort of cute," I admitted.

"My dad has this saying," he continued, not noticing how I startled when he said the word *dad*, how it seemed like such a normal word in his mouth, like *dad* wasn't the thing that had brought such catastrophe into our lives.

"He says, 'nervous like a long-tailed cat in a roomful of rocking chairs.' That's Maur—my mom right now. I feel like if I blink too many times in a row, she'll worry about me."

"Wait," I said. "Your dad said that? *My* dad says that." It sounded strange that our dads would have anything in common—even a dumb saying. His dad was a criminal; my dad's biggest crime was putting the empty milk container back in the refrigerator.

Oliver laughed. "Are you serious? Huh. Maybe they got it from each other."

"Well, *your mother* kind of spent the last ten years worrying about you, wondering if you were even alive," I pointed out. "It's a hard habit to break. Just ask my parents. They worry about me all the time and I never disappeared."

"But I'm *fine*," he insisted, crossing his arms over his backpack and resting on top of it. "I just want to go surfing."

"So go surfing," I said more dismissively than I meant.

He paused a moment, staring down at the wood grain of the table. "I want to go surfing with *you*."

Je ferais was still balanced between my fingers. "Why?"

He shrugged. "Why not?"

"*Wow*. I feel really appreciated right now."

"Okay, fine. I want to go surfing with you because we had fun last time," he said, then added, "And I like talking to you. You listen."

I could feel my cheeks turning a little pink and I tried to will the color away. "Sometimes, I think, I just don't know what to say." We were both whispering now, and probably would have been even without the librarian's eyes on us. "I don't want to say the wrong thing, so I don't say anything at all. That's not the same as being a good listener."

"That's actually exactly what it means," he replied. "So will you go?"

"Fine," I finally agreed. "I'll go, on one condition."

"Sold. Done. What?"

"*You* figure out my cover story for my parents."

"Where are we going?" Caro came strolling over, either

blithely unaware of or not caring about the librarian's sotto voce rule. (I was leaning toward Option B.)

"Oliver wants to go surfing this afternoon," I told her. "I told him *he* has to come up with an excuse for me so that my parents won't wonder where I am."

"Tell them you're spending the night at my place." Caro shrugged, then her eyes glinted, full of mischief. "Oh, that's perfect! Then you can go to Drew's party tonight, too!"

"I was going to go, anyway," I started to say, but Caro let out a guffaw that raised everyone's attention, not just the librarian's.

"Uh, yeah, sure," she said, then turned to Oliver. "Do you know what her curfew is?"

I could tell that Drew had gotten to Caro and told her about how Oliver was worried about them. She had an easy smile, though, and she patted Oliver's arm as she talked to him, like their friendship didn't have a ten-year-long gap in it.

"I'm sitting right here," was all I said, though.

Caro just ignored me. "Nine o'clock. In the *evening*. Including *weekends*." Caro shook her head like she had just announced a casualty list. "Drew's parents will probably still be backing out of the driveway at nine o'clock. She isn't going to any party without me as an alibi." She turned back to me, leaning up against the back of my chair. "Just tell your parents you're coming to my place after school and then sleeping over." She returned her gaze to Oliver. "They love me."

"Oh, now you're talking to me?" I asked. "I wasn't sure. I

thought I might have been invisible."

Oliver smiled at me, then Caro. "Well, that was easy. Thanks, Caroline."

"Caro," she corrected him. "Nobody's called me Caroline since the second grade. So you're coming, right?"

"Where?"

"Drew's party. Just show up, this isn't a formal invite thing. BYO-whatever."

"And by 'whatever,' she means 'alcohol,'" I explained.

"You speak Caro-ese better than you do French," she said.

"What about you?" Oliver asked her. "What's your story for your parents?"

Caro blinked. "I'm the youngest of six. My parents stopped raising us after Kid Number Four. They don't care where I go."

"They *care*," I interrupted her. "It's not like you're Eloise living in the Plaza."

"On my island," she sighed dreamily. "Anyway, text your parents. Tell them now."

The bell suddenly rang, startling everyone in the room, and Oliver stood up. "I'll ask Drew about borrowing his wet suit again," he said. "Do you think he'll mind?"

"Nope!" Caro said, grinning so wide that I could see her back molars. "Drew is *totally* fine with you and Emmy hanging out." Then she winked. Actually *winked*.

"Caro," I groaned, covering my eyes with my hands. "Stop. Please. I'm begging you."

"See you tonight!" Caro said as Oliver hoisted his backpack onto his shoulders.

"Meet you in the parking lot?" Oliver asked me, and I nodded, my face still buried in my hands.

"You are so embarrassing," I told Caro as soon as Oliver was safely out of earshot. "You are the *worst*."

"I am the *best*, and here's why." Caro plunked herself in Oliver's empty seat. "I just got you date number two with your childhood sweetheart–slash–tragic love story—"

"My what?" I uncovered my face to look at her.

"—and you get to go to the party afterward and hang out with both of your cool friends and Oliver."

"Don't call him that."

She frowned. "That's sort of his name."

"No, my 'childhood tragic love whatever' thing you just said. Don't say that. It's not funny, Caro." I hadn't meant my words to sound that vehement, and judging from her expression, neither did Caro.

"Fine, sorry. But you know what I mean."

I did and I didn't. I didn't know what any of it meant, or even if I wanted to.

"Um, Emmy?" she said, then glanced down at my now-shredded note card, pieces of *je ferais* still between my fingers. "What did the French language ever do to you?"

CHAPTER SIXTEEN

After school, Drew's wet suit and surfboard slung into the back of my car next to mine, my parents texted about my change in plans ("have fun!! Thank u for telling me and BE SAFE!" my mom wrote back), and Oliver in the passenger seat next to me, I peeled out of the school parking lot and headed west.

"So what'd you tell your mom?" I asked him. The windows were down and the wind made it hard to hear, so I just yelled louder instead of rolling them up. The fresh air smelled good, like clean laundry and salt, a reminder that we were only a few minutes away from the ocean.

"I just said I was hanging out with you," Oliver said. His elbow was resting on the car door, and his hand was cupped against the wind, forcing his fingers apart.

"No, you did not!" I gasped.

"What?"

"Oliver!" I screeched. "My mom talks to your mom, like, every five minutes! If she—"

Oliver grinned wickedly at me. "Kidding."

I tried to stop a smile as I punched him in the arm. "You have a real violent streak, you know that?" He laughed, trying to block my fist as I socked him again. "Ow! Okay, uncle, I'm sorry."

"You're a weenie," I told him.

"Weenie? Wow, my delicate ears. Ow, okay! Sorry again! Eyes on the road, by the way. You're operating heavy machinery with me in it. And I asked Rick, not my mom. I just said that Drew and some guys and I were going to the movies."

I glanced at him. "Is Rick, you know, cool about that?"

"I guess. I don't know, he's cooler than my mom sometimes. He doesn't act like the roof is going to cave in every five minutes."

I sat back in my seat, putting both hands on the wheel once again. "Do you know what would happen if my mom found out I was at a party?" I asked him.

"Is that rhetorical?"

"Yes. But just so you know, they would lock me in the basement forever."

"I don't believe that," Oliver scoffed, sticking his arm out the window once again. "That's not even possible."

"Oh, trust me, it would happen. And then you would feel bad for me."

"It wouldn't happen," Oliver insisted. "You don't even have a basement."

"Fine. The attic, then. They would lock me in a cold, dark place and feed me nothing but gruel. Like a mash-up of *Jane Eyre* and *Oliver Twist*. My mom was an English major, she could make it happen."

Oliver looked at me, tucking his hair behind his ears.

"What?" I asked, glancing at him before checking my mirrors and turning right.

"You're just a weirdo," he said. "That's all." But his voice was soft, probably muted by the wind. He looked at me for a few more seconds before sticking his head out the window like a dog, smiling into the air when I laughed at him.

"Now who's the weirdo?" I yelled, but either he didn't hear me or he just agreed, because he smiled again and didn't say anything more.

Oliver and I had both been right about the swells: they were just baby waves that day, the hot weather and dry wind making the horizon look both still and shimmery at the same time. They were perfect for Oliver.

Unfortunately, he was still a far from perfect surfer.

"Paddle, paddle, paddle, PADDLE!" I screamed, sitting astride my board as I watched him try to get ahead of a wave. His arms moved fast like propellers, but as soon as the wave caught up to him, he planted his feet on the board . . . and immediately fell over.

"Have you considered a different sport?" I asked him, once he had gathered up his board and swum back out to where I was waiting. "Badminton, maybe? You would be great at shuffleboard."

He grinned and splashed water in my direction. "We can't all be superhero badass surfers," he said as I splashed him right back. "Think of it this way: I make you look even better."

"I don't need you to make me look good!" I protested, sending a huge amount of water his way. "I looked good before you showed up."

The double entendre hung between us and I was grateful that the sun was in Oliver's eyes so that he couldn't see me blush. "I mean——you know what I mean. Right?"

Before he could answer, though, a round of catcalls started up from the beach. Three guys were walking toward a spot farther down, but all of their heads were turned in our direction. "You don't need that wet suit, baby!" one of them yelled, sending his friends into a round of hysterics.

I raised my middle finger at them, making them laugh even harder, and if I had been blushing before, now my face was ablaze. "Assholes," I muttered.

Oliver's spine was straight, his head turned resolutely toward the shore. "Who are they?" he asked, his voice sharper and harder than before. "Do you know them?"

"No, they're just tourists." I waved my hand in their direction as if to sweep them away. "Dudes. Jerks. Whatever. Most guys around here aren't like that, don't worry."

Oliver was still staring at them, though. With his damp hair and Drew's wet suit just a little too tight on his body, he reminded me of a panther in an old storybook I used to have, poised in the trees and ready to pounce. "Oliver, seriously," I said. "Ignore them. Please don't do something stupid like avenge my *honor* or whatever."

He finally looked away. "I'm not," he said. "You can probably avenge yourself much better than I could, anyway."

I smiled despite myself. "Well, yeah, duh. Your upper body strength is terrible."

"Does that happen a lot, though?" Oliver said.

"Not really. I mean, once in a while, yeah. But not really." I ran my fingers back and forth in the water, watching the sand particles and seaweed strands dance between them. "Like, if you're wearing a wet suit instead of a bikini, they say shit. If you wear a bikini instead of a wet suit, they say shit. But it doesn't matter. They just do it to make up for the fact that they suck and I'm better than them."

"How do you know they suck?" Oliver asked.

I gestured to the empty water around us. "Do you see anyone else out here besides us today? These waves are baby waves, everyone good is probably up at Newport."

Oliver had ducked under the water to smooth back his hair, but came up sputtering, mock-indignant. "Wait, are you saying *I* suck?" he said. "Is that what you're saying?"

"No!" I cried. "Wait, don't—!" But it was too late. He pulled me off my board and straight into the water, me laughing so hard when I went under that I came up coughing, eyes and nose stinging with salt water.

"Is that any way to speak to your teacher?" I gasped, trying to wipe my nose in the most discreet way possible. "Disrespectful!"

Oliver laughed at me trying to push my wet hair out of my face. "You look like you got attacked by seaweed," he said, then reached over and tried to help me. "Here, sorry. But you had it coming."

I let him move a lock of wet hair out of my eyes, his thumb just brushing my forehead as he swept it back. I had a comeback on the tip of my tongue, but when he looked at me and smiled again, it melted away in my mouth, leaving nothing but a smile behind.

"I don't think I'm gonna go to Drew's party," he said.

"Wait, what?" The conversation had suddenly taken a drastic turn. "Why? What just happened here?"

"I don't know." Oliver shrugged and looked over his shoulder toward, I realized, the same guys who had harassed me a few minutes earlier. "I just . . . I'm not really good at parties. With, you know, other people."

Realization dawned. "Oliver, how many parties have you been to?"

"Um."

"That's what I thought," I replied. Of course, Oliver hadn't been going to ragers while his dad kept him hidden from the world. For years, even though he was living in the biggest city in the world, it was probably Oliver and his dad—*only* Oliver and his dad.

"You have to come tonight," I told him. "It'll be fun, and Caro and Drew and I will all be there."

"Yeah, but I don't know anyone else." He scratched at his arm and looked down at his board, avoiding my gaze. "I mean, I barely know *them*."

"Well, you're not going to get to know them if you stay home with your mom and Rick and the twins," I pointed out. "And they're great, but I can't lie, it's not exactly Social City over at your house."

Oliver stared out at the horizon.

"Just come on," I urged. "You said yourself that you didn't want to be stuck at home with the twins watching you. Look, if you hate it, we can leave. If people are mean to you, I'll beat them up." I lifted my arm and flexed my muscle. "See? I'm pretty strong. And intimidating, too."

"Really." Oliver seemed both amused and deeply unimpressed.

"Really," I told him as we bobbed in the water, listening to the small waves crash behind us.

"Fine," he finally said, then pushed himself back up on his board. "You win. I'll go. Now c'mon, the towering surf awaits!" He gestured toward the (very flat) ocean and I hopped up on my board next to him.

"You really do suck at this," I teased him as we started to paddle out farther. "I'm just taking pity on you."

"We shall see!" he yelled. He paddled faster, just out of my reach, the way he always seemed to be.

CHAPTER SEVENTEEN

After surfing, we went over to Caro's so I could give her a ride to the party. "Come up!" she yelled from her balcony, half her head in hot rollers and only one eye completely made up. "I'm not ready yet! Tell David to let you in!"

"Caro's older brother," I filled in when Oliver gave me a questioning look. "He's cool. He's mostly stoned."

"Ah," Oliver said as David opened the door. His eyes were heavy, like a basset hound who desperately needed a nap. "Hey, dudes," he said to both of us. "Oliver! Cool. Good times."

Oliver looked at me again but I just brushed past David, grabbing Oliver's wrist and dragging him behind me. "Hey, David," I said, then whispered to Oliver, "Hurry, before he starts a conversation."

"He can *have* a conversation?" Oliver asked.

We went upstairs to Caro's room that she shared with her

older sister Heather. There was a pile of laundry in the hallway, right next to an empty laundry basket. We stepped around it and went into Caro's room.

It was always easy to tell Caro's side of the room: it was organized to an alarming degree. Drew once asked Caro if she used a ruler to make sure everything was at right angles. When she just blinked at him and said, "Obviously," we became a little worried. But if you shared a room with Heather, you would probably be a complete neatnik, too.

Because Heather, like I said before, is a natural disaster disguised as a human being.

"Welcome to hell!" Caro said cheerfully, waving us in and around a pile of shoes, none of which matched. She gestured to a bottle of hand sanitizer that was on her desk. "Use it if you feel like you have to," she told us. Oliver was still in the doorway, his eyes wide as he took in the scene. "I know," Caro said when she saw his face. "It's a lot to contemplate."

"It's like watching two movies at the same time," he replied.

"*Right?*" Caro cried. "I mean"—she gestured to Heather's side of the room, where there was a huge pile of sheets and blankets that presumably hid a bed—"she could have a family of kangaroos under there and I wouldn't know. If I don't show up to class next week, just assume that it's because I've been stampeded by kangaroos."

I gingerly stepped around the shoes and went over to Caro's side, sitting on the floor next to her desk. (The bed was so neatly made that I was afraid of mussing the hospital corners.) There were pens and pencils lined up in alternating order on her desk and highlighters in ROYGBIV formation in a plastic cup next to them. I didn't need to open the drawer to know that her Post-it notes were organized in the exact same way.

"So, are you so psyched?" Caro said, heading back to the bathroom. "First school party, Oliver. Get ready for . . . well, nothing really. We just hang out. It's not like the movies."

"Can't wait," he said. I could tell he was still a little freaked out by the difference between the two bedroom halves and I patted the floor next to me. "It's safe down here," I said.

"I'm actually afraid to touch things anywhere," he whispered, stepping around the shoes. "Do any of those even match?"

"Nope!" Caro called from the bathroom without even looking to see what he was talking about. "If Heather's limbs weren't attached to her body, she would just leave them lying around wherever. It's a little frightening. And she has a driver's license, so steer clear."

"No pun intended," I added, tracing a circle with my fingertip into the worn carpet. The room had been Caro's older brothers' before they moved out, and it showed. There were even some Batman stickers on Caro's bed frame, which she had artfully hidden with pillows.

"I'm counting down the days until one of us moves out of here," Caro called from the bathroom, then stuck her head out the door and pointed at me. "You plus me plus community college equals apartment."

I rolled my eyes. "Please. Like my mom would ever let me move out. You should hear her speech about how dorms are dangerous because of meningitis. It's a party-killer."

"Your mom loves me," Caro said, ducking back into the bathroom. "Tell her I'll have hand sanitizer in every room. No one's getting meningitis, not on my watch."

Oliver was still making his way through the room and I started to say something when I saw him pick up Caro's old baby doll. Alice had been around since Caro's first days on earth and it also showed: there was a skid mark on her nose from where one of Caro's brothers had used her in a game of catch (and missed); a coffee stain on her cloth arm; and one button eye completely missing, thanks to their old Labrador, Noodle, who apparently had a thing for buttons. Caro never said this, but I knew she put Alice on the bed with her good eye facing Caro's side of the room, sparing her the indignity of having to spend eternity staring at Heather's disaster area.

"Alice," Oliver said.

Caro immediately stuck her head out of the bathroom door, her eyes wide as she looked at me, then Oliver. "You remember Alice?" she asked.

Oliver nodded, carefully smoothing down Alice's threadbare dress before setting her back down. "You brought her to show-and-tell," he said, then huffed out a little laugh. "Sorry, I just made things super weird, didn't I?"

"No, no," both Caro and I started to say. And he hadn't, but

I still felt a tiny chill run across my arms, like a seven-year-old Oliver had hovered in the doorway for a second and I had only just missed seeing him.

"It's not weird," Caro continued. "It's sweet. Alice appreciates it."

It's weird, Oliver mouthed to me as he sat down on the floor. "Sorry."

"It's fine," I whispered back, making room for him. "Don't worry so much."

"What happened to her other eye?" Oliver asked, but before I could answer, Caro came back in the room.

"Ems, what are you wearing?"

I looked down at my jeans and top. "This? We just got back from surfing and I already know everyone at this party, so I don't have to dress to impress."

Caro gestured to her closet. "Feel free to borrow something. Please."

I sighed and got up. At least she wasn't saying anything about my hair, which was still damp with salt water and up in a bun. "Fine. Where's that sweater you got last week?"

Caro poked her head out of the bathroom again, this time with an eyelash curler clamped around her left eyelashes, and jabbed a finger in the direction of Heather's bed. "Don't even talk to me about it," she muttered.

"What is *that*?" Oliver suddenly asked.

We turned to look at him as he gestured to Caro's eye. "Are

you, like, plucking out your eyelashes or something?"

I was the first one who started laughing. Caro, out of self-preservation, waited until she had released the curler. "What?" Oliver said, smiling a little like someone who suspected there was a hidden camera nearby. "Is this something I should know?"

"It's an eyelash curler," Caro told him. "It makes your eyelashes . . . swoopy."

"It's sort of redundant to define 'eyelash curler,'" I pointed out. "It's pretty evident what it is from the name."

Oliver got up and walked over to take it from Caro. He was taller than both of us and in the bathroom doorway, he seemed impossibly large. Didn't she feel crowded? "This is medieval," he said, opening and closing it. It looked a lot smaller in his big hand than it had in Caro's. "You actually use this? What if you blink?"

"You don't," Caro and I chorused.

"What if, like, someone slams the door while you're using it and you blink just because that's what you do when someone slams the door?"

"Then your eyelid is bald and you have a psychopath living in your house," I said, taking it back from him and giving it to Caro.

"That is some *Game of Thrones*—level shit right there," he said.

"You've seriously never seen one of those before," I said. "How is that possible?"

He shrugged. "Two guys living together for ten years without a mom or sister. You do the math."

"You had a mom!" Caro called out from the bathroom. I could

tell from her voice that she was applying mascara now, blithe and oblivious to Oliver's small wince. "You just didn't know where she was!"

Time to intervene.

"Can I borrow that after you?" I yelled to her, examining my nail polish.

"My mascara?"

"Yeah!"

"You're not supposed to share eye makeup! What if I have pinkeye?"

"It'd be an honor to share pinkeye with you, Caro."

The tube came flying out of the bathroom a few seconds later.

"Thank you!"

Finally, after Caro had finished her eye makeup and I found a shirt in her dresser (folded as neatly as an envelope, of course), we were ready to go. "What about me?" Oliver teased, holding out his arms. "Now I'm really self-conscious about how straight my eyelashes are."

I tugged at his shirt and rolled my eyes as we left behind the half-Pollock, half-Mondrian bedroom. "Embrace your uniqueness," I told him. "And watch out for those shoes."

CHAPTER EIGHTEEN

The thing with Drew's house is that it's sort of ridiculous.

It's in Canyon Crest, which is this really nice neighborhood set on a hill a few miles away from my and Oliver's neighborhood. My dad's theory is that they set it on a hill so that no matter where you are in our town, you can see the mansions, which sounds about right to me. "We enjoy watching the serfs," Drew said when I floated that theory past him, and I've known Drew long enough to recognize the sarcasm in his voice.

I can't say that's not how other Canyon Crest residents actually feel, though.

We drove past Drew's driveway, which was U-shaped and long, and Oliver glanced up at the Tudor-style windows that seemed to be glaring down at us. "I feel like I should be remembering this," he said.

"You don't?" I asked.

"Nope." He shook his head as he looked out at the neighborhood.

"Where are you going?" Caro asked from the backseat, where she was struggling to buckle her open-toed high-heeled sandals.

"I'm not going to park my car in the driveway!" I told her. "What if my parents drive by and see it? Or friends of my parents?"

"You live your life like you're under surveillance," Caro muttered, now propping her foot up on the passenger seat.

"Those look painful," Oliver commented, trying to avoid Caro digging her heel into his shoulder. "Why does everything you do look like it hurts?"

"Because!" Caro huffed with a final shove. "You guys want us to look natural and there's nothing natural about looking natural."

I could see the confusion cross Oliver's face and stifled my own smile.

"Those shoes don't look natural," Oliver pointed out.

"Yes, but they're three-inch heels, which make me look like I'm an average height of five five. See?" she explained. "Natural."

"Why do you want to be *average*?" I asked her, scanning the street around the corner for a place to park. I wasn't the only person who had had that brilliant idea, apparently. I recognized more than a few cars from the school parking lot.

"I said *natural*, not average."

Oliver and I exchanged glances, both of us trying to hide our amusement.

"How far away are we?" Caro looked out the window as I parallel parked the minivan. (Which, might I add, is not easy to do, considering that the trunk is big enough to hold a few surfboards.) "Do I have to hike in these spikes?"

"Naturally," Oliver said, earning himself a gentle shoulder shove from Caro.

"But it's dark and there's gravel! What if I trip?"

"Just act natural," I told her, and Oliver cracked up as we both climbed out of the car. "Here," he said, bending down a little. "Climb on."

Caro looked wary, but jumped up on his back and wrapped her arms around Oliver's neck. "This is both super weird and really helpful," she said, trying to pull down her skirt in the back so that she wouldn't flash half of Canyon Crest.

"You're welcome," Oliver said. "Can you, um, loosen your grip a little, though? My neck." He coughed and winced.

"Oh, sorry, sorry." Caro readjusted herself, then looked down at me and grinned. "You look so little from up here."

"You're, like, six inches away from me," I pointed out as the three of us (well, two and a passenger) trekked it toward Drew's house. The last time we had all gone to Drew's house, it had been for Drew's fifth birthday party, but I could still picture Oliver, Caro, and I trudging up the driveway, gifts in hand.

"It's a dramatic change," Caro told me, unaware of what I had been thinking. "You don't understand because you're average height."

Oliver just hefted her higher onto his back. "Caro, your shoes. Ow."

"Oh, sorry, sorry." She dug her heels out of his sides. "My bad."

We hiked up Drew's driveway (empty, of course) and I almost slipped in the loose gravel, grabbing Caro's ankle at the last second to steady myself and almost pulling the three of us down to the ground in the process. "If I die . . ." Caro warned.

"If *you* die?" Oliver said, trying to right both himself and me. "Who makes driveways like this in real life? Why is it so long?"

"Because if you can afford this driveway, you can afford the car that's good enough to drive on it," I said. "It's a show-off thing."

"Well, where's Drew's car?" he asked, looking around.

"In the garage," Caro said, gesturing a little without actually letting go of Oliver.

"Stop talking, we're almost there," I said.

Drew gets a little twitchy when people talk about his parents' money. "It's not even *mine*," he says whenever someone brings it up, then he changes the subject.

Sometimes, the things people *don't* say are louder than the words that come out of their mouths.

"You should've seen the moat they tried to put in," I whispered to Oliver in a not-very-whispery voice as we climbed up the (massive, seriously) front steps. "Zoning laws and all that, but trust me, it could have been epic."

"Well, an alligator is one thing," Oliver said without missing a beat. "But when you need five or six, that's a different story." He grinned down at me as Caro slid off his back.

Caro noticed, though. "He's picking up what you're throwing down," she whispered to me as Oliver started to knock on the door. "Wait, no, what are you doing?" She interrupted him, reaching up to stop his hand before he knocked again. "This is a party, you just go in."

"Lead the way," Oliver said, but Caro took an extra second to give me a Meaningful Look before plowing through the front door.

It looked like things were already in full swing. I could hear Drew's brother, Kane, laughing from somewhere deep inside the house—or maybe it was just in the next room. Drew's house was so large and the ceilings were so high that it made the acoustics weird, like that whispering spot at the US Capitol. (We took a field trip in eighth grade. And yes, my mom was a parental chaperone. No surprise there.)

"Hey!" I heard Drew yell, and he appeared at the top of the stairs, already on his way to very drunk and with a bottle of something in his hand. It was actually a double staircase, one on either side of the foyer that met at the landing at the top. We recorded ourselves acting out a scene from *Romeo and Juliet* on that balcony for an English assignment back in freshman year, when Caro swooned so much that she nearly fell over the railing. "A-plus for effort," our teacher had said when he saw the footage, but we ended up with a B-minus, anyway.

"Remember?" I grinned, turning to Oliver. It was instinctive and accidental, like my brain could place him there even though he hadn't been there at all.

"Remember what?" he replied. His eyes were sort of wide and I realized that Drew's house was probably a smidge overwhelming, what with the staircases and the noise and the total strangers.

"Nothing," I said. "We should get something to drink."

"A-fucking-*men*," Caro echoed, and we went past some of Kane's friends and into the kitchen, where a keg was sitting on the kitchen floor, with dozens of beer bottles and red cups scattered on the granite-topped island.

"I see Kane brought the refreshments," I said, taking stock of everything. There was a bowl of Cheez Doodles on the counter next to a spilled cup and I grabbed it and held it to me. "Grab snacks when you see them," I said to Oliver when he raised an eyebrow at me. "Otherwise they become victims of beer-pong games gone wrong."

"Ah," he said, then took a bag of chips that still hadn't been opened.

"Good, you learn fast," I said.

"Too bad I'm a Cheez Doodle kind of guy."

"Yeah, that is too bad," I teased. "Because these are mine and they're going to be delicious and—"

"Hiiiiiiiiiii!" Drew said, suddenly draping himself over both Oliver and me. "You made it!"

"It wasn't exactly a treacherous drive," I pointed out, then gave him an awkward one-arm hug while protecting my Cheez Doodles.

"Did you have to go into Caro and Heather's bedroom?" Drew asked, and I nodded. "Then trust me, it was treacherous. But you survived. You're here now! You're alive!"

"It feels like everyone's here," Oliver commented as two people jostled past him.

"How drunk are you?" I asked Drew. "Here, have a Cheez Doodle."

"He gets one?" Oliver cried.

"I get two," Drew announced, then popped them into his mouth. "Sorry, dude, I live here. I get preferential treatment. And to answer your question, Ems, I am somewhere between that one bonfire last summer and that time that you and Caro and I went to Steve's party before finals week."

"So, kind of drunk but on your way to very, very drunk?"

He bopped my nose. "Exactly." He let go of both of us to greet someone else. Oliver, sensing his opening, immediately dove for the Cheez Doodles.

"Hey!" I yelped. "You have tortilla chips!"

"They're boring! And unsalted!" Oliver shook the bag in my face. "Besides, fake orange cheese is meant to be shared with friends." He dug his hand into the bowl and ate a huge handful, then smiled at me with a huge, cheesy (no pun intended) grin.

"That is so gross," I said, trying not to laugh and trying not to show how I didn't think it was that gross at all, not really.

"Hey! Want some *milk* to wash those down?" Someone bumped into Oliver and I heard snickers over the music, which was suddenly loud and thumping and probably making the chandelier in the foyer dance on its axis.

Oliver swallowed quickly, then shook his head. "No, man, thanks. I'm good."

The guy turned to me. "Hey, Emmy."

I took a deep, inward breath. Brandon Mills. The last person I wanted to see at this party.

"Hey. This is Brandon," I said to Oliver. "He went to our school, but he graduated last year."

"We surf together," Brandon added.

"I don't think being in the Pacific Ocean at the same time counts as 'surfing together,'" I said. "He goes to UC Santa Barbara," I told Oliver. "Hopefully he'll be going back there soon. Like, in the next ten minutes or so."

"Aw, don't be so jealous. Maybe one day you'll be on the surf team, too." Brandon tried to put his arm around my shoulders, but I shrugged him off. If I could, I would have shrugged him all the way out the front door and back up the coast.

Oliver was watching us both very carefully, his eyes shifting from me to Brandon and back to me. "Nice to meet you," he finally said, even though his eyes were locked on mine.

"Hey, man, saw you on TV," Brandon said, shaking his hand. Both of their grips looked tight. And painful. "Good interview." He was still smiling, the way people smile when they want you to know that they're talking shit about you, that they didn't really see your television interview and don't really care whether or not you've returned home after disappearing for ten years.

"Thanks." Oliver sounded the same way that he had in the interview, clipped, not sure of the right words to say.

"So." Brandon turned back to me. "Did Kane teach you any new moves? While I was away?"

"Oh, shut up, Brandon," I said, rolling my eyes and taking Oliver's arm to lead him away.

"What? It was just a question!" he yelled as we walked past, but he was laughing and so were a few other people in the kitchen.

"What was that?" Oliver asked. He was still holding the Cheez Doodles, bless him. "Are you *friends* with that guy?" The way he said "friends" made me think that he didn't really mean "friends" at all.

"Um, absolutely *not*," I said. "He's just a douche bag. I mean, he's in college but still goes to high school parties? It's ridiculous. Where's Caro? She always hangs out with the cool people."

"Emmy!" Caro waved from the second-floor landing, a red cup already in her hand. "Wherefore art thou, Emmy?"

I waved at her, then looked at Oliver. "Do you know what we need?"

"A drink."

I tapped my nose. "Bingo."

A few hours later, the party had progressed (or de-gressed, depending on your point of view) nicely. And by that, I mean that I was drunk.

So was Oliver. So were Caro and Drew and pretty much every person I had seen since leaving Brandon behind. I was sticking to beer, but Caro and Drew were both doing shots and inventing some sort of complicated drinking game that involved a basketball, a feather duster, and some refrigerator magnets, and made no sense to anyone but them.

"You have to do the thing!" Caro screamed at him, waving the feather duster. "Shot!"

We had moved back down to the kitchen, but half the party was in the backyard, smoking weed and playing music. Someone had produced an acoustic guitar, as well, and there was an odd, drunken version of "Hotel California" being played.

"Ugh," Caro said, dropping down onto my lap. I was sitting because, frankly, standing seemed too complicated. I had slumped into Oliver at some point, as well, his arm propping me up.

"Here," Caro said, then put the feather duster on top of my head. "It's a hat!"

"Why, thank you!" I said, then modeled it for her and Oliver. Drew was still kneeling on the ground, trying to figure out the magnets. "What do you think? Couture?"

"Ooh la la," Oliver said. His words were a little sloshy, a nice change from earlier in the night. "You can wear it when you surf."

"Impractical," I told him, then plopped it down on his head. "It matches your eyes."

"Picture! Picture!" Caro cried, then dug her phone out of her pocket and took a few staggered steps back. "Smile!"

We smiled. "Whoa, why is it—?" Caro squinted at the screen, then held it out in front of her. "I can't tell if I'm blurry or if the picture's blurry. And oh my God, who brought that goddamn guitar? I want to kill them. Do you know how you can tell who the douche bag is at the party? It's the guy who starts playing the acoustic guitar." She took the feather duster back from Oliver and jabbed it in the direction of the backyard. "Take *that*! And *that*!"

"Is it Brandon playing?" I asked her and she turned and pointed it at me.

"Oh God, *probably*. Brandon's not even a douche bag. He's a douche CANOE. A whole *canoe*, Emmy!" She sat back down in my lap and dropped the duster on the floor. Drew quickly snatched it up and took it back to the magnets. "Is he tripping or just really drunk?"

"He was hitting on Emmy," Oliver said, his chin now resting in his hand.

Caro frowned. "Drew was?"

Drew just laughed from the floor, then started stacking the magnets.

"No," Oliver said. "The douche canoe."

"He was not!" I protested, trying to turn around, but my limbs were perfectly comfortable where they were and had no intention of moving.

"Oh, he *totally* was," Caro said to Oliver. "I mean, I didn't see it, but he always hits on her. What did he say to you that one time, Em?"

I reached for my beer, then took a sip and passed it to Caro. "'You're not like other girls,'" I said in my best dude-bro voice.

Oliver frowned a little. "Is that bad?" he asked. "I thought you were gonna say something way worse."

"It's bad!" Caro and I both screamed at the same time, then immediately jinxed and unjinxed each other, crossing our fingers and rapping our knuckles against the wooden table. "It's just a stupid thing to say," Caro added after we could both speak again.

"Like, what's *wrong* with being like other girls?" I added. Just thinking about Brandon and his stupid comments was getting me riled up, killing my buzz, and I sat up from Oliver and immediately felt a little cold. "Why, because I surf? Plenty of girls surf. It's not exactly a rare thing here. I'm not, like, this dinosaur fossil that he discovered. And girls are awesome! Caro's a girl and *she's* awesome."

"I am." Caro nodded to herself, then jabbed a thumb into her chest. "More people should be like me!"

"Agreed!" Drew announced from the floor. "Who are we talking about?"

"Brandon," I told him.

Drew made a jerking-off motion. "That fucking acoustic guitar."

"*Right?*" He and Caro high-fived.

Oliver was suspiciously quiet next to me, and when I finally turned my head to look at him, I realized that he was staring at all of us with the fondest look in his eyes. "I missed this," he said.

"Missed what?" Caro said as Drew slid back to the floor, propping himself up on my and Caro's legs.

"This," Oliver said, waving his arm so that some beer sloshed out of the bottle and landed on the floor. "You guys. This."

Drew, Caro, and I all exchanged glances. "Uh, dude, sorry to ruin your moment, but right now is not that great," Drew said.

"Nope. We are incredibly, off-the-charts normal right now," Caro slurred. "This party? All a terrible cliché."

"Hey!" Drew yelped.

Caro gave him a peck on the cheek. "You know what I mean, lovebug."

"I didn't ever have normal," Oliver said. "I mean, I thought I did, but now . . ." He shrugged a little. "I just wish I had known you all longer. All those years. Without the ten-year gap in the middle. It would have been nice."

Caro stared at him a moment, then burst into tears.

"Oh, shit." Oliver's face, already solemn, immediately shifted to panic. "Caro, no. Oh God. What is she doing? Did I break her?"

Drew and I just shook our heads. "She always cries when she gets drunk," Drew explained as he pulled Caro off my lap and down onto the floor with him.

"I can't help it," Caro wept, wiping at her eyes. "I'm tenderhearted! And this isn't waterproof mascara. Fuck."

"It would have been nice," Drew told Oliver as I patted the top of Caro's head and Drew passed her some napkins that looked . . . not very fresh. "But you're back *now*, right? We get a do-over."

"No, we don't," I said without thinking. (I don't cry when I'm drunk, the way Caro does. I just talk.) "There's no way to do over what happened. And even if there was, all of the pieces fit differently now. Oliver's not the same person he was when he was kidnapped. *I'm* not the same person. *None* of us are. It's not a do-over. It's a start-over."

"You can't step in the same river twice," Caro sniffled.

Drew just rolled his eyes, even as he continued handing her napkins. "Caro, we get it. You like *The Great Gatsby*. You don't have to keep quoting it."

"It's not my fault I do the reading and you don't!" she told him. "And it's a classic line. Please educate yourself. And don't cheat off of me, either."

"It was ONE time!" Drew protested.

"I need some air," I said, nudging Oliver with my elbow.

"Good call," he said, then helped me stand up. I was drunk enough that it took my head an extra few seconds to catch up to my body, but once I was upright, walking wasn't too difficult. Oliver took both of our beers in one of his hands, then used the other to steady me as we stepped over Drew and Caro ("Take a jacket," Caro mumbled from the floor, her voice already starting to sound far away and sleepy) and made our way outside.

Brandon was still playing the acoustic guitar, strumming out Bob Dylan's "Don't Think Twice, It's All Right" with a bit more competence than I expected from him, and I led Oliver through the shadows so we wouldn't have to deal with him. One encounter with Brandon was enough to fill my quota for the next year.

"Here," I said to Oliver, leading him toward a gazebo that Drew's parents had built on their property soon after they bought the house. The wood was old now, the white paint starting to peel and revealing spots filled with dozens of potential splinters. "Drew and Caro and I used to have 'secret meetings' in here," I told him, sitting down on the steps. "Though I don't know how secret they were in a gazebo. Lots of potential for enemy surveillance and infiltration."

Oliver smiled as he sat back down next to me, then handed me my beer. It was warm and flat, though, and didn't taste as good as the ones at the beginning of the party had. "Can I ask you a question?" he said.

"Is that the question?" I nudged his shoulder when he raised an eyebrow at me. "I need a better audience for my sense of humor. And yeah, of course."

He traced his thumb around the beer, wiping off the condensation in one clean stripe. "Why *don't* you join the surf team?"

I blinked at him. "*That's* your question?"

"Because you flinched when Brandon said that maybe one day you would. You're good enough, right? It's not a big secret or anything that you're good. I bet you could make the team, no problem."

"Dude, my parents. I told you, they'd freak out. Like, werewolves during a full moon freak out. And the surf team costs money. There's fees, meets, equipment, signed permission slips. There's no way. No."

"But how do you know?"

"Look, Ollie, you don't—" I started to say, but the look on his face stopped me. "What is it? What's wrong?"

"No, it's just, no one's called me Ollie in, like, forever." He smiled a little.

"I was—I *am*—the only one who was allowed to call you that," I told him. "I guess it's still habit. Is that okay?"

"No, it's fine, it's fine. Sorry, go on."

"You don't know, okay? When you disappeared, my parents, they changed. They would've smothered me in Bubble Wrap if they could have."

"Well, that wouldn't have been very safe."

"You know what I mean." I nudged him with my knee.

"But they want you to be happy?"

"Yeah, I guess. But sometimes happiness means different things to different people. And if they found out and said I couldn't do it anymore?" I shivered at the thought, the idea of not cutting through glassy water in the morning, not riding out the wave and having it take me somewhere that I didn't know I could go, that first sweet gulp of air after wiping out and resurfacing. "Maybe when I go to college. Maybe then. I'll be eighteen and I won't be here anymore."

"You won't?" Oliver asked. Neither of us were looking at each other: he was pulling paint chips off the gazebo's front step and I was plucking grass out of Drew's parents' immaculate lawn, one blade at a time. If the conversation kept going the way it was, we were going to cause some serious damage to the backyard.

"I, um, I actually applied to UC San Diego," I said. "No one knows that, though. Not even my parents—or Caro and Drew." Just saying the words out loud made my heart start to race. "They have a surf team. It's like, second-in-the-nation good. And even if I don't make it, I could still surf at Black's Beach. That's a good place to go. If I get in, I mean. I probably won't, but if I do, then yeah." I hugged my knees to my chest. "Don't tell anyone. Okay?"

"I won't tell," Oliver promised, looking down at his lap. "I, um, I lied to my dad, too. About school."

"You did?"

"Yeah. You know how they found my fingerprint in that forensic science class? I didn't actually tell him that I was taking it. I signed up behind his back. It was a Saturday science class through this local college. He was always so weird about me doing things outside of the house, so I just didn't say anything. I forged his signature and I went."

"You liked science so much that you were willing to give up your Saturdays?" I teased him. "Nerd alert."

Oliver huffed out a little smile. "So now I'm home and it's your turn to leave. I see how it is."

"Oh, please." I shoved at his arm. "It's not like I'm going anywhere right *now*. We still get to have our do-over. I mean, our start-over." I sprinkled a handful of grass over his shoes, then shivered again.

"Cold?" Oliver asked.

I wasn't sure what I was. Yes, I was cold, my hair still damp from surfing and the sea air starting to creep over the hills and drift into the suburban yards. But it was his knee pressing against mine, the fact that neither of us moved away or acknowledged it, the warmth of his skin under his jeans and the way it felt so new and so familiar at the same time.

"Yeah," I said. "Really cold."

"Here." He started to slip out of his hoodie.

"Is this new?" I asked him as I tugged it over my head, fixing the sleeves so that they came down past my fingertips.

"Yeah. My mom got it for me."

She had bought it for him, bought it so he could fit in and look "cool," bought it so he would talk to her and not hate her for taking ten years to find him.

I thought of Maureen watching Oliver walk up the front steps to school on his first day back, her face so tight and scared that it was hard not to feel the same way when you looked at her, and when I thought of my parents watching me the same way, I suddenly wanted to go back inside and cry on the floor with Caro.

Instead, I grabbed the strings and tightened the hoodie around my face so Oliver couldn't see my eyes. It smelled like the twins' shampoo again, but also like Oliver, soap and salt air and just *him*.

"You're a weirdo," he laughed, trying to pull the strings out of my hand so he could see my entire face. "You look like a hobbit."

"It's my disguise," I told him, blinking fast to keep the tears at bay.

"Well, considering that I just gave it to you, it's a pretty terrible disguise." Oliver tugged at the strings again and this time I let him unravel them so the hoodie opened back up. The moment had passed and I was okay again.

"Better not go into the FBI," he said. "You'd suck at that job. No offense."

"Like that was ever a plan," I scoffed, then fixed the sleeves again. "Your mom has good taste."

Oliver gave a half nod, half shrug, then looked back to the party. "So those are your friends," he said, gesturing back toward the noise and light.

"Some of them. But Caro and Drew more than anyone, though. And, well, you," I added hastily. "You're my friend, obviously."

"Yeah?" Oliver turned to look at me and in the faint light from the party, filtered through the gazebo's lattice, his eyes seemed grayer, softer.

"Of course we're friends, Ollie." My voice was scratchier than I meant it to sound and I coughed a little. "I've had this . . . thing."

"Thing?" Oliver repeated. "What thing?"

Stop talking, Emmy. Stop. Talking.

"It's this note. I've had it since you . . . since your dad, that day."

Oliver frowned a little and scooted even closer to me. "What note?"

"Caro gave you a note that day. She passed it to you in class."

"What did it say?"

I smiled, suddenly embarrassed. Why did I keep it for ten years? We were just dumb little kids, it didn't matter. Why was I even bringing it up?

"It said, 'Do you like Emmy, Yes No?'" Now I couldn't even bring myself to look at Oliver, I was so mortified. I was never drinking again, not if it made me start blabbering about ten-year-old memories.

Oliver, however, had a curious smile on his face, almost like he was fond of this note he didn't even remember. "Well, what did I say?" he asked.

"You circled yes," I whispered. "I mean, it's stupid, it's so stupid. We were seven years old, it doesn't—"

"It matters," Oliver murmured. "You kept it?"

I nodded again.

"I'm glad I circled yes, then," he said.

I smiled back at him, and I realized that our faces were closer than they had been before, and the party sounded more muted, almost like we were drifting away from it. The stars tilted, the moon spun, and then my mouth was on his and we were kissing.

He tasted like beer, like warm apple cider. I realized that my hand was moving on its own, up to his sleeve and then cupping his shoulder. I hung on to Oliver as we kissed again because this time, he wasn't going anywhere.

"Sorry," was the first thing he said when we parted. "I'm sorry, Emmy, I didn't—"

"Why the hell are you apologizing?" I whispered. My heart

was a pinball trapped in my rib cage, my lungs a broken accordion.

"Because we're friends. I don't know. I don't want to screw this up." He was leaning in again, though, his pulse strumming like a hummingbird's heart under my fingertips, and I leaned up to kiss him again before he could say anything else.

After a minute, I climbed into his lap. I had kissed a couple of boys before, but those kisses had been perfunctory and self-conscious. A quick peck for Josh back in seventh grade because everyone else was making out during the slow dance and I didn't want us to be left out. A weird, clumsy make-out session on the bus on the way home from a field trip with Brian G. (We had seven Brians in our class that year. It got confusing. Not that I made out with all of them. Whatever, you know what I mean.)

But kissing Oliver? That was different.

Oliver had always been different.

His hands held my waist like I was going to fall, his arms locked around mine and kept me steady as I cupped his face in my hands. "Still sorry?" I whispered to him, and he laughed against my mouth.

"Not really, no," he admitted. "This isn't high on my list of regrets."

"Good," I said, then kissed the side of his mouth. "Can I ask you something?"

"Sure."

"Did you get jealous about Brandon? Because he's, like, nothing. He's nothing to me. I didn't want you to think that."

"I wasn't jealous," Oliver said. "But I didn't like that he was making you feel bad about something you like to do. That's a shitty thing to do to anyone, but I didn't like that he was doing it to you."

"So you didn't make out with me because of Brandon?"

"Um, no. I kissed you despite the douche canoe."

I laughed, loud and sharp against the quiet night air. "I thought you were really cute when I saw you on TV, that first night." The words sounded odd when I said them out loud, like I had a tabloid news fetish. "I mean, I was glad you were home, not that—"

His fingers intertwined at the base of my spine. "I know. I thought you were cute, too. You stuck your tongue out at me."

I groaned and dropped my head against his shoulder, hiding my face in shame. "I felt like the biggest dork in the world after I did that. Ask Caro. She'll tell you. I was in agony."

"I don't think Caro can answer too many questions right now," Oliver said, then shrugged his shoulders so I had to sit back up again. "At least, not while she's asleep on the floor."

"She'll wake up soon," I told him. "She gets her second wind after about thirty minutes or so."

I slipped off his lap so I could curl up against his side. He put his arm around me, like a hug, like a wing, like a home. "That's what I meant earlier," Oliver said, "about wishing I could have been here. You know things about one another. They know things about *you*."

"Too much," I groaned.

"No, I'm serious. I don't have that with anyone except . . ."

When I looked up, Oliver was staring straight ahead, his jaw tight, his face suddenly a secret to me. "Your dad," I finished for him.

"Yeah," Oliver said after a few seconds had passed. "My dad. We were——" He cleared his throat. "He's my best friend. Or he was. I don't really know what he is—or was—anymore."

I pulled his arm around me even tighter, then put my arm around his waist. "I'm sorry," I whispered.

He hugged me against his side, then kissed the top of my head. "Thanks," he said. "No one else has said that."

"But your mom . . . ?"

"My mom doesn't know what she wants." I could hear the anger as it reverberated in his chest, low like a drum. "I think she spent so much time looking for me and now that I'm home, she doesn't know what to do with me. I disrupted her life. She was totally fine without me."

I shook my head, more to myself than Oliver. "When you went missing, she never stopped looking for you," I said. "She didn't focus on anything else except you."

"Yeah. Except for getting remarried and having more kids."

"Hey!" I sat up. "That's not fair."

"Yeah, well. Sometimes I don't feel like playing fair. Nobody was playing fair with me."

"Your mom had one focus, one cause. And that cause had such momentum, you know? It's all she did. It's all she thought and breathed. And now suddenly, you're back. It's over. She got you back. But, if you're driving a semi at sixty miles an hour, you can't just stop on a dime, you know?"

"Did she say that?"

"Well, no, but I've known her longer than you have. I watched her, Ollie. I saw . . ." My voice trailed off as I remembered Maureen's panic, how she used to walk with her arms out in front of her, as if to break a fall or embrace a child that was just out of reach. "Everyone's different because of what happened," I finally said. "Especially her. And you."

"I feel like even if I did talk to her, she wouldn't want to hear what I really have to say." Oliver had rested his head on top of mine, his words rumbling down through my skull.

"Well, *I* do," I said. "You can say anything to me." But I didn't carry it further. I didn't ask what he really wanted to say. Because the truth was that I wasn't sure I wanted to hear it, either.

"Emmy!"

Oliver and I jerked apart, our arms suddenly back against our own bodies and not wrapped around each other's. "Yeah?" I yelled, even though the person was in silhouette against the lit-up patio and I couldn't really see who it was. "Who is that?" I asked.

"I have no idea who *anyone* is," Oliver replied. "Except Caro and Drew."

"Caro's ready to go home!" the person—male—yelled back.

"Of course she is," I muttered, starting to stand up. Sitting outside with Oliver had sobered me up and this time when I stood, my head managed to keep up with my body. "Coming!" I yelled. "Who are you?"

"Kevin!"

"Oh my God! It's Kevin!" I whispered to Oliver. "That's Drew's boyfriend!"

Oliver squinted, trying to see better. "They're dating?"

"Well, I don't know if they're dating yet, but Drew wants to make out with him and I think Kevin feels the same."

"Got it." Oliver held on to my arm as I climbed down the stairs, then we navigated our way back to the house, our shoes making soft *swish-swish-swish* sounds against the dewy grass.

The party had definitely wound down, and people were either half asleep on couches and chairs or, like Caro, standing up and slumped against whatever upright objects could keep them steady.

For Caro, that object was Drew.

"Hi," she said when she saw me. "I'm ready to go." Then she pointed at Drew. "He totally made out with Kevin." She announced it in a stage whisper so that both Drew and Kevin blushed.

"Um, yes, you're ready to go," Drew said, trying to shove her off onto me. "Please leave my house and come back when you can be discreet." But his cheeks were pink and Kevin was smiling in that way you smile when someone you like kisses you back.

"Well played," I murmured to Drew.

"Hi, I'm Oliver," Oliver said to Kevin, waving a little.

"I know," Kevin said. "I'm Kevin. We went to preschool together."

"Oh, cool. Yeah."

"Call one of your siblings," I said to Caro. "I can't drive like this."

Caro pulled her phone out of her hoodie pocket, her finger hovering over the screen. "Which one should I call?" she muttered to herself.

"Grumpy, Happy, Dopey, whoever," I told her, then leaned against the kitchen table. "Just pick one."

She eventually called Jessica, her oldest sister, and the two of them had a quick conversation that seemed to focus on all the times Caro had covered for Jessica in the past. "You owe me," Caro kept saying, and apparently she won the argument because she hung up and said, "Jess'll be here in five minutes."

"Great," I said. "Let's wait outside. I need fresh air."

"M'fine," she mumbled. "Sleepy. Home. Bed. *Heather*." That last word sounded more like a threat and she frowned.

"Yeah, okay." I pulled Caro back from Drew, who seemed more than happy to shove her away and get back to more important things, like a boy who showed up at his house just to spend time with him.

Oliver and I got Caro around the corner and into the backseat of Jessica's car. "If you puke, you're dead to me, Caro," Jessica said, but Caro just ignored her and said, "But I want to ride in the front."

"Drunk people in the back," I told her. "It's a cardinal rule."

"I've never heard of that rule," Oliver said with a grin.

"Yeah." Caro was now trying to lie down, even as Oliver and I were climbing in next to her. "You made that up."

"Shove over," I told her. "Your shoes are taking up way too much room."

"They have a big personality," she slurred, and I saw Jessica giving us all the evil eye in the rearview mirror. I couldn't blame her, though. If I had a sister who woke me up in the middle of the night to pick up her and her drunk friends, I'd be pissed, too.

"Do you have enough room?" I asked Oliver once we left Drew's neighborhood, back down the hill toward our boring, everyday suburban sprawl, the mansions in the rearview mirror. Next to me, Caro's eyes were closed and she was propped up against the window.

"I'm fine," he said. The window was open a little, making his hair dance across his forehead. "You can move closer if you want," he added, gesturing to Caro's feet. "You could get hurt."

I curled up next to him, my knees tucked into my chest and my head against his shoulder. "For safety's sake," I said, and felt him smile against my hair as he wrapped his arm around me. The streets were empty and we watched as the buildings and houses flew past us.

I had Jessica pull up a few blocks away from our houses so she could let Oliver out. I was pretty sure my parents were asleep, but I didn't want to risk being seen. "Sorry," I said again to him. "Curbside service next time."

"Byyyyyye, Oliver," Caro said from the backseat. "Did you have a nice time? I hope you had a nice time."

"Caro," he said, "this was the best party I've ever been to in my life."

It was the only party he'd ever been to in his life. And I was the only one who knew it. I looked away to hide my smile.

"Text me later?" he asked me.

"Okay," I said. "Sleep well."

"Yeah. You too."

He didn't shut the door, though. "Bye," he said.

"See you later."

"Okay." He slammed the door and I rolled down the window so I could lean out. I could hear Jessica's annoyed sigh, but I ignored her.

"Get home safely," I told him.

"Yeah, sure." He smiled back. "Hey, um, this might not be the best time to say this . . ."

My heart plummeted. "Okay?"

He tapped his fist against the car door a few times, then looked at me. "I'm glad you never moved."

It was the nicest thing anyone had ever said to me.

"Well, I'm glad you finally came back," I said, and when we finally drove away, he never moved from under the streetlight, his image growing smaller and smaller until I couldn't see him anymore.

But I knew he was still there.

Back at Caro's, her brother David was playing *Mortal Kombat* and didn't even acknowledge us as Caro and I came in through the front door and started up the stairs.

"Shh, my parents are sleeping," she whispered, but we all knew that Caro's parents slept like the dead. (To be fair, they had six kids. They were probably exhausted.) My parents, on the other hand, slept like nervous birds. I once got up to use the bathroom and came out to find both of them in the hallway, my mom behind my dad, each of them clutching one of my mom's high heels.

"What are you doing?" I cried.

"We thought you were an intruder!" my mom yelled as my dad flipped on the light.

"An intruder who breaks into the house and then stops to use the *bathroom*?"

That was just one example of why sneaking into or out of my house was not an option. I don't want to get impaled with an Easy Spirit pump. I don't know how I plan on dying, but it's not going to be like that.

Caro and I took turns in the bathroom and she loaned me some clean pajamas. "You're like a paper doll," she giggled as I came into the bedroom. Heather's side was still empty. Either that, or she was just asleep under the clothing explosion and it was impossible to see her through the debris.

"I'm like a what?" I said.

"You keep borrowing my clothes."

"Well, yours are all nice and clean. Scoot over."

Caro turned off the light as I climbed into her bed. Sleeping over at Caro's always meant a foot kicking me in the arm or a hand draped over my face. Back when Caro had her cat, Mr. Pickles, he used to sleep on top of my head, only he'd eventually slide down so that I'd wake up and find myself being smothered by a ten-year-old cat who had no interest in moving.

I don't really miss Mr. Pickles. Don't tell Caro.

She was asleep within minutes, but I lay awake, listening to the crickets. It's funny how, even though Caro doesn't live on my street, it still sounds the same outside, bugs and distant cars and a silence so loud that it can wake you up, or worse, keep you from falling asleep.

Caro rolled over next to me and slung her arm over my shoulders. Mr. Pickles 2.0. "Caro?" I whispered.

Nothing.

"Caro, get off." I gave her a shove and she just snuggled down against my arm. I sighed. The things I do for our friendship. "Caro?" I whispered again. "Are you awake?"

She wasn't, of course, which made it easier to confide in her. "He kissed me," I murmured. "Outside at the party."

Caro just snuffled.

"Well, congrats for you," came a sleepy voice in the direction of Heather's bed. "Now will you shut up, please?"

"*Sweet dreams*, Heather," I said, hoping that my sarcasm was able to reach her through her dirty sheets and probably bedbug-ridden pillows.

"Whatever."

I rolled over, away from Caro so that I was on the very edge of the bed, my arm pressed against the mattress seam. "But he did," I whispered, this time to myself, and it was there, dangling on the precipice between awake and asleep, that I finally tumbled over the edge.

CHAPTER NINETEEN

"Guess who's invited us over for dinner next week!" my mom said the second I walked in through the back door on Saturday. It was lunchtime, at least I thought it was. We had all—me, Caro, Heather, Heather's bedbugs—slept late the next morning, then Caro's oldest brother, Michael, made blueberry pancakes, which we ate while watching cartoons. The fact that we were hungover went unsaid, but the pancakes and coffee had helped.

A little.

"Who?" I said, wincing at her too-perky tone. "The queen? Do I get to wear a tiara?"

"You're always so cranky after you sleep over at Caro's," my mom replied. "What time did you go to bed last night?"

I shrugged. "Dunno. Two?"

"That is WAY too late," she said. "Caro's parents are okay with that?"

I shrugged again as my dad strolled into the room. "What's too late?" he asked.

"She stays up way too late when she goes over to Caroline's house," my mom informed him.

"All we did was watch movies," I said. "It's like sleeping with your eyes open. And it's rude to talk about someone like they're not there." I reached for a banana out of the fruit bowl. "Manners matter."

Both of my parents gave me a Look. "What, exactly, are you learning at school?" my dad said, shaking his head. "My tax dollars at work, I swear."

"*Our* tax dollars," my mom corrected him. "Promise me you'll take a nap later today, okay?"

"Twist my arm," I replied, not bothering to mention that taking a nap was already on my Short List of Priorities that day.

And so was talking to Oliver.

I had checked my phone the minute I woke up, waiting to see a text or missed call or something from him, but I just had junk emails from SAT prep programs and a few "Don't you want to apply HERE?" colleges. (Those colleges were like clingy boyfriends or girlfriends. No one wants to go to school there when they're so desperate to get people to do just that. They needed to start playing hard to get, I thought, or no one was going to ask them to prom.)

I had deleted everything, but Heather caught me checking my phone three separate times at breakfast. "No word from Lover

Boy?" she asked around a mouthful of syrup and blueberries, which was exactly as attractive as it sounds.

Caro, however, dropped her fork. *"Who?"* she asked me. "Who's she talking about?"

Michael flipped another pancake at the stove, the sudden sizzling sound reminding me of an old torture technique. "Can we, um . . . ?" I nodded my head in the direction of Caro's siblings.

Caro didn't need to be told twice. She grabbed our plates, napkins, and silverware. "Get the syrup!" she called to me as she ran upstairs, and since I happen to love both syrup and Caro, I obeyed.

"Are we seriously going to eat in your room?" I asked as I ran up the stairs after her.

"What? No! Are you insane?" She beckoned me into the bathroom, then shut the door behind us.

I looked around. "You want me to eat breakfast in the bathroom?"

"I don't care if you eat breakfast in here or not. I just want you to talk and this is the most private place in the house. What am I hearing? You told Heather something important, but not me?" She punched me twice in the shoulder. "Slugbug Betrayal!"

"I don't think that's how the game works," I said, reaching for my pancakes. "And I thought I was telling *you*, but you were already asleep. Heather happened to be awake and I didn't even know she was in the room at first."

"Ugh, she's the worst. So, anyway. Lover Boy." Caro narrowed her eyes at me and managed to look intimidating even with a drop of syrup on her chin and pancake batter in her hair. "Did you . . . kiss Oliver?"

I nodded, no longer interested in eating. "Outside. Last night, when we were sitting in the gazebo."

"You kissed him in the gazebo? Oh my God, what kind of weirdo romantic are you?" But Caro was grinning from ear to ear. "Was it good? Is he a good kisser?"

I guess my hesitation and smile told Caro everything. "Get OUT!" she cried. "Do you think he remembers it? How drunk were you?"

"He better remember it!" I said. "We were just talking and then . . ." I brought my hands together. "It just happened. It wasn't like we were planning it."

"Yeah, you just lured him into a gazebo at a mansion." Caro wiggled her eyebrows at me. "Well played, Emmy, well played."

I pretended to curtsey, which is hard to do when you're holding a plate full of pancakes and your borrowed pajama pants are too big. "Thank you, thank you," I said. "But I haven't heard from him yet."

"Well, it's not like you live next door to each other or anything—OH, WAIT."

I checked my phone again. "What if he *doesn't* remember it?"

Caro shrugged. "Then Drew and I will burn his house down."

"You're very loyal."

"Make sure to say nice things about me when they arraign me for arson."

"Emmy." My mom's voice cut through my thoughts. "Are you listening?"

Nope.

"Yeah, totally," I said, then hopped up on the island countertop. "Down," my mom said, pointing at the floor, and I hopped back off. I had forgotten that I wasn't at Caro's anymore. "So who's dinner with?"

My mom raised an eyebrow that told me that's what I just missed. "Maureen invited us over for next Monday night," she said. "You and me and Dad and then her and Rick and the girls and Oliver. Isn't that nice?"

It sounded like a nightmare. "Awesome," I said. "But the girls have a million food allergies. What are we eating? Tofu?"

My dad made retching sounds.

"I think they're grilling," my mom said, ignoring him. "But we're supposed to bring the salad, which means that I have to find that recipe. . . ." She fluttered off to her laptop, where she organized recipes by food group, holiday, event, and season. It's an Excel spreadsheet straight from foodie heaven. "Are you in the mood for feta?" she called to me as she disappeared.

"Possibly!" I called back. I had finished eating that banana in record time. "Can I go hang out with Drew today?"

"Ask your father," came the reply, so I turned to look at my dad. "Can I?"

"You and Drew have been spending a lot of time together," my dad said in a non-nonchalant (or perhaps, chalant? is that even a word?) way.

"Dad, Drew's gay," I told him, just as my mom yelled, "Drew's gay!" from her office. I swear, she's installed hidden microphones in every room in the house.

"I know," my dad said, then tapped me on the head with the newspaper as he walked past. "Your old dad may know a little more than you think he does."

"What?" I said, but he just waved the newspaper at me and went out to the garage, leaving me alone in the kitchen.

"So is that a yes?" I called to no one in particular, and when no answer came, I decided it was definitely a yes, and went to call Drew.

CHAPTER TWENTY

Drew picked me up in his van an hour later, barely stopping at the curb before I was already opening the door and swinging myself in. "Hello, hello," he said, adjusting his sunglasses. "The Drew Express has arrived safely and on time. Please feel free to give our fledgling business five stars on Yelp."

"I'll tell all my friends," I said, fastening my seat belt. I couldn't help but notice that Oliver's driveway was empty and that the blinds in the front window were pulled shut. Where had they gone?

"Where's your board?" Drew asked me.

"Parents," I replied, jerking my thumb over my shoulder. "They're both home right now, watching my every move."

"Just as well. The waves are super flat today." Drew hit the gas harder and I made a mental note to prepare for my mother's eventual discussion about how it's a "safe neighborhood" and Drew needed to be "more cautious." (Talking to her is like playing Mad Libs sometimes. You just insert the appropriate phrase into its proper slot.)

"So!" Drew said, grabbing my knee for emphasis. "Guess what we are doing today?"

"Surprise me." His smile was so wide that it made me smile, too.

"We"—he squeezed my knee again—"are going to Starbucks."

I just stared at him. "Wow," I finally said. "Because those are *really* rare and we *never* go to them. I'm so glad we're hanging out today."

"Could you please stop dripping your sarcasm all over my car's interior? And I could give a shit about Starbucks. I like the place next door better, you know that. But Starbucks has the best *employees*." He wiggled his eyebrows at me.

The pieces clicked together.

"Kevin works at Starbucks?" I guessed, and Drew nodded. "So I get to go to Starbucks and watch you flirt with the barista?"

"Feel free to live tweet the experience!"

"Drew!" I banged my head against the headrest. "This is going to be so boring! And aren't you supposed to play hard to get? This is definitely not playing hard to get."

"Okay, first, thank you for being an amazing, supportive friend. I'll totally buy you something that involves whipped cream and I'll love you forever."

"And?"

"And the time for playing hard to get is over because I have been *gotten*." Drew looked so pleased that the tips of his ears were turning red. "Kevin stayed over after the party last night."

"You had sex with Kevin?!" I dove for my phone, ready to text Caro.

"No, no, not *that*. God, calm down. I just . . . we kissed and . . . you know, we actually cuddled."

"You do like to snuggle."

"I am a first-class snuggler, let's be real. And so is Kevin." Drew held up his hand, made a V with his index and middle fingers, then brought them together. "Compatible."

"Is he a good kisser?"

He signaled to turn left out into the main intersection. "Do you think I'd be this excited if it was like making out with a mackerel? He was amazing. *He* is amazing. And he"—Drew honked at the person in front of him to move—"said he likes me back. *What* is the holdup here?" He honked again.

"You literally look like you're starring in a romantic comedy right now," I said. "You're almost glowing. I need sunglasses to look at you."

Drew handed me his and I put them on. "Do I look stupid?" I flipped down the car's visor to look in the mirror, but there wasn't one.

He glanced at me. "No, you're adorable." He honked again. "I mean, seriously. How hard is it to press a gas pedal?"

"You know Caro and I still have to vet Kevin, though. He

needs to be group-approved for our official seal of approval."

"Caro already gave him the thumbs-up last night, even though she was so drunk, she couldn't even spell her name. Which is more than I can say for you and your disappearing act. *Why* are we just sitting here?" Apparently, Drew had no problem keeping two conversations going at the same time, one with me and one with the traffic jam.

"Well, I was a little busy last night," I said, suddenly feeling my ears turn as red as Drew's.

But he was too distracted by the traffic jam to notice. "Are you *kidding* me?" he cried, sticking his head out the window. "The sign says STOP!" he yelled. "Not GIVE UP!"

"I thought making out with someone was supposed to *lower* your blood pressure," I mentioned as he settled back in the driver's seat.

"You know I have road rage," Drew replied, like it was the simplest answer imaginable. "Now, sorry. What?"

"What what?"

"You were saying?"

"Oh, just that I was busy last night." I tucked my hair behind my ear.

"Nervous tic!" Drew cried. "Tell me everything. Especially because we're not going anywhere anytime soon." He glared at the traffic jam.

"So, um, me and Oliver sort of made out last night."

"Shut up!" Drew slapped the steering wheel in delight. "You did not!"

"Oh, but I did."

"Okay, can I just say? Oliver is way cuter than the last guy you kissed."

"Ethan was totally fine, dude, I—"

"Rabbit teeth. There, I said it."

"He was going to get orthodontia eventually," I protested. "But I don't want to talk about Ethan."

"Yes, okay. Redirecting back. *Thank you!*" he suddenly screamed at the cars in front of us as they began to crawl forward. "I was starting to worry that I should have packed a snack and a canteen just so I could drive three miles to Starbucks. So where did you make out?"

"The gazebo, of course."

"Naturally. Did you initiate?"

I hesitated just long enough for Drew to say, "It's totally fine if you did, you know. You have to be a take-charge woman, Emmy. No one likes a doormat."

"No, I'm just trying to remember," I told him. "I think . . . I did? Or maybe it was . . . ?" I frowned and tilted my head, like it would dislodge the stuck memories and send the correct one to its rightful place in my brain. "I think we sort of just met in the middle." I brought my hands together. "Like this. But, you know, better."

"And he's a good kisser?"

I nodded, blushing again. "He's no mackerel."

Drew gave my shoulder a gentle shake. "You're so cute!" he

said. "You and your childhood love, back together. Someone needs to call Oprah. Or Ellen. Whoever has a daytime talk show that will get you a movie deal."

"He's not my 'childhood love,'" I told him, making air quotes around the last two words. "He's Oliver. He's just a dude—"

"—that you made out with last night. You're welcome, by the way, for throwing that party."

"Thank you, Drew," I intoned. "Best friend ever. You're the best."

He nodded approvingly. "I think you and I should stick together more often," he said. "We can make out with half of California if we play our cards right."

I just laughed and moved my hair again so it would stop blowing in my face. Drew's car was amazing, but it had no air-conditioning, and all the windows were down. "He still hasn't texted me," I said.

"Did you text him?"

"No. That's why I wanted to hang out with you. Because I wasn't sure what to do."

Drew patted my hand. "You've come to the right place."

CHAPTER TWENTY-ONE

As happy as I was to see Drew happy with Kevin, canoodling at the register over the chocolate bars and day-old bananas, it wasn't exactly my ideal Saturday afternoon. Still, Drew made good on his promise to get me some sort of frosty mocha whipped-cream thing that was delicious. It eased the pain of hanging out at a table mostly by myself, checking my phone for a text that never came.

"You should text him," Drew told me when there were customers, and Kevin had to take their order. "Just do it."

"Well, what do I say?" I ran my thumb over my phone's screen. "Like, 'Good making out with your face last night? Let's do it again.'?"

"Text Caro and ask her. You need all the help you can get."

I made a face at Drew but texted Caro, anyway. Her response came through a minute later:

Just say what's up or whatever.

I told Drew when he wandered back to me.

Drew sounded annoyed. "'What's *up?*' *That's* her answer? God, she bugs the hell out of me sometimes. I love her but I want to kill her, you know?"

"I know," I said, because I did. "That's friendship, dude. Kevin's free again, by the way."

Drew glanced over his shoulder. "Be right back. You better have texted him by the time I return." He pointed his finger at me, then tapped me on the nose and went back to Kevin, who hadn't stopped blushing in the hour that we had been there.

I rolled my eyes in their general direction, then texted Oliver before I could stop myself. It took a few minutes to figure out what to say, but in the end, I went with something safe, just in case Maureen was checking Oliver's phone. "Hey," a voice said, and I looked up to see Kevin holding a duplicate of the drink Drew had bought me earlier. "Thought you might want another. On the house."

"The service here is amazing," I said, then smiled and took it. "Thanks."

Kevin sat down next to me. "Drew went to use the bathroom but he said I had to check and make sure that you texted Oliver."

"So you're up to speed?"

"You made out with him last night but now you're too scared to text him and he hasn't texted you yet?"

"Impressive. You are up to speed. And I did text him. I said"—I held up the phone so Kevin could read it—"'Had a great time last night.' What do you think?"

Kevin shrugged. "A little boring, but it'll do. Better than Caro's response, that's for sure." He grinned at me and I could see why Drew was starry-eyed over him. "Thanks for hanging out here, by the way. I know it's not exactly exciting just watching us talk to each other."

"No worries, dude. I like when Drew's happy and he seems happy with you."

Kevin blushed even deeper and tried to hide his smile by playing with his apron strings. "Is this the part where you tell me you'll break my legs if I break his heart or something?"

"No. I thought that was already implied. Besides, I figured Caro might have already covered that."

He nodded. "Last night. She mentioned something about a crowbar . . . ?"

"That's my girl."

"Did you text him?" Drew came hurrying over. "Did he text you yet? What did I miss?"

"Had a great night," Kevin reported. "I told her it was meh."

"Six out of a possible score of ten," Drew agreed. He nudged Kevin's hip with his own. "How long is your break?"

Kevin just smiled and took Drew's hand in his own. I couldn't help but watch as Drew laced his fingers between Kevin's and pulled him a little closer.

I knew my cue to leave.

"Well, thanks for the drinks," I said, standing up and gathering my phone. "I'm gonna go, though."

"No, stay!" Drew said.

"There's scones," Kevin added. "The blueberry ones, not the gross currant ones."

"Ugh, currants." Drew shuddered.

"I don't even know why we sell them," Kevin admitted.

"Bye," I said pointedly, then stood on my tiptoes to kiss Drew's cheek. "See you on Monday. Use protection."

"I assume you mean an *apron*," he muttered in my ear, but kissed me back. "Be safe walking. Don't take any rides from strange men."

"I'll keep it in mind," I said, then stole his sunglasses off his head and took a sip of my drink as I headed out. He and Kevin were already halfway out the back door, tripping over each other's feet and giggling.

I checked my phone. Nothing.

Time to head home.

I was halfway there, waiting for the light to change at the intersection, when Maureen's SUV suddenly pulled up next to me. Rick was at the wheel and Maureen was talking to someone in the backseat, motioning with her hand about something. The windows were tinted, but I could make out the outline of the twins' car seats in the middle seats, and farther back, the tousle of Oliver's hair.

My breath caught before I could stop it.

"Oh, hi!" Maureen said, her voice muffled by the window. *Open it, open it,* I could see her mouthing to Rick, who dutifully did just that. "Hi, Emmy! What are you doing out here?"

Protest noises started to come from the backseat, and then Rick rolled down those windows, as well. "Hi!" the twins yelled. "We went mini golfing!"

"I hit the windmill!"

"I drank lemonade and threw up!"

"Cool," I said, desperately trying to get a glimpse of Oliver without being desperate about it. (Way easier said than done.)

He leaned forward when he heard my voice, just so I could see half his face in the window, the other half still stuck in the backseat. "Hey," he said.

"Hi," I said, and before I could figure out what else to say, Maureen interrupted us.

"We're heading home now! C'mon, we'll give you a ride! Open the doors, Rick, let her in."

"Careful in the backseat," Rick said as I started to climb in. "There's some random golf balls rolling around back there."

"Thanks," I said, trying to climb over the twins without actually touching them, since I wasn't sure which one had been sick, and also without tripping over myself in front of Oliver.

"There's room next to Oliver," Maureen said, directing me from the front seat.

"I think she's got it, hon," Rick said.

"Well, I'm just making sure." Maureen threw me a grin in the rearview mirror. "Enough room back there?"

I fell into the seat next to Oliver, squeezed in by bags of supplies: extra clothes, snacks, books, and tiny pink shoes. He looked like a giant next to all of it, but when I sat down, he smiled at me and grabbed my hand, squeezing so tight that all I could do was squeeze back just as hard.

"Hi," was all he said.

"Hey," I replied. Our voices were cool, like we said hello to each other all the time, like we weren't holding hands in the backseat of his mom's car, hanging on for our dear lives. "Did you get a hole in one?"

"I got a hole in one!" Nora screamed, trying to turn around in her car seat despite the harness, and I casually threw my bag over Oliver's and my hands before she could see. Oliver laughed, then hid it with a cough.

"You okay, sweetie?" Maureen asked from the front. "There's water in the cooler if—"

"I'm fine, Mom," Oliver said.

"I got a hole in one, Emmy!" Nora finally settled for just craning her neck around at a terrible-looking angle. "It went in!"

"Awesome!" I told her. "Did you get a sticker?"

"Yeah, but it's on my shoe."

"Of course it is."

Oliver's grip on my hand hadn't let go and I knocked my knee against his, raising my eyebrow in that subtle, universal gesture that means, "You okay?" He just nodded, so I let it go.

"Did you get my text?" I asked him. "Because I, um, I texted you. Today."

"Hey, Mom?" he called.

"Yes, sweetie?"

"Did I get Emmy's text today?" There was an edge to his voice, like this wasn't a question he should be asking.

Maureen sighed heavily from the front seat. "Honey, you'll get your phone back on Monday before school. We talked about this. He missed his curfew last night, Emmy."

"Let him explain it, Mo," Rick murmured from the front seat.

"No phone until Monday," Oliver told me, his voice cheerful but his eyes anything but happy. "So no, I did not get your text. And I couldn't text you, either."

That last sentence went over everyone's heads but mine, and I smiled despite myself. *"Oh,"* I said. "Oh."

"Right?" Oliver asked. We were speaking our own language at this point, grinning like idiots at each other. "What did your text say?"

"Oh, I just wanted to know if you had a good time last night, that's all."

"I had a great time," he replied. We sounded like we were performing a skit about the two most blandly cheerful high school students in America. "Really great."

"Emmy, can you please tell Drew that next time Oliver needs to be home by eleven?" Maureen looked at us again through the rearview mirror, her "mom face" firmly in place. "I don't know what his parents think is appropriate for a Friday night, but Oliver's curfew is eleven o'clock."

Oliver knocked his knee into mine this time. I didn't need a body-language expert to explain what he meant. "Yeah, of course," I said. "Drew's not great with time."

"You just don't know *what* could happen," Maureen said, and the double meaning in her words made everyone, even Molly and Nora, go quiet for the rest of the ride.

Oliver never let go of my hand.

Once we pulled up into their driveway, I had a plan. "Hey," I said as the twins started to frantically unbuckle themselves like their car seats were on fire. "Do you have that book that I loaned you for English?"

Oliver didn't miss a beat. "Oh, yeah, totally," he said. "Come on up, I'll get it for you."

"You're so sweet to loan him your things from last year," Maureen said. "Molly, no, do not eat that Cheerio from the floor. I said *no*."

"Of course," I said. "It's not a problem."

As soon as we were out of the car, and while Rick and Maureen fumbled with the girls and empty juice boxes and bags, Oliver and I disappeared inside and ran up the stairs, taking them two at a time. "I am so sorry!" he whispered, even though we were the only ones in the house. "She went ballistic when I came home last night."

"What'd you say?"

"Just that Drew and I met up at the movies." We hit the landing and booked it into his room. "And it let out later than I thought it would. Don't worry, I didn't mention you at all."

"God, thank you. My mom would—"

"I know, I know. Basement, Dickens, gruel."

"Exactly." I closed the door behind us, then turned around and smiled at Oliver. "Hi."

"Hi," he said, then gathered me up and kissed me hard.

It took all the coordination in my body to hang on to his sweatshirt sleeve, but I managed to stay upright. He tasted even better than he had the night before, this time without the fog of alcohol between us, and I wrapped my hand around the back of his neck and pulled him closer, dizzy with the sort of longing that was now hitting me like a freight train.

"I was kind of freaking out," I admitted when he pulled away for a second. "I thought . . ."

"You thought I was a douche canoe," he finished.

"Yeah, kind of," I giggled. "But not anymore. Quick, hurry, before they find us."

Oliver pulled me closer, tighter than ever this time, and kissed me again. The only way I could describe what kissing him felt like was, like the last day of school, knowing that months of freedom and sunshine lay before you, the feeling that you could do anything you wanted and time stretched out in endless possibilities. That's how I felt in his arms, like the future was limitless just because he was there. He was finally there.

We heard the door from the garage slam open, followed by, "Girls, do *not* slam the door!" We pulled apart once again. "Quick, which book do you want?"

"I don't care, anything," I said, and he shoved a copy of *Mrs. Dalloway* at me. "Wait, wait!" I whispered. "Come here, your mouth." I pressed my thumb against his lips, wiping away my lip gloss. "Bonne Belle Lip Smacker in Dr Pepper just doesn't match your skin tone," I teased, and he kissed my thumb.

"Tastes good, though," he said.

"Oh my God, you need to shut up right now." I kissed him again, then pulled away and straightened my shirt. "You good?"

"Um, *yeah*." He laughed. "This is way better than miniature golf."

"Glad to know where I rank," I told him, then clutched the copy of *Mrs. Dalloway* to my chest. "See you at school on Monday?"

"Absolutely," he whispered back, then I left his room and went back downstairs, dodging Maureen and going out the front door, only letting the empty cul-de-sac see my face-splitting smile, my ridiculous happiness.

CHAPTER TWENTY-TWO

Over the next week, Oliver and I kept to a pretty steady routine of going to school, going to the beach for more surfing lessons, kissing, making out in the backyard, and basically lying to our parents about all of that. (Except for school. That, unfortunately, wasn't a lie.) Caro came to the beach a few times with us, since Drew was busy hanging out with Kevin at Starbucks or at soccer practice, but after the second time, she got bored. "I'm the third wheel," she said on the way home. "I'm turning your bicycle into a tricycle."

"Or we could just be three unicycles," I replied. Oliver was in the front seat next to me, his hand on my leg as I drove with the window down, trying to dry my hair as fast as possible.

"Or we could be a penny-farthing," Oliver said. "Maybe we could put Caro in a sidecar."

"A penny what?" Caro and I both said at the same time.

"You know, that old-fashioned bike that had one big wheel up front and then a little wheel behind it?" Oliver mimed riding a bike, which, let's be honest, didn't help to clear up the confusion.

"Yeah, no, I'm not that," I told him. "Can you roll your window down? I need more air."

"You were saying about the sidecar?" Caro yelled, her voice nearly being drowned out from the sudden gust of wind. "It'd probably be less windy out there than it is in here!"

So after that, it just became Oliver and me. His surfing wasn't really improving, but we spent most of the time bobbing up and down on the boards, talking instead of practicing.

But on Friday, when our parents thought we were doing another group project for AP Civics at Caro's house but Oliver and I were actually down at the beach, he was subdued, almost tired. His eyes were heavy, his words soft. "Hey," I said as we floated next to each other, our legs churning in the water. "What's wrong?"

"I'm fine," he said absently.

"You're doing the dude sulk," I told him.

Oliver laughed. "The what?"

"You guys always get pouty and sullen." I poked my lip out and slouched down, trying to make him laugh for real this time. It worked. "What's wrong?"

Oliver, though, just looked behind him and watched as a wave started to form. "You think I can get this one?"

I glanced at it. "Probably. You're getting good." And he was.

He had already ridden to the shore several times that day, hooting and hollering with each successful wave.

"I'm taking it," he said, then swung his legs out of the ocean and back onto the board as he started to paddle.

"Oliver, wait," I said as he started to move, and he deliberately reached out and splashed me, leaving me sputtering.

"Oh, you're going down," I said, racing to catch up to him. It wasn't too difficult—his arms were longer and stronger, but I had three years' worth of experience—and we rode in together, almost like we were moving as the same person.

Afterward, we sat on the beach together, our wet suits drying on a rock next to us as we huddled together underneath a blanket that we found in the back of the minivan. "Your car needs a name," Oliver said. "Something with personality."

"Stealth Fighter," I offered. "Secret Mission."

"Barely Running," Oliver said, and I laughed and pretended to choke him.

"Get your own car if you don't like mine!" I cried.

"Oh, Emmy, I would if I could," he said, and the sadness I had seen in the water was back now, clouding his eyes like a storm.

"What is it?" I asked. "What happened?"

Oliver shrugged and picked up some sand to run through his fingers. "I guess some national crime show called yesterday. They want to do a feature on my dad and . . . you know, everything." Oliver brushed the sand away, then waved his hand, the kidnapping just a pesky fly that could be swatted away. "My mom thinks they could find my dad that way. 'National exposure,' that's what she said."

"And you don't want to," I guessed.

"It's, like, I can move on or I can stay stuck here. I can't do both. She wants me to adjust to school, to her new family, to be *normal*—whatever the hell that even means—but then she wants me to go on camera and talk about how my dad kidnapped me ten years ago? I just want to let it go."

"You don't want to find your dad, though?"

Oliver looked down at me, his face as sad as I had ever seen it. "I want that more than anything in the world. But not like this."

He trailed off. "I just can't hate my dad the way everyone wants me to."

"Ollie, no," I said. I reached for his arm but he pulled away. "We don't want you to hate him."

"You know what I mean," he replied. "I had a life with him. He taught me how to do things, how to ride a bike and catch a pop fly. We went to movies, museums. He showed me the constellations." Oliver laughed a little. "One time, he even used a flashlight and a grapefruit to explain the phases of the moon. It wasn't awful. Except for the fact that my mom wasn't there, I mean. That part sucked."

I sat quietly, realizing that I had never asked him about his dad, about their life together. "I'm sorry we never talked about him," I said quietly. "I just thought it would upset you, that's all."

"I'm not mad at you," Oliver corrected himself, then put his hand over mine, pressing it into the sand. "But everyone acts like I stopped growing up at seven years old. They act like the past ten years didn't happen to me, too."

"It was just so terrible here," I said. "It was scary, not knowing where you were for so long. Your dad just took you, Oliver. We didn't know what happened."

"I didn't know what happened, either!" Oliver said. "Everyone has spent the past ten years thinking that my *dad's* the monster, but I've spent the last ten years thinking that my *mom* left *me*. I spent all that time being mad at her, and I can't just flip that. I don't work that way, Emmy. My brain, it doesn't . . ."

I tangled my fingers through his, feeling the sand rub between our skin.

"My mom and Rick and the twins, they have this perfect family, you know? And I just came in and fucked everything up. They're fighting all the time and I know it's because of me. And I can't go back to where I was, and this town is just so fucking . . ." Oliver shook his head at me. "I don't even know what I'm saying anymore. We should go."

"No, we should stay," I said. "I'm sorry. I didn't realize."

"Even you and Drew and Caro, you have all these in-jokes and you talk the same and know all the places and people that I don't know anymore. But I had places and people and in-jokes, too."

"People?" I asked.

"A few friends," he clarified. "I even had a girlfriend when I was fifteen." He glanced down at me. "Sorry."

"Why are you sorry?" I said, then thought, *I'll kill her if she hurt him*. The jealousy passed after a second, though.

"I'm not. I just mean that I had a life before I came back. And no one ever wants to hear about it. I feel like if I talk to my mom, she'll just use it against my dad."

"Like on a TV news show," I said.

"Exactly."

I tightened the blanket around my shoulder, pulling Oliver and me closer together. It was freezing now, but I didn't dare move. "Maybe we should talk about it more," I said. "About both of us during the past ten years."

"Can I ask you a question?" he asked after a few more minutes of silence, and I nodded against his shoulder. "What happened after I left? I mean, after my dad and I . . . ? Maybe we can start there."

I sat up a little, trying to organize my thoughts. "Um, there were police. A lot of them, in your house talking to your mom, in my house talking to me and my parents, Caro and Drew. They took your clothes, your shoes, your toothbrush—anything that would help try to find you. But your dad, he already had a three-day start, you know? You can go anywhere in the world in three days."

"Chicago," Oliver murmured. "You can go to Chicago."

I looked at him. "Really?"

He nodded, splaying his hand over mine so that his fingers reached all the way past my fingertips. "We were there for the first six months. He said we were having a vacation, that we needed some father-and-son-bonding time." Oliver's voice was as soft as his touch and he traced my fingers as he spoke. "But I wanted to go home after a while. Chicago is loud and we were in this tourist area and it wasn't like here at all. And he said that we couldn't go home because my mom had left, that she didn't want to be with us anymore."

Hearing him say the words so matter-of-factly made me wince, but he didn't notice. "And I cried and I cried because I just wanted to see my mom, you know? And I didn't understand why she would just leave like that because we were supposed to make cookies for Halloween. That's what I kept telling my dad, that we had to make cookies, and I couldn't stop crying. And he just held me and he just kept saying how sorry he was, that he was so, *so* sorry." Oliver huffed out a laugh that didn't sound funny. "And now I know what he was really apologizing for. But all I really remember was missing my mom.

"And then he said we needed a 'fresh start.' That's what he said, a fresh start. And that he had always wanted to call me Colin so we should change our names." Oliver shrugged. "I guess I was afraid of pissing him off, not because he was mean or abusive or anything like that, but just . . . I was already down a mom, you know? I didn't want to lose my dad, too."

"You should tell your mom this," I whispered. "Oliver, you need to tell her."

"What kind of kid doesn't call his mom, though?" he murmured, looking down at the ground so that his hair fell down around his face, hiding him. "Why didn't I just call her?"

"You were *seven*," I whispered, brushing his hair back behind his ear with my free hand. "You were a little kid, Ollie, and you thought she didn't want you. No one could ever blame you."

He glanced up at me, and I suspected that he didn't quite believe me. "I'm serious," I told him. "No one has ever or will ever blame you. Your mom never has. She never *did*."

"Yeah, but now . . ." Oliver's jaw tensed before he said the rest of his sentence. "The problem is that now I miss my dad just like I used to miss my mom." He glanced back at me, waiting for judgment.

"I would miss my dad, too," I admitted.

"Even if he lied to you for ten years about everything?"

"Even then," I said, because it was true. "I'd hate him and miss him at the same time."

"That's . . . pretty much what it is. And it sucks." Oliver took another deep breath, then looked toward the purpled sky and exhaled. "Fuck. I am so tired of paying the price for something I never did and didn't even want in the first place!"

I sat and I thought of surfing, of college, of ten years spent in a gilded cage. "I understand," I said, then curled back up against him. "I really, really think I do."

He wrapped his arm around my knees so that we were huddled together, and I tucked my hands into his hoodie pocket. We sat in silence for a long time, listening to the waves and seagulls and distant traffic. *The world continues to spin even when we want it to stop*, I thought. *Especially then.*

CHAPTER TWENTY-THREE

After that, we talked.

He told me about his dad, how he had once organized an at-home movie festival just for Oliver so that he could learn about the great directors and count it toward homeschooling. ("The movies were kind of boring," he admitted, "but the popcorn was good.") He talked about how they went fishing in Illinois, hiking in Vermont, and once even to Disney World, when Oliver was eight. "It was the greatest day of my life," Oliver said, still smiling at the memory, and I smiled, too, wondering where the day he finally came home ranked on that list. I almost didn't want to know.

He also mentioned different things, like the fact that he was lucky that his adult teeth grew in straight because his dad would never have let him go to an orthodontist, and that he never was allowed to have sugar or candy because they never went to a dentist. It didn't make sense at first, but then it hit me. "Dental records," I said, and Oliver tapped his nose as if to say, *Bingo*.

"I mean, I don't know if anything would have happened," Oliver clarified. "But I didn't care. I was just excited that I didn't have to go to the dentist. And of course, it was one of the first places my mom took me."

"Did you have any cavities?"

He grinned at me, and yeah, he was lucky his teeth grew in so nice and straight. "Not a one," he said.

In return, I told him about what it was like growing up here, me and Caro and Drew becoming our little triangle of friends. I told him about the police, the yearly updates on the news, how the interest had been so big for a month or so and then tapered away. "That's when things really got bad," I told him one night, when we were driving around in the car. "I think when everyone was focused on the kidnapping, it was more helpful to your mom. But when interest waned . . ." I shrugged. "It's hard when everyone else moves on, but you can't."

"Did she ever have to . . . ?" Oliver trailed off, but I knew what he was asking. No one could ever ask that question directly.

"Identify a body?" I asked, and he nodded. "Not directly. She sent dental records a few times, but they never matched. I think it got to the point where she just wanted to know even if it was bad news, but then the police would call and ask her to send them and she would just . . ." I shook my head. "It was bad."

I told him about how protective my parents were, not even

letting me get my license until I was seventeen. "That was huge," I admitted. "Like, monumental. I thought they would just keep saying no, but they finally said yes."

We were sprawled in the grass at a park near Drew's house for that conversation, listening to crickets and general nighttime noises. It's always easier to talk in the dark when you can't see the other person's face, when you don't worry about how they're reacting to what you say. You can just . . . talk.

Oliver found my hand across the damp grass, then gathered it up in both of his and placed it on his stomach. It felt solid and warm. "You should tell them about surfing," he said. "I think they'd actually be proud of you."

"No way!" I snatched my hand back and rolled to sit up. "Are you crazy? They'd freak out for a million different reasons. No. Just no."

"Maybe not, though. Maureen would probably talk to them—"

"You told your mom?"

"No! Emmy!" Oliver sat up, too. We were supposed to be studying at Caro's house for a group project that didn't exist. "I didn't tell anyone, okay? Relax!"

But my heart was pounding. "If they find out, then I can't surf anymore, and they probably won't let me move out and go to school, either."

"I know, I know. I'm sorry, okay?" He reached for my hand again. "I was just saying that sooner or later, they're going to find out."

"Later," I said. "Absolutely later. Like, when I'm a retiree who lives in Boca Raton. Then they can find out."

My parents figured out something else in the meantime, though. "Emmy?" my mom called up the stairs one evening. "Can you come down here for a minute?"

Never good.

My mom and dad were both sitting on the couch. I knew this meeting venue all too well: if my mom is trying to act like it's no big deal, she sits on the couch. If it's a serious "you are in so much trouble" scenario, then they sit at the dining room table. So far, so good.

"Emmy," my mom began once I sat down, "we can't help but notice that you and Oliver are spending quite a lot of time together."

"Yes?" I said, because I wasn't sure if it was a question or if I was about to say the wrong answer. "We are?"

"You are," my dad said.

"Are you two dating?" my mom asked.

"Mom," I groaned, covering my eyes with my hand. "People don't really date anymore, they just . . . I don't know, hang out together."

"Is that the same as 'hooking up'?" my dad asked.

"Oh my God!" Now I covered my ears with both hands. "Am I grounded? Can you just ground me? Hearing you two talk about 'hooking up' is cruel and unusual punishment."

"Emmy, relax," my mom said. "You're not in trouble, you're not grounded, and your dad is joking."

My dad winked at me and calmly took a sip of his water.

"Revenge will be sweet," I muttered to him.

"But you and Oliver are 'hanging out,' yes?" my mom asked.

I nodded, picking at one of my ragged cuticles. I had scraped the side of my hand on my board earlier that day and it was starting to ache. "Yes," I finally said. "We're hanging out."

My parents glanced at each other. "We know you've been a wonderful friend to Oliver," my mom started to say, but to my surprise, I cut her off.

"We're not just friends," I told her. "It's more than that."

"Oh," she said. "Okay. I know we haven't talked about this before since it hasn't come up, but your father and I would prefer that you not seriously start dating until you're eighteen. That being said"—she rushed on before I could protest—"because we know Oliver and his family, and since they live right next door to us, and because we *trust you*, we think it's okay if you two want to keep . . . hanging out." I could tell that it pained her to say that phrase.

"But no closed doors," my dad quickly added. "No being alone in either of our houses without a parent home—the twins *absolutely* do not count as responsible chaperones, so don't even ask—and no sex."

"Subtle," my mom murmured as I started choking.

My dad shrugged. "It's not like she doesn't know what the word means. You okay, Em?"

I nodded as I tried to get myself under control. I couldn't wait to text Oliver and see what Maureen's version of this conversation sounded like. If she used the word *intercourse* like Drew's dad had, Oliver was probably going to fling himself out the window.

"I'm fine," I managed to say. "And got it for all of those rules. Can we stop talking now, though? If I promise to do everything you say, can we end this and promise to never speak of it again?"

"One last thing," my mom said. "Oliver is going through a lot right now, honey. Just . . . keep that in mind."

No one knew that better than me, though.

THE TREES

It's two days before Emmy and Oliver's third birthday.

They're planning a party. Well, they're not planning it, their moms are, but it doesn't matter because it's going to be so much fun and they're having their party together. At first, Emmy didn't like that idea because she thought it meant they would have to share presents, but then Oliver pointed out that the birthday cake would be bigger if it was for both of them, so that helped. Oliver is smart like that.

And right now, at the park, while their moms are sitting in the shade and talking about party plans, Emmy can't see Oliver anywhere. He's not on the swings or the slide, and he's certainly not sitting next to her in the sand, making a sand castle that always seems to slide out of her bucket and into a heap on the ground. It never looks like a castle the way it does at the beach. Emmy likes the beach a lot better than the park.

She stands up and looks at their moms, who are so busy talking that they don't see her quizzical expression, wondering where Oliver is. She looks past them toward the street, but she knows Oliver isn't there. They're not allowed to cross the street by themselves, not yet. Emmy can't wait to do a lot of things when she's older, especially crossing the street without holding a grown-up's hand. She can't wait to do things by herself.

She turns and looks toward the trees. That's always been a scary part of the park, where the ground gets damp and smells like dirt and darkness. She never goes over there, but she sees the sun splash across Oliver's hair, lighting him just for a second, and she hurries over to him.

"What are you doing?" she calls when she's close enough.

"I saw a frog!" Oliver cries, pointing toward one of the trees. Emmy has never seen a real live frog before. She wonders if they're slimy. They look slimy.

"C'mon!" Oliver says, scampering forward. "He can be our pet!"

Emmy looks back over her shoulder. Their moms feel so far away and it's kind of scary. She almost wishes they would see her and Oliver and call them back, pull them back into the familiar orbit of snacks and parks and sand castles that always crumble. But then Oliver disappears behind a tree and Emmy turns back around. The sun ghosts across her hair, warming her for a minute, and she does what she's always done before.

She follows Oliver into the dark.

CHAPTER TWENTY-FOUR

Sunday was "Family Day" for Oliver, and my parents needed my help cleaning out the garage, which meant no time to sneak away for surfing that day. And then, true to form, I had to do all the homework I had left until the last minute while my mom walked into my room every fifteen minutes explaining, "If you'd just do a little bit every day, Emmy, then it wouldn't build up so much. You can't keep leaving things until the last minute."

After the fourth time this happened, I finally set down my pen. "Mom. Every time you come in here, you interrupt me and keep me from doing the homework that you want me to do! Is that really a good idea?"

"Well, I'm just saying," she said. "What are you going to do when you go to college in a couple of years?"

I knew she didn't mean anything by it, but her comment bit me in exactly the wrong way. "You know, some high school seniors like to go to college right after graduating. They even move away and live in dorms! Can you believe it?"

"We've talked about this, Emmy," my mom said.

"*You* talked about it," I muttered. I knew that the idea of me moving out had nothing to do with me and everything to do with my mom.

"What was that?" she asked.

"Nothing." I smiled at her. "I love you. Best mom ever!"

She just raised an eyebrow at me, but finally left me alone. "Bed at ten thirty!" she yelled as she went downstairs.

I waited for Oliver's light to come on in his bedroom, but it never did. I texted with Caro for a while, who mostly told me about how terrible Heather was and how she hoped that she would smother to death in a pile of laundry, then I went to bed. Oliver's room stayed dark.

It was nearly impossible to see him at school the next day, since he was a junior and I was a senior and we didn't share any classes together. "Hey," Caro said, bumping into me in the hallway. "So can I move in with you? Because I might murder my sister."

"Remember? If you're patient, she'll just suffocate in a pile of laundry," I said.

"I don't have that kind of time," Caro said, "because I am losing my mind. Seriously. I need my own room."

"You really want to sleep in my mom's office?" I said, raising an eyebrow at her. "Think carefully before answering. My mom will have your entire life planned out on an Excel spreadsheet if you do that."

Caro's eyes glazed over with happiness. "That sounds like heaven," she sighed happily. "Tell me more about spreadsheets and organization and cleanliness!"

I was about to answer her when I saw Oliver walking down the hall. It looked like he was heading in a straight line toward me, his eyes never looking away from my face, and I grinned despite my effort to stay cool, to look cool.

"Oh God, you are a mess," Caro whispered.

"Shut up, I know."

"Hey," Oliver said when he was close enough. "Hi, Caro."

"Hey, dude. How's surfing?"

"Great." He nodded. "Good times, good people. Uhh . . ."

Clearly, he wanted to talk. "Caro," I said, "can you, um, give us a minute?"

"I'll give you *three*," she said magnanimously. "Because that's when the bell's going to ring, anyway." She tapped Oliver on the arm as she walked away. "Later, my friends."

Oliver watched her go, then put his hand on my upper arm. "Hi."

"Hi," I said, still grinning like a fool. A happy, happy fool. "Are you ready for a fun day of learning?"

"No. But I hear you're coming over for dinner tonight."

"We are," I said. "My parents and I plan to take blatant advantage of your hospitality and delicious food and generous cable TV package."

"Hmm." Oliver leaned in a little closer. "That's *all* you want to take advantage of?"

"Oh my God, you are *not* playing fair right now," I said. "Not at all." I closed my eyes as he kissed my forehead.

"Let's ditch and go surfing," he whispered, so close that I could feel his breath on my skin.

"I can't. I mean, I would if I could, but I can't. My parents—the school, they have that online thing where they can see if I attended classes or not and my mom checks it every day." I reached up and twirled a lock of his hair around my finger, still damp from his shower. "Your mom probably checks it, too."

"Every *day*?" Oliver repeated, his eyes widening. "Doesn't it bother you that you're under lock and key like that?"

"Sometimes," I admitted. "I guess I'm just used to it."

Oliver nodded thoughtfully, like he was filing that information away for future reference. "So see you tonight?"

"Absolutely," I said. "We'll be the ones with the salad. You can't miss us."

He smiled and I leaned forward to kiss him again, fast before we got caught. "Rebel," I whispered. "We're not supposed to do that on school property."

"Is this where I make a comment about how you should be bringing dessert instead? Because I can do that!" Oliver continued as I wrinkled my nose and shoved him away. "Not a problem, Emmy, really! If you need a cheesy joke, I am *here* for you!"

"Don't forget to chill my water glass!" I yelled back, then blew him a kiss as I turned the corner. I saw him catch it, turning the corner with his fist aloft, holding my heart in his hand as he disappeared.

CHAPTER TWENTY-FIVE

When my parents and I got to Oliver's house that night, though, his mood was different, like someone had dimmed a switch. "Hey," he said, opening the door. He was wearing a collared shirt like the one he had worn on the TV interview, but a different color this time.

"Hi, Oliver!" My mom beamed. "Here's the salad, but it needs to be chilled because otherwise the lettuce will wilt and . . ." She trailed off as Maureen came around the corner. Oliver glanced down and took the bowl from my mom without saying a word, ducking back toward the kitchen as Maureen bustled toward us. Her face was tight, her mouth pursed, and she gave us a smile that wasn't exactly convincing.

"Hi," she said. "C'mon, come on in. Sorry, we were just . . . getting ready. You are so sweet to bring the salad! Oliver, can you—?"

"Got it!" he yelled back, and I glanced up at my dad. I could tell from the look on his face that he felt the same way I did: *this is going to be a long, long night.*

Not quite sure what to do with myself, I followed Oliver into the kitchen while Rick came in with a beer for my dad and our moms disappeared around the corner. "Hey," I said to his back, since he was making room in the refrigerator for my mom's (unnecessarily enormous) salad bowl. "What's up?"

"Nothing," he said, but his face was as smooth as Maureen's had been pinched. He wasn't quite looking at me, either, his eyes going over my head or past my arm.

"Hey," I said again, this time softer, and I reached out to grab his hand. "What's wrong? You're being weird."

"You are," he said, trying to duck away from the question, but just as I was about to press the subject, the twins came bounding into the room, a hyper duo of wet hair and *The Little Mermaid* pajamas.

"Emmy! Emmy!" they cried, and I dropped Oliver's hand just as he turned away. "Emmy! We got a new Barbie!"

"She has brown hair like us!"

"Emmy Emmy Emmy!" Nora pulled at my shirt. "Play Barbies with us, 'kay? You can have the new one."

"I can't, twinsies," I said. "I have to eat dinner and hang out with Oliver. I'm off the clock tonight."

"You not s'posed to call us 'twins' anymore," Molly informed me, even as she wrapped her skinny arms around my waist and tilted her head back to look up at me. "We're not twins, Mommy said. We're *invididuals*."

Out of the corner of my eye, I saw Oliver hide a smile, which made me feel a little better. "Oh, really?" I said. "Invididuals, huh? You sure about that?"

"Mommy *said*," Nora repeated.

"Nora, Molly." Maureen came bustling into the kitchen. "Come on now, it's bedtime."

A chorus of protests rose up, but Maureen just flapped her hands at them, like they were baby birds in a nest. "No, no, you know the rules."

"But our friend is visiting!" Nora cried, pointing at me.

"Don't point," Maureen said. "It's rude. And you can see Emmy tomorrow."

I nodded at them. "Totally. Besides, you two see me all the time. I'm *boring*."

Molly and Nora both glared at me as they started to slink away, a betrayer to their cause. "But Oliver has to read the story!" Molly suddenly said, turning around and pointing at him.

"Don't point!" Maureen cried. "Does anybody listen to anything I say anymore?"

"Kind of hard not to," Oliver muttered, but Maureen was too far away to hear him.

"Oliver! You do the story tonight!" The twins (excuse me, the "invididuals") had let go of me and were now hanging on to him, and over their heads, Maureen gave him a pleading, tired look.

"You do the voices!" Nora said to him, and Oliver gave the same look right back to his mother. It startled me a little to see how similar their reactions could be. I don't think either one of them realized it, though.

"Oliver, do you mind?" Maureen murmured. "Please?"

Oliver looked at me. "Mom, what's Emmy going to do while I'm up there?" he asked, even as Nora started to climb him like a tree.

"Set the table," Maureen replied. "See? A solution for everything."

Oliver sighed and rolled his eyes, then shot me an apologetic look. "Okay, monsters," he said, and they cheered. "First one upstairs gets to pick the book." The girls took off, their feet making thunder-like noises on the stairs as they raced to their room.

"You do the voices?" I asked him, not even bothering to hide my smile. "Are you just a big mush?"

Oliver blushed. "This isn't the sort of detail that I wanted to be made public," he said.

"I might die of adorableness," I said. Maureen had followed the girls upstairs, yelling about brushing teeth and washing hands, and now it was just Oliver and me in the kitchen. I tangled my fingers together with his, pulling him a little closer. "Do a voice for me," I said. "Go on."

"No way in *hell*." He laughed and started to pull away when I leaned in. "Forget it. Nope."

"Come on!" I teased. "Is it cute? I bet it's really cute. Do you do

Olivia's voice? Angelina Ballerina's? Oh my God, you do *Angelina*?" I said when he blushed. "This is too cute! I'm dying. No, wait. I have to text Caro and then I'll die."

"Do *not* text Caro!" he said, diving for my hand as I reached for my phone. "Come on, Em. I need some dignity. Please."

"Oli-*ver*!" one of the twins yelled from upstairs. "We're waiting!"

"My audience is really demanding," he said, pulling away from me even as I continued to giggle. "You're not really going to text Caro, are you? Tell me you're not."

"I won't," I said. "I promise. Your Angelina Ballerina secrets are safe with me."

He hesitated just before leaving the kitchen, then ran back to me and kissed me fast. "Hi," he whispered. "Didn't have a chance to do that yet." Then he disappeared, yelling, "I hope you *invididuals* are happy now!" as he took the stairs two at a time. I pressed my hand to my mouth, waiting for a moment in the now-quiet kitchen, and then went to find some place mats.

CHAPTER TWENTY-SIX

Oliver and I ended up not sitting next to each other at dinner. "Sit at the head of the table," Rick said to Oliver. It was pretty obvious that Rick was trying to be nice to Oliver, being generous and treating him as "man of the house" or whatever, but Oliver just sat down and didn't respond. Rick looked like he expected Oliver to say *something*, but when he didn't, Rick's face fell a little and he turned away. Maureen sat down at the opposite end, closest to the kitchen, and my mom and I sat on one side while Rick and my dad sat on the other.

I have to say this about the twins: they may be small, little, and noisy, but when they're around, there are rarely any awkward silences, and suddenly I found myself wishing that they were at the table with us.

"I hope you all like chicken," Maureen said, reaching for the salad bowl as my mom started to pass the main course. "I know, it can be so blah. I really should have just let Elizabeth cater this one," she added, nodding at my mom.

"It's nice to have a night off!" my mom said.

Oliver and I shared a quick, desperate look. Adults making small talk for the next two hours. Joy. I'd rather be doing homework.

We made it through most of the chicken and salad. Oliver ate silently, nodding his thanks when my dad passed him the basket of rolls, and glancing at me every so often. I did the same on my end. "So, Emmy," Rick said, "how are college applications going?"

I looked up mid-chew. So did Oliver.

No one else seemed to notice, though. "Rick," Maureen laughed. "Honey, most kids are starting to hear from the schools they applied to. The application process was a while ago."

"And Emmy's going to community college for at least the first year," my mom added. "I'm not sure I'm ready for an empty nest, to be honest!" Everyone laughed at that, even as her words made the chicken start to rise back up in my throat. Another year with a nine o'clock curfew, another year of lying to my parents about surfing, about sneaking out and staying at Caro's. Even though I was already living that life, another year of it felt unimaginable.

Maureen said something about Oliver starting to get college information already ("I guess the publicity is good for something, right?"), but Oliver's eyes were locked on me. He raised an eyebrow and gestured a little with his fork, and when I just shook my head in an "I'm fine" gesture, he paused for a minute, then spoke up.

"I think Emmy should go away to college."

My fork fell to my plate.

"Well, it's a little late now," my mom said, laughing.

Oliver just shrugged. "I dunno. I just mean, she's smart, you know? Like, *really* smart. And she's responsible. She could go away to school. And you know, maybe she should."

I sat frozen. If he said anything about UCSD, I would kill him and then the whole discussion would be a moot point because I'd be going to prison, not college.

"Oliver." Maureen didn't even try to hide the edge in her voice. "You don't tell people how to raise their kids." She smiled at my parents. "Sorry, you two."

"I'm not," he said, and Oliver wasn't hiding the edge in his voice, either.

Maureen just gasped. I hadn't realized that the two of them shared the same stubborn streak, but now, sitting across the table from each other, it was like an invisible current connected them. For the first time since Oliver had come home, ironically, they seemed just like mother and son.

"I'm not," Oliver said again. "I just think Emmy doesn't need to be so protected, that's all."

The conversation was taking a dangerous turn and I instinctively gripped the edge of the table, hanging on for the ride.

"Are you doing this because I grounded you?" Maureen finally exploded. "Is that what this is? You want to embarrass me in front of our friends because you think I embarrassed you?"

"That's right, *Mom,*" he said. "It's all about *you*. I forgot."

"You were late!" Maureen cried. "You were late coming home, and Keith is still out there somewhere and—"

My mom started to stand up. "Maybe we should go," she started to say.

"No, Elizabeth." Maureen gestured to my mom to sit down. "Please, stay. Sit down. This conversation is over."

But now Oliver was standing, too, his napkin balled up in his hand. "Do you *really* think he's gonna kidnap me again? Is that what you think?"

"I don't know!" Maureen yelled, and now she was standing, too. My mom sat back down reluctantly, then reached for my hand under the table. "I didn't think he would take you the first time, but guess what? He did!"

"I'm almost eighteen!" Oliver said. "What, do you think he's just going to drag me away somewhere? I'm five inches taller than him!"

"You are?" Maureen blinked. She seemed to sag a little and her lower lip trembled for a second, but then she regained her composure. "Oliver, listen to me. Keith committed a crime, a big one. He is a *criminal*. He is not to be trusted. You need to accept that."

"Stop talking about him like that's all he did!" Oliver shouted. "He raised me, okay? He taught me how to ride a bike, he took care of me when I was sick!"

"He was an alcoholic!" Maureen cried. "I had no idea if you

were *hungry*, if you were *starving* . . ."

"Dad never drank!" Oliver said. "You think you know everything and you don't! I was *fine*!"

"What if you got sick? Do you think he would have taken you to an emergency room or a hospital? He didn't even take you to the *goddamn* dentist!"

"He and I were there, Mom. You weren't!"

"I looked for you!" Maureen screamed, and now she was crying. My dad's face was pale and Rick was standing up now, too, a reluctant referee. My mom's grip on my hand was iron tight, and I was pretty sure I was hanging on to hers the same way.

"I spent every day looking for you!" she continued. "All of my money! All of my time! I tried to find you!"

"Yeah, well, you *didn't*."

"Hey!" Rick said sharply. "That's enough, Oliver. You're putting your mom through hell, you know that?"

"Why is this always about *her*?" Oliver yelled back. "Everyone acts like it was *my* idea to disappear but actually, I'm the one who decided to come *home*!"

Maureen froze. So did the rest of us.

"Every time I asked Dad about you, he would just say he didn't want to talk about it!" Oliver yelled, his face flushed. "And then one day, I went to the library, the big one with the lions, and I tried Googling you, and there were all of these articles about *me* and I saw your picture for the first time in ten years, Mom, okay? *Ten years!* And I knew then what Dad had done so when they asked for fingerprint volunteers on that stupid field trip, I said yes. And now sometimes I wish I hadn't because I just fucked everything up for you, didn't I?" Oliver's eyes started to fill with tears. "You had this perfect life with the twins and Rick and I just messed it all up."

"Oliver, no, honey—" Maureen said as she started to cross the room to him. I was still in my chair, and my mom's hand felt clammy in mine.

"No!" Oliver yelled, and Maureen stopped in her tracks. "Just don't, okay? You still love the kid that left, but I don't think you like the one that came back! I don't think you—"

But he stopped talking when we all heard the tiny sobs coming from the corner. Molly and Nora were standing in the doorway, huddled together, both of them crying as they watched the fight.

That current between Maureen and Oliver suddenly severed, and Maureen seemed to crumple as she buried her face in her hands. "Shit," I heard her whisper.

Oliver, for his part, looked sick, like he wanted to throw up, and he closed his eyes and said something to himself that I couldn't make out. Then he opened his eyes and stalked away from the table, coming back a few seconds later with his hoodie in his hand, the same one he had been wearing in the gazebo the night we kissed. Had that really been just last week?

"I'm sorry," Oliver said, and I wasn't sure who he was talking to until he knelt down in front of the twins and hugged them both, their small arms reaching up to wrap around his neck. "I'm sorry, okay?" I heard him say again. "I didn't mean to scare you. I'm sorry." Then he was kissing their heads and standing up, heading toward the door and almost running out.

The rest of us sat at the table in stunned silence. My entire face was hot, but my hands were cold, like I had a fever. My mom let go of my hand and started to go around the table to Maureen, Rick went to the twins, and I sat back in my chair and looked at my dad, who was watching me very, very carefully.

"Dad?"

"Go," he said, answering the question that I didn't even know how to ask.

I stood up. My legs were shaking. "I have my phone," I told him.

"It's okay, Emmy. Go."

I pushed my chair back and grabbed my coat, then walked out the still-open door and pulled it shut behind me. I had no idea where Oliver had gone, or even where to look, but when I went out to the front yard, I saw a small figure stalking up the street, illuminated by orange streetlights and the ever-present coastal fog. He looked like a ghost, lost and alone, floating away.

"Oliver!" I called. "Wait!"

He didn't acknowledge me, though, and I dashed through the wet grass after him, my sneakers squeaking when I hit the street. Three years of surfing had its benefits, it turned out, including some pretty good cardiovascular skills, and I caught up to him in less than a minute. "Oliver, please!"

"Emmy," he said, and he stopped so fast that I went running past him and had to double back. "Emmy, look. I appreciate you coming after me, that's really nice of you but—"

"I'm not going back," I said, and he just looked at me and started walking again. "Wait," I said. "Stop walking, okay?"

"Just go back and stay with my sisters, okay? I didn't mean to upset them."

"I know. They know that, too." His legs were longer than mine and I had to hurry to keep up with him. "Where are you going?"

"I don't know!" he finally cried, coming to another screeching halt. "I have no idea, Emmy, okay? I don't know where the fuck I am or where the fuck I'm going! I probably couldn't even find my own house on a map." He ran his hands through his hair, balled it up between his fingers, then let it go with a huge sigh. "Sorry. I'm not mad at you."

"I know," I said again, because I did. I felt like I knew everything he was about to say, like that electric current that had snapped between his mom and him had snaked over and wrapped itself around me.

I ignored him, though, and led him to the curb. "Sit," I said, and he plopped down next to the streetlight and leaned against it. I sat down next to him, then wrapped myself around his arm, holding him there. He took a deep breath, then let it out and rested his head against the top of mine.

We sat there in silence for a few minutes, our ribs rising and falling in opposite waves, like we were breathing for each other.

His pulse was racing under his skin and I ran my thumb against the veins in his wrist, waiting for him to calm down. "What happened?" I asked after enough time had passed.

"I think you saw what happened," he said, but there wasn't any bite to his words. He sounded deflated, like the fight had sapped his energy.

"I mean before. Did you and your mom have a fight or something? Because that was . . . sort of out of the blue."

"Not really, not if you live in our house. It's been coming for a while." Oliver ran his thumb over my knuckles, smoothing the skin. But his eyes looked wild, feral, like the coyotes that sometimes snuck through our backyard in the middle of the night. "I just can't stand it sometimes, you know? Like, I know my mom suffered a lot. I know that and I don't mean . . ."

"Why didn't you tell her, though?" I asked. We were standing next to each other now and I reached out and took his sleeve in my hand. He just glanced away, looking so defeated under the streetlight.

"Because how do you tell your mom that you knew your dad took you away from her and you didn't do anything about it?" He didn't phrase it as a question. "What kind of kid does that?"

I pulled him over to the curb, where we sat down together, Oliver falling with a heavy sigh onto the concrete. "Fuck," he muttered, pressing the heels of his hands into his eyes.

"You didn't do anything," I told him, fumbling for the right words. I felt like if I said the wrong thing, he would wither up like a flower, cave in on himself and disintegrate. "You were a kid, Oliver. It's not up to you to fix what your dad did."

"Yeah, but now I have to fix what *I* did," Oliver said, then laughed to himself. "I get so mad at my mom for not realizing I'm not that seven-year-old kid anymore, but she's not the same person she was, either."

"None of us are," I said softly.

Oliver kept talking like I hadn't said anything. "I didn't know what to do at first because I didn't want to turn my dad in, y'know? Like, this wasn't my perfect scenario or anything. But he had let me take this forensic science class through the local high school and we had a field trip to the local precinct and they asked for volunteers to do the fingerprinting and I . . . I thought if it was true, that this way I would be able to see my mom without turning in my dad." He shrugged and then laughed, high-pitched and a little hysterical. "And so I volunteered and the next day there were two police officers at our house. My dad wasn't home, but I was." He shrugged. "And that was it. Gone again."

I didn't say anything. The words I needed to say probably hadn't been invented. A car drove past us, its lights flashing across our faces and making us both duck away from the brightness. When it passed, we came back together.

"Remember last week, when we were talking?" I said. "You said, what kind of kid doesn't call their mom? But you *did*, Ollie. You did what you could when you could. And yeah, it's not easy now but it won't always be this difficult. It'll get better."

Oliver looked down at me. "Is that what everyone said when I first went missing? That it wouldn't always be this difficult?"

I nodded. "Something like that, yeah."

"And did you believe them?"

I smiled, my eyes filling with tears. "Nope. Because it never did get better. Not until you came back."

Oliver kissed the top of my head and I curled up against his arm, wrapping my hand around his. The street was quiet around us, most of suburbia tucked away for the night.

"I'm sorry I was a jerk to your parents," Oliver finally said after a while. "They're always really nice to me."

"You weren't a jerk," I said. "I was just nervous that you were going to out me for applying to UCSD. Whatever, it's fine, I don't care. But we should probably go back. Our parents might get worried."

"Yeah, I know." He squeezed my hands through the hoodie. "Thanks for coming after me."

"Yeah, well, I needed some cardio, anyway," I said, then wished I hadn't made a joke.

He just wrinkled his nose at me, though, then stood up and pulled me to my feet. "Onward," I said.

"Just so you know," he said, "I'm probably going to be grounded again. So don't expect a text or anything for a while."

"Got it," I said, but I didn't think Maureen would ground him, not this time.

I thought that she would probably just be happy to see him come home.

When we got back to the house, Oliver kissed me quickly under the shadow of a bougainvillea tree, its pink petals brushing against the tops of our heads as we met in the middle. "You going up to your room?" he asked, and I could feel the words form on his lips.

"Soon," I said. I could see my parents moving in our kitchen, their bodies casting long shadows out onto the backyard grass. Oliver followed my gaze, then nodded. "Okay. I'll wait for you to turn off the lamp, then."

"You don't have to wait for me," I said. "You're probably exhausted. You should go to bed."

"Oh my God, Emmy, one mom is enough right now." But he was smiling as he said it, and I smiled back and then stood on my tiptoes to kiss him again. "Good night," he whispered. "See you tomorrow."

"'Kay," I said, and we split up into our separate yards, our hands staying together until the last possible second, until just our fingertips touched. He swatted playfully at them as we parted, a brief smile crossing his face as if to let me know that he was all right, that everything had just been a joke, a gag to pass the time until something actually interesting happened.

I smiled, too, but I didn't believe one bit of it.

CHAPTER TWENTY-SEVEN

When I finally managed to open the sliding-glass door and step into our living room, neither of my parents were in the room.

In fact, the only person sitting on the couch was Maureen.

She had her hand wrapped loosely around the stem of her almost empty wineglass, swirling it around in slow motion so that the wine climbed the sides of the glass and then oozed back down. The rivulets winding their way down to the bottom made it look as though the glass was crying. When Maureen heard me come in, she stopped.

"Emmy," she said, but she didn't sit up or even look at me. "I'm sorry you had to see all that."

Her mascara was smudged, and so was her lipstick, which I later realized was just the red wine staining her mouth. "It's okay," I said automatically.

"No, it's really not," she sighed. "But you're a polite girl, I know. You've always been very polite."

"Thank you." I glanced around for my parents, wondering if they could come rescue me from this conversation. I had seen Maureen break down in our kitchen many, many times, but I had never been alone with her. My parents had always buffered the situation.

I wondered if this was what adulthood was supposed to feel like, suddenly needing my parents and having them be just out of reach, leaving me to fend for myself.

"How is he?" Maureen asked. She started swirling the wine again, then took a sip.

"Okay," I said. I put my hand on the back of a chair. "He's home now if you want to talk to him."

Maureen just laughed through her nose, a sound of disbelief. "Talk to him," she repeated. "Oliver and I don't talk. Or rather, he doesn't talk to me." She laughed again, but it sounded more like a sob. "You know, I've thought of a million different scenarios for him coming home, but not one of them ended with him hating me."

I sat down in the chair across from her. If my parents weren't going to steer this boat, then it was time to grab the oars. "Oliver's in so much pain right now. He doesn't . . . I don't think he knows how to talk to you, or even what to say, you know? Everything is so different for him. It's like . . . it's like he barely knows who he is, much less who he is supposed to be." I was trying to explain things without betraying his trust, but all I could do was fumble for words. And Maureen was a woman who had been given a lot of platitudes in her life.

"I don't even know how to help him," she sighed. "The guilt he must feel, the *responsibility*—"

"You have to ask him about who he is now," I said. "Trust me. He has a lot to tell you. He doesn't think you want to hear it, though."

Maureen blinked away tears. "I don't think he wants me to listen. I don't think he wants anything to do with me at all."

"Look," I said, my voice sharper than I meant it to be. "When I was eight, my parents wouldn't let me go to this slumber party because they said I was too young to stay over at someone else's house. And I was so mad at them because everyone else was going, even Caro, but they wouldn't let me. So I wrote this note and put it under their bedroom door. It said, 'Dear Mom and Dad, I hate you. Love, Emmy.'"

Maureen smiled a little. "Like you would ever hate your parents."

"But see? That's my point. I didn't really hate them, but I got mad at them because I knew that no matter what I said, I was safe with them. I could tell them I hated them in a thousand notes and they would still love me because they're my mom and dad. I think . . . I think Oliver's taking it out on you because he knows that, deep down, you're not going to leave. You never really did. You just have to wait for him to come back around to you."

Maureen's eyes were filling with tears and I sat back in my chair, suddenly nervous. I wasn't sure where "making Maureen cry" ranked on the list of things my parents didn't want me to do, but I imagined it was pretty high up there.

"No, no, sweetheart," Maureen said when she saw my face, quickly wiping her eyes and reaching for my hand. "It's all right, I'm not upset. Well"—she laughed a little to herself—"I am, obviously, but not at you. You're just very smart."

"I feel like that's still up for negotiation," I said, and then glanced up as my mom (*finally*, oh my God) came into the room.

"Everything all right?" she asked as Maureen started to stand up. "Maureen, do you—?"

"I'm fine," she said. "I should probably go home. Emmy says that Oliver is there, so . . ."

My mom wrapped her arm around my shoulder as Maureen gathered her things, and I let her keep it there. Usually, it feels like a trap, like maybe this time she's not going to let me go, but for the first time in a long while, I wanted to stay close to her.

It had been a long, long night.

"I'll walk you home," my mom said to Maureen, giving me a final squeeze, and my shoulders felt cold when her arm left them. "Just to make sure you get there safely."

Maureen nodded, then took two quick steps forward and grabbed me in a hug. I suspected that its fierceness and strength was meant for Oliver, not me, but this wasn't the first time I had felt that way. For the first few months after Oliver went missing, she would hug me so hard that it made me wince.

It was just frightening to think that even now, with Oliver home and safe in his bedroom, Maureen still reached for me instead of him.

"Your daughter is very smart," Maureen said to my mom as she pulled away, then rubbed her thumb across my cheek.

"Yes, she is," my mom said, then gave me a wink as she pulled the sliding door open for Maureen. I could hear Maureen say something to my mom, but she was already outside, and I waited until my mom shut the door behind them before making a hasty escape out of the room.

I found my dad in the kitchen. Or, to be more exact, I found my dad's socked feet standing behind the open refrigerator door. There was a lot of muffled shuffling sounds, followed by a clatter. "Dad?"

He poked his head around the door. "Oh, hi," he said, like I had been there all along. "Are you starving? I'm starving. I don't know about you, but that wasn't the most relaxing dinner."

"Are there leftovers?" I asked, coming into the kitchen and boosting myself up on the countertop. Unlike my mom, my dad didn't shoo me down.

"Are there leftovers?" he repeated. "Is that a joke? Have you *seen* your mom's organizational skills?"

"I caught her using the label maker once," I told him. "She said she wasn't, but I know she was."

"She was," my dad agreed. He rummaged around, then pulled

out a Tupperware container. "What do we think this is? Guess correctly and you win it."

I looked at it. "Chicken salad. The Waldorf one, with grapes and walnuts."

My dad opened it, gave it a sniff, then handed it to me. "Congratulations, you get to eat with your father."

"Yay," I said, then leaned down to get a fork out of the drawer. "What are you having?"

He found another container. "Mac and cheese, apparently," he said.

"That's a pretty good consolation prize," I said, passing him a fork.

"Not too shabby," he agreed.

We ate in silence for a minute. I hadn't realized just how starving I had been and the chicken salad was really good. "So," my dad finally said. "Tonight."

"Tonight," I repeated, still shoveling in food. He passed me a napkin. "Thanks. Yeah, tonight was . . ."

"Tonight sucked," my dad said, and I started to laugh hearing him say that. "What?" He smiled at me. "Isn't that the *slang* you kids are using? The *lingo*? Do I sound hip?"

I just shook my head. "The only hip I hear is the sound of yours breaking."

"*Ohhhh!*" he cried, like I had just made a three-point shot from the free-throw line. "That's a good one. Let no one say that my daughter doesn't have a few zingers in her back pocket."

"Yeah, well, I get it from my dad."

"Yes, you do, kid."

I took another bite of salad and chewed. Hearing him call me "kid" reminded me of what Oliver had said about his dad. "Maureen wants to do this TV show," I said. I hadn't been planning to say anything, so I was as surprised as my dad was to hear me say that. "To find Keith. Oliver's dad. It's like a crime show or something, but Oliver doesn't want to do it."

My dad just nodded and shoved the food around in his container. "Did he tell you that?"

"Yeah. He says, um, he says he really misses his dad. Like, as much as he missed his mom back when he first disappeared." It was getting a little more difficult to chew and I set the salad down, suddenly not as hungry as I had been.

"What do you think?" my dad asked me.

"I think that Keith should go to jail or whatever. I mean, he did a really bad thing. But at the same time . . ."

"Punishing Keith punishes Oliver, too?" my dad guessed, and I nodded.

"It's just hard to see him feel this bad," I said. "Like, he didn't do anything but he keeps getting hurt, anyway. I don't like watching him go through this."

My dad set down his food, too, then hopped up on the counter next to me. "So. You and Oliver."

I looked up at him, surprised. "Me," I said. "And Oliver."

"Those are two very different sentences, Emmy. Look," he

added quickly before I could protest. "I saw you two at the table tonight. I know there was a lot going on, it got chaotic there, but I saw you two looking at each other. And I know what I saw."

I was blushing furiously now, untucking my hair from behind my ear so my dad couldn't see my face. "He's always been my friend," I said. "Even when he wasn't here, okay? And he still is, even though we're . . ."

"No, I know, sweetie. But Oliver has a lot of pain right now, and I don't want you to take his burden on yourself." My dad stroked my hair, eventually uncovering my face, and I let him.

"Dad, it's, like, ten years too late to worry about that," I said.

"I know," he said again. "You saw a lot. Your mom and I tried to protect you from most of it, but Oliver was your friend and he disappeared and there aren't many ways you can hide that from your kid." He was still stroking my hair. "But I don't want you to stay in that place forever. And I don't want Oliver to stay there, either. You kids have a chance to move on."

"It's sort of hard when . . . when you don't know how." The words hurt even as I said them and realized how true they were. I couldn't remember a time when I hadn't been worried or scared for Oliver. How do you move on from that? I could feel tears pricking at my eyes. *Do not cry,* I told myself. *Do not cry, do not cry, do not cry.*

"Well, that's growing up, isn't it?" my dad said. "You don't always have to know. And things aren't always fair. You just have to keep moving forward. A step in one direction."

"Do you think Maureen should do the TV show?" I asked after a few minutes, while my dad rubbed my back.

"I think." My dad thought for a minute. "I think that both Maureen and Oliver want answers that they might never get. And they need to figure out how to deal with that."

I looked up at my dad. "Tonight, when Oliver and I were talking, I said I'd still love *you*, even if you kidnapped me. I really would. I get how he feels."

My dad smiled. "That's the nicest and most sociopathic thing anyone's ever said to me."

"That's what I'm here for," I said, then wrapped my arms around his neck and hugged him tight. I suddenly wanted to tell him everything—UCSD and surfing and kissing Oliver at the party—but I stopped myself.

One thing at a time.

CHAPTER TWENTY-EIGHT

The buzz at school started quietly at first, like one tiny mosquito that kept floating around near you, but always just out of reach so you couldn't squish it. Then it got progressively louder after lunch, and by the time school ended, it was like someone had smashed a wasps' nest full of gossip onto the floor.

"Why's everyone freaking out?" I asked Drew once I ran into him. I mean, literally ran into him. He was wearing his soccer uniform and carrying his cleats in one hand.

"UCs are notifying people!" he yelled as he kept running. "Sorry, the bus is leaving! Away game!" He blew kisses in my general direction as he turned the corner, and to be honest, it was a good thing he couldn't talk.

Because I had gone numb.

The admission letters had arrived. The yes or no I had been waiting for for four months—no, actually, more like four *years*—

was sitting in an in-box somewhere for me, and I suddenly felt terrified no matter what the answer would be.

What was I supposed to do? I immediately started to text Caro, just out of pure instinct, but stopped before I could even start. I couldn't tell Caro, not yet. She didn't even know that I had applied to UCSD. In fact, only one person in the entire world knew what I had done, and I needed to find him immediately.

Oliver was coming out of the guidance counselor's office when I bumped into him. He was scowling a little and had a tight grip on both straps of his backpack, but he smiled when he saw me. "Hey!" he said. "Why are you still—wait, what's wrong?"

I just shook my head and Oliver bent down and grasped my shoulders. "Em. You're totally white right now. Are you okay? Did something happen?"

"Acceptance letters are in," I whispered, and Oliver's eyes grew as wide and round as I knew mine were.

"They are?" he whispered back. "What did it say?"

"I don't know!" I was starting to feel a little hysterical. "I haven't looked yet! And I can't go do it at home because my mom's there and she . . ."

"Got it," he said. "What about the library?"

I shook my head. "No. I don't know what the news is, or how I'm going to react, but either way, I don't want to have my reaction in the school library!"

"Okay, okay, calm down." Oliver squeezed my arms again and I took a deep breath. "You can't just check it on your phone?"

I glanced at my phone. "I have two percent battery—wait, now it's one percent battery—left."

"Okay, what if—oh, wait! Oh my God—ballet!"

"Oliver, only one of us can have a meltdown right now, and I don't know what you mean by—"

"No, I mean, my mom took the twins to ballet class and Rick's up in San Jose on a business trip! No one's home! You can check on my laptop there."

"But we're not supposed to be alone in the house together," I said.

"Emmy!" Oliver gave me a small shake. "Are you serious right now?"

"No. Yes. I don't know! Let's go!"

I drove back to our houses in record time, my hands shaking even as they gripped the wheel. "I think I'm going to throw up," I told Oliver.

"No, you're not," he said.

"No, I really think I am. What have I done? Why did I think this was a good idea?"

"Because you're smart and want to join the surf team and move out of your parents' house."

"Those are pretty good reasons," I admitted.

"They are," he agreed.

I parked my car around the corner so my mom wouldn't see it, then Oliver and I ran down the street and let ourselves in through the back door. The house was quiet, with some pink plastic cups sitting half full on the countertop and a small purple hoodie left slung over a chair. "Oh no, Nora forgot her jacket," I said.

"Worry about it later," Oliver told me, hustling me up the stairs to his room. It smelled different from the rest of the house, like Oliver. Maureen's scented candles from Anthropologie hadn't made it this far, apparently. "Okay," he said, opening up his laptop. "Type. Do whatever."

I sat down at the keyboard, then froze. "Emmy," Oliver said, his voice softer this time as he knelt down next to me. "The answer's not gonna change now. You might as well open it."

"Good point," I said, but I didn't move my hands. "Can you, um? Do you mind just standing over there?" I gestured toward his bed. "I want to read it by myself first, whatever it says."

He moved without even questioning it and I took another shaky breath, let it out slowly, then typed in the admissions address. A few clicks later and I saw the letter waiting in my in-box.

I opened it and read it.

Then read it again.

Then read it once more just to make sure.

"Emmy?" Oliver sounded hesitant. "Are you . . . is it . . . ?"

"Dear Emily," I started to read out loud, then stopped for a second so I could catch my breath. "Dear Emily, Congratulations! I am delighted to offer you admission to the University of California, San Diego for fall—"

"YESSSSS!!!!" Oliver grabbed me out of the chair and up into his arms and I squealed with laughter, a sound of pure delight.

"Oh my God!" I cried against his shoulder, and then I couldn't hang on to him tight enough. "I got in!"

"You got in!" He swung me in a circle and I laughed again. "You're going to college!"

"I'm going to college!" I cried, because in that moment, I didn't care what my parents said, I didn't care what anyone said. I had done it all on my own. This was all mine.

"C'mere," Oliver said, and then he was kissing me while still holding me up. I kissed him back, dizzy from happiness and adrenaline and the spinning. Eventually, we made it back to his bed and I collapsed into the sheets, still kissing him, not letting him go anywhere.

Oliver had no problem with that.

"Good thing you're a better kisser than a surfer," I teased him in between kisses, moving his hair back so that it wouldn't get in the way.

"Well, college girls turn me on," he replied, then leaned in again as I started to giggle. He kissed my jaw instead, then right below my ear, and I instinctively turned toward him.

That's when we heard the garage door start to mechanically grind open.

"Shit!" I cried, and we sprang apart. I slammed the laptop shut and grabbed my car keys while Oliver straightened the bed and then his shirt. We were both breathing hard, both flushed, and even though I was a minute away from being busted by Oliver's mom and two prima ballerinas, I couldn't stop smiling.

"Hurry," he said. "Use the back door again."

"Okay," I said, then grinned at him.

"Are you trying to get us both grounded?" he hissed, but he had a pretty dopey smile on his face, too. "Go! Get out of here! Go research dorm rooms or something."

I grabbed his hand and kissed it one last time, then disappeared down the stairs and out the back door just as the laundry room door started to open. "I'M SO COLD—" I could hear Nora start to say as I slid the door shut behind me, and I turned and went past a row of sago palms, tall enough to hide me from the windows.

"I'm going to college," I whispered to myself once I was back in the car, and when I adjusted the rearview mirror, I didn't recognize the girl in the reflection.

But I liked what I saw.

CHAPTER TWENTY-NINE

I managed not to text either Drew or Caro that night, and at dinner my mom said, "Why do you have a funny little smile on your face?"

"Oh, just happy," I said, shoving around some rigatoni on my plate. *Did they have rigatoni in the campus cafeterias? Maybe I should try being a vegetarian.* "No big deal."

My mom eyed me, but said nothing more. I could tell she thought my smile was Oliver related, and I decided that that was probably safer than her realizing the truth. I was going to have to tell my parents at some point, but I was hoping it could be in the future. Like, the way future. Possibly once I was a grandmother.

By lunchtime the next day, though, I couldn't keep it in anymore. "Caro!" I said when I saw her in the hallway. "Caro! Best friend for life! I have to tell you something!"

She stopped in her tracks and pulled out her earbuds so I could hear the tinny music blasting. How she doesn't go deaf is beyond me. "Well, you can tell Drew, too," she said, gesturing over my shoulder to our friend as he came walking over.

"Hallway meeting!" he said, flinging his arm around my shoulder. "I'm thinking of inviting Kevin to my grandmother's big seventy-fifth birthday party extravaganza. What do you think?"

"Snore alert," Caro said.

"Can't you just take him to a nice dinner instead?" I asked. "And yeah, what Caro said."

"Duh, we've already been to dinner, like, *three* times. I don't know how much more unlimited salad and bread sticks I can handle."

"I love the bread sticks," Caro said dreamily. "God, I'm starving."

"I just want my family to meet Kevin," Drew said, and underneath the eagerness of his voice, I could hear everything he didn't dare say out loud: *I want my family to want to meet Kevin.* "And everyone will be there at the restaurant and Kane will be there, so it's not like I'm going in alone and . . ." He stopped and took a breath. I realized that he was wringing his hands in front of him.

"Drew," I said, putting my hand on his arm. "You should invite Kevin. If everyone else is bringing a guest, you should be able to, too."

"Oh, I'm not worried about that," Drew said, waving my words away. "I'm just worried that Kevin doesn't want to meet my family."

"Well, he's already met Kane," Caro pointed out. "That's about as exciting as it'll get."

"True," Drew said. "And there will be alcohol."

"Tell him it's like a booze cruise, only no boat and your grandmother will be there," I suggested. "That's a good sell."

"And cake!" Caro added. "Who doesn't love cake? Oh my God, seriously, can we go eat lunch now?" She looked pained.

"Wait, I still have news!" I said.

"Let's walk and talk," Drew said. "I have to head over to yearbook."

"Can you ask them to cut back on all the picture taking, by the way?" Caro asked as we started to make our way through the hall and toward the quad. "Not every aspect of high school life needs to be commemorated."

"Not every student hates school the way you do, Caro," I told her, linking arms with her. "Some of us might want to remember it."

"If Caro had her way, the yearbook would be a pamphlet," Drew added.

"On my island," Caro muttered. "Okay, Emmy, hit it. The big news."

I stopped walking and turned to face them. Caro looked pained that we weren't heading in the direction of food anymore.

"The big news——" I started to say.

"Oh my God, you're pregnant!" she said.

"You're *pregnant*?" Drew said in the loudest whisper possible. "Is it Oliver's?"

"What?" I cried. "No, I'm not pregnant! What the hell, Caro? Do you really think I'd be announcing that in the hallway at school?"

Caro shrugged. "I don't know. You've never told me you're pregnant before. I don't know what the rules are."

"I'm not pregnant!" I said again. "This is how terrible rumors get started! Talking to you two is like playing a sick game of telephone!"

"If you are, though," Drew said, "then you should be on *16 and Pregnant* because then Caro and I will get airtime as your supportive best friends and then you'll probably end up on *Teen Mom* and make some really good money." He nodded sagely, the oddest and youngest financial planner ever.

I just stared at both of them. "You two are the worst best friends in the history of existence."

Caro just grinned and hoisted her backpack up farther onto her shoulders. "Well, whatever you're going to tell me is going to be really disappointing now."

"Thanks," I said, then took a deep breath. "Okay, here's the actual news. I got into UCSD."

"Oh my God!" Drew said, then reached forward and grabbed me up in a hug. "Congratulations! Wait. Did I even know you applied?"

"No," Caro said, but her voice was oddly flat. "I didn't know you applied, either, Emmy."

I hugged Drew back, then pulled away to see Caro's stony

face regarding me with . . . well, I don't know what it was, but it wasn't exactly pride or happiness. "I didn't tell anyone," I said. "I just did it to see if I could get in. And I did!"

"And you did," Caro repeated. "When were you planning on telling me, though?"

I glanced at Drew, who gave me the "you're on your own with this one" look. "Um, right now?" I said. "I couldn't obviously tell you that I got in until I knew whether or not I *had*, Caro."

"Because it's not like we had plans to go to community college together for the next two years or anything?" she replied.

"Plans?" I asked. "I don't remember having *plans*. We talked about it, yeah, but we didn't—"

"Did you tell Oliver?" Caro continued like I wasn't even speaking.

"He knows that I got in." Why was I starting to feel so defensive about this? Wasn't Caro supposed to be happy for me? That was Rule Number One in the Best Friend Handbook, right?

"No, I mean, did you tell him you applied?"

I swallowed hard. "Yes. But Caro—"

"Fucking forget it," she said, then started to walk away.

"Caro!" I yelled after her, but she waved her hand at me and kept walking.

I looked at Drew. He looked at me. "I'm out," he said, holding up his hands. "This is between you two, not me."

"Great, thanks," I said, still watching Caro as she slipped around the corner. "I guess I have to go after her now."

"Probably a good idea," Drew agreed. "You shouldn't let Caro stew for too long or she gets . . ."

"Yeah," I sighed. I knew what he meant. Caro was an excellent stewer. She could turn a splinter into a redwood if she thought about it long enough. "Talk to you later?"

"Go, before her head explodes," Drew replied, and I hurried off after Caro. "Hey, Emmy, wait!"

"Yeah?"

Drew smiled at me. "Congratulations."

"Thanks, Drew." I smiled back at him. And then it hit me. In six months, we wouldn't see each other every day, that we'd be in separate schools—separate parts of the state—for the first time in our lives.

"Now go get Caro," Drew said, gesturing off into the distance. "Before she turns into a fire starter or something."

When she's mad, Caro becomes an expert speed walker and I eventually had to jog to catch up to her. "Caro!" I screamed. "Would you just stop? *Please?*"

She stopped so fast that I almost ran into her. "What?" she asked, and the venom in her voice made me take a step backward. "Is there more exciting news? Let me guess, you—"

"Oh, knock it off, Caro!" I yelled. "I got into college and you're mad at me? That makes zero sense! You're supposed to be happy for me! That's what friends do!"

"You know what else friends do?" she said. "They tell each other things! Important things, like the fact that they're, oh, I don't know, applying to colleges, maybe?"

"I applied to *one*!"

"You should have told me!" Caro yelled. "I thought we would get an apartment together, take the same classes!"

"Get an apartment?" I repeated. "Caro, do you really think my mom would let me do that? There's no way! We talked about it, yeah, but there's no—"

"Yeah, well, I didn't know you were planning this whole new life!" Caro said. "Everyone seems to be doing that, though, making all these new plans without me. Drew's got his scholarship and a cute barista and you've got San Diego and Oliver."

I tried to interrupt her, but she didn't stop. "I'm *really* glad you told Oliver, though. He's been home, what? Two months? Six weeks? And yet he knows more about you than I do."

"Oliver? *Seriously*, Caro? Is that what this is about?"

Caro stalked over until we were less than a foot apart. "It is *always* about Oliver," she said, her voice low and venomous. "It's been about him for *years*. I thought now that he was home that maybe we could move on, that we wouldn't just be 'Oliver's old friends,' or whatever the fucking press used to call us. But it's still all about him." Caro held up her hands like she was dropping the past ten years at my feet. "So fine. He wins."

"This isn't a competition!" I cried. "I'm still friends with you and Drew. I'm just . . . dating Oliver. That's all."

"Then why didn't you tell me about college? Why didn't you mention it to me? You're not the only one who wants out of here, Emmy!"

"I didn't even think I would get in!" I cried. "It just happened!"

"Okay, then here's another question. Why don't you call and ask me to do something? Or—crazy thought—ask me how I'm doing!"

I didn't have an answer for that. It was no secret that I hadn't been spending as much time with Caro and Drew now that Oliver was home. With Drew, it hadn't really mattered because he was spending all of his free time with Kevin. But Caro . . .

"Caro," I said. "Why don't you hang out with us this afternoon? We were just going to go to the Stand and get dinner, but you should come with us."

Caro just turned around and started walking away again. "You'll have to forgive me if I pass on your pity date," she called over her shoulder. "I know where I'm not wanted."

"Caroline!" I yelled. "You can't just walk away in the middle of a fight. That's not fair!"

"Look who's suddenly upset when things aren't fair," Caro yelled, and kept walking. She walked until she was just a speck in the distance, then she seemed to melt into the horizon. I watched her go, defeated, then turned around and trudged back to school where Oliver was waiting for me near the concrete statue of our mascot, a giant, soaring bird that looked like it was constantly deciding which student to gobble down first. (Go Hawks.) At that moment, I sort of wished he would pick me.

"Hey!" Oliver said. It had gotten cloudy out and he had tugged his hoodie up over his head so that just a few strands of hair were peeking out. "Where'd you go? I saw Drew and he said something about Caroline and stew?"

"Yeah, well," I said, "Caroline's not exactly happy about me getting into UCSD."

"What?" Oliver frowned. "Why? She's, like, your best friend. I thought she'd be running around the school, yelling at people and lighting firecrackers."

"Yeah, well," I said again. "Apparently not." I didn't feel like explaining that the problem had everything and nothing to do with him. "Ready to go?"

Oliver eyed me, then slung his arm across my shoulders. He didn't answer my question; instead, we walked toward my car, with only one place to go: home.

CHAPTER THIRTY

The silent treatment from Caro went on for a week. My phone had never been so quiet. "Are you *still* not talking?" Drew said when he saw me at school on Monday, after a weekend with no Caro. "How am I supposed to have two best friends who are fighting? This doesn't work for me."

"Learn to adjust," I told him. "And I'm happy to talk to Caro. She just doesn't want to talk to me."

Oliver, while understanding, was equally clueless. "Can't you just, like, text her?" he said. We were both studying in his room while Maureen made approximately twenty-three separate trips from downstairs to the linen closet, which meant that she passed Oliver's room every time. "No closed doors, you two!" she said the first time, in a teasing voice that all parents use when they actually mean, "No, seriously, we will strip the skin off your bones if you close that door."

Luckily, one of the floorboards on the second floor squeaks, so we could always hear her coming. With the twins fast asleep in their room and Rick watching TV downstairs, it was pretty easy to make out between laundry trips. "How many sheet sets do you even *have*?" I whispered to him as the floorboard squeaked and we sprang apart.

He just shrugged and picked up his pencil. "Yeah, but so then why does cosine . . . ?" he said as Maureen passed. "I have no idea," he whispered once she was gone. "You know she's spying on us."

"No, you want to figure out the tangent," I said as she walked back, then waited to hear her footsteps on the stairs. I was supposed to be tutoring him in pre-calc since I had taken it the year before, but Oliver didn't need too much help.

"Did you talk to UCSD yet?" he asked once the coast was clear.

"I have until May first," I told him. "I don't have to decide until then."

"So when are you going to tell your parents?"

"Um, hopefully as my car pulls out of the driveway on the way to San Diego." I wrapped my hand around his, still holding on to the pencil. "That should be a good time, right? They can't run as fast as the car."

"I think a lot of people can run as fast as your car," Oliver said.

"What it lacks in speed it makes up for in personality," I said. "Besides, all the sand probably weighs it down."

He laughed and leaned in to kiss me. Who knew pre-calc

could be so romantic? "No, but seriously," he said after a minute. "You need to tell them."

"Dude, I know. I will. Just . . . I have to do it on my own time. I know my parents, I know when it's a good time and when it's not."

Oliver regarded me with suspicion. "You weren't joking about that driveway comment, were you?"

"ANYWAY," I said. "Focus on math."

"What do I get if I get the next one right?" His breath was warm on my neck, making goose bumps raise up on my arms as I shivered.

"You get a gold star," I whispered back, then turned around to kiss him.

"Is that a metaphor?" he asked.

"Get it right and see," I replied, and started to kiss him.

Cccccrreeeeeeaaaaaaaakkkk!

"Laundry time," Oliver muttered as we flew apart again.

"Worst chore ever," I added, and he could only nod his head in agreement.

Oliver was right, though. The clock was ticking and I had only three weeks before I had to tell UCSD whether or not I would accept their offer. Which meant, of course, that I had only three weeks to tell my parents that there was even an offer to accept. I tried a few times—at dinner one night, while we were all in the car the next—but every time I started to say something, the words seemed to fall apart in my mouth and all that came out was a cough. "Are you getting a cold?" my mom finally asked after the third time at dinner. "You sound a bit wheezy."

"I'm fine," I said automatically.

"You're not eating very much," she said. "I thought you liked this pasta?"

It was bow-tie pasta with cream sauce, my mom's secret recipe that she wouldn't even give to my grandmother. (And if you don't think *that* caused a ruckus at Thanksgiving last year, then you would be very wrong.) And yes, I did love it, but between Caro and school and college and Oliver, it felt like the anxiety boulder in my stomach left no room for food.

"I'm fiiiine," I said again, suddenly aware that I was whining. "I'm fine," I repeated, trying to sound like an almost college student and not a three-year-old. "I just have a lot of schoolwork and Caro and I . . ."

Both my parents froze with their forks to their mouths. "Caro and you what?" my dad said. "Don't leave us hanging. Caro and I are joining the circus? Caro and I have decided to become neurosurgeons? Caro and I have decided to reimburse our parents for the eighteen years' worth of room and board that they've so lovingly provided us?"

"Honey, she and Caro are *fighting*," my mom said. "Don't be ridiculous."

"How did you know we were fighting?" I asked.

"Because you're only sending a million texts a day, rather than two million," my mom said, but I could tell that she was trying to be nice about it. "What happened?"

She was clearly dying for more information. I wonder if she and Maureen had discussed this at all. "We just had a stupid fight," I said. "She said some things and I said some things, that's all. No biggie."

"You and Caro have never fought before," my dad said.

"We argued over that My Little Pony doll when we were four," I pointed out. She won. I was still bitter.

"Well, I'm sure you'll make up," my mom said. "You and Caro have been friends forever."

"Can I be excused?" I asked, wiping my mouth with my napkin in preparation to flee. "Oliver and I wanted to do some homework together."

My mom raised an eyebrow at me. "Where? Here or there?"

"There," I said. Our house didn't have any squeaky floorboards.

"Two more bites," she said, and I swallowed them in one, relieved to be off the hot seat.

For now.

CHAPTER THIRTY-ONE

The high school had an open house on Wednesday night, one of those things where all the parents and their kids can come to the school and show off their work and talk to the teachers about how great/wonderful/abysmal their little darlings are. It's a big community to-do, and my parents, of course, haven't missed one ever. Even when my mom had bronchitis, she managed to make a miraculous recovery and show up to discuss my B-plus grade with my eighth-grade history teacher. (My mother thought it should have been an A-minus. She thought wrong.)

Oliver's mom, on the other hand, hadn't been able to attend one for ten years, so she was over the moon. "Come on, we're going to be late!" I heard her yelling that evening as she herded everyone into their cars. I heard this because I was being herded by my parents into our car.

"Emmy, step on it," my mom said. "If we don't get there

soon, there's always a line to talk to your AP Bio teacher." Mr. Hernandez was thirty years old and very, um, in demand by most of the moms in our school. Not that my mom wanted to hit on Mr. Hernandez. She was probably the only mom who actually wanted to discuss my participation in class with him.

"Aren't you tired of talking to my teachers?" I asked them as I fastened my seat belt. "I can just reenact the conversation for you."

"You're a poor man's Mr. Hernandez," my dad told me.

"Oh my God. *Dad.*"

"Fasten your seat belt," my mom said.

"It's fastened." Like it always was every single time she asked.

Oliver and I both looked at each other as our respective cars backed out of the driveways. I was about to wave when he suddenly crossed his eyes and stuck out his tongue at me.

I had to laugh. That's what I had done to him back on his first day of school, back when I could barely imagine talking to him, much less sitting on his lap or wrapping my arms around his neck or sprawling on the warm sand, my head resting against his shoulder as he ran his fingers up and down my back. He had been a friend, then a stranger, and now something more.

And going to UCSD meant that this time, I would be leaving him.

School always seemed so weird on open house nights, lit up in the dark and suddenly filled with parents. It was even weirder hearing your parents refer to your teachers as Mr. or Mrs. So-and-So, like they were students, too. My parents were pretty much on a first-name basis with every other parent there, and my mom shouted "Oh, hell-*lo*!" at five other families even before we got inside.

I managed to hang in there for about thirty minutes, showing my parents where I sat in French class ("Why are you so far back?" my mom wondered), introduced them to my calculus teacher and let her talk about what a great math student I was, and waited with them in line for the famed Mr. Hernandez. "Emmy is an excellent diagrammer," he told my parents, smiling at them, and I swear I heard half the moms swoon.

I looked at my dad. He looked back at me. Then we both tried not to laugh.

"How long does this go on for?" someone said into my ear as we headed toward my civics classroom and I turned around to see Oliver standing next to me as our parents all greeted one another. (Rick was at the twins' future elementary school, probably taking copious notes for Maureen.)

"Forever," I whispered back, then found his hand and squeezed it. "Hope you didn't make plans for the next three days."

"Does this seriously happen every year?" he asked.

"Look at my eyes," I said, then widened them dramatically. "Does this look like the face of someone who would joke about this?"

"You look deranged," he said, and we both leaned forward a little before we remembered where we were, and more important, who we were with.

"You must be so happy to be here," my mom said, and Maureen could only nod as her eyes filled with tears.

"Mommm," Oliver said. "You promised you wouldn't, not here."

"I know, I know," she said, then waved her fingers in front of her eyes as if to fan away the tears. "I just haven't been to one of these since first grade, you know?" She started to tear up again, then stopped herself. "It just feels good to be back in the swing of things." Maureen smiled at Oliver, then reached for his hand. "We're just . . . we're trying."

Oliver nodded, but didn't let her hold his hand. "Mom," he said again. "We're at school, okay?"

"Sorry, sorry," she said again, then rolled her eyes at my mom as if to say, *Teenagers.* My mom smiled back and luckily for her, didn't try and hold my hand, either.

"Do you wanna go walk?" I asked Oliver. "Unless you want to see all of your teachers for a second time today, that is."

"Um, no," he said.

"Is it okay if we . . . ?" I asked, pointing down the hall. "We'll stay on campus."

My mom raised an eyebrow at me. *"Only* walking," she said. "No funny business."

"Got it," I said, even as I linked hands with Oliver. "No telling jokes or making humorous observations."

"Oh, get out of here," my dad said, swatting at my head as I ducked past, and I giggled as Oliver ran to keep up with me.

I don't know why my mom thought we'd spend our time kissing

on campus. To be honest, high school isn't the most romantic setting. It smells like dirty linoleum and tempera paint, along with paper and burnt coffee and gym socks, and besides, there were probably a thousand students and their parents wandering around. Still, it was nice to wander with Oliver and not have to listen for a creaky floorboard or keep an eye out for the twins, who were forever curious about why we were always studying together.

"It's gonna be weird to be here next year without you," Oliver said. "Who's going to eat lunch with me?"

"Don't say that," I said. "I'll still come back and visit. And who knows, I might not even go."

Oliver glanced down at me. "You don't mean that."

I shrugged. "Maybe. I don't know. It's scary, you know? Moving. Leaving my bedroom. Leaving my parents." I took a deep breath. "Leaving you."

"Well, I left you," he pointed out. "Think of it as payback."

"You didn't leave," I started to say, but just then Caro came running up. I had seen her at school, but both of us had been going out of our way to avoid talking to each other, and I actually took a step back when she came closer. "Caro?" I said.

"Yeah. Hi. Look, Drew's upset."

"Drew is? About what?"

"You should probably just come with me."

My heart was starting to pick up pace. Drew never really got upset. He had always been the peacemaker between me and Caro, between Kane and his parents, between his parents and himself.

"Okay," I said, then gestured to Oliver to follow me.

"Wait, no," Caro said. "Just you, Emmy." She looked at Oliver, her face a protective shield. I knew what she was thinking: *Oliver isn't one of us anymore.*

I was about to protest, but to my surprise, Oliver spoke up first. "Caro, wait," he said, and she sighed and turned to face him, her arms folded over her chest. The campus lights had come on, bathing us in a watery yellow light. Under them, Caro looked tired and concerned and unsure, so unlike her normal self. "What?" she asked.

Oliver glanced at me before taking a deep breath and turning back to Caro. "Look, Caro, I know that I came back and sort of changed everything, especially for you and Emmy and Drew. I get it, okay? But we were friends once before and it'd be cool if we could try to be friends again. Not, like, re-creating what we had when we were seven, but as who we are now."

Caro's eyes filled with tears before she hastily brushed them away, and I realized that Oliver's return had impacted more than just my family and his family. We weren't the only people who had known him. Caro and Drew had been there the day Oliver's dad drove off with him. The police had questioned them, too. And when Oliver came home, they had been standing right next to me.

"Fine," she said. "Come on, Drew's waiting."

We followed her out to the parking lot, where Drew was standing near his parents' Escalade. It loomed in the near darkness and made Drew look even smaller. "No, I don't know," he was saying into his cell when we arrived, his back turned to us. "Okay . . . yeah, okay. Love you, too, Kane. Okay, yeah. Bye." When he turned and saw us, his cheeks were wet, and Caro immediately went to his side and wrapped her arm around his waist.

"What's wrong?" I asked, shivering a little as the fog started to roll in. Next to me, Oliver pulled on his hoodie and zipped it up a little more in front.

"It's stupid," Drew said, shaking his head. "It's just . . . so stupid. It doesn't matter."

"It matters," Caro murmured. "It matters a lot."

"What happened?" I asked again. "Is it Kevin? Did you break up?"

"No, no," Drew said. "At least, not yet."

"Dude," Oliver said. "Just tell us what happened." His voice was kind, though, and I thought it was a good thing that he was there, because I was about ready to shake the answer right out of Drew.

"I asked my parents if I could bring Kevin to my grandma's birthday party," Drew said, his voice trembling a little. "And at first they said they had to think about it, and then tonight before we came here . . . they said they thought it wouldn't be a good idea." He was twisting his own hoodie strings around his fingers so that they cut off the circulation. It looked painful but I didn't move to stop him.

"Wait, why?" I asked as Caro rubbed his back. "I thought they were cool with this. I mean, not cool, but . . ."

"Yeah, well." Drew laughed a little. "They say they're cool with it, but my grandma's a different story."

"So tell your grandma to fuck off," Caro spat, and Drew gave her a one-armed hug.

"It's a little hard to do that when she controls the money," he said, then took another deep breath. "I guess my dad's business isn't doing so well?" He said it like a question, like he wasn't even sure if it was the truth or not. "And she's been helping my parents out with, like, mortgage payments and stuff like that."

"And they think she'll cut them off if she finds out you're gay?" I cried.

"Apparently, Grandma's old school," Drew sighed.

"Apparently, Grandma's a homophobe," Caro corrected him. (I hoped for Drew's grandma's sake that she and Caro never met in a dark alley.)

"Whatever she is, it means that I can't bring Kevin to the party."

Oliver, who had been very still, suddenly spoke up. "It's not about the party," he said quietly. "You want your parents to stick up for you."

"I just want to know I'm worth more to them than some fucking mortgage payment!" Drew said, then quickly wiped his eyes on his wrist cuff. "Like, this was all just fine in theory. But now that they actually have to tell people and deal with that, they're just bailing. And I don't get to bail because this is my life, you know? And I don't want to bail, I don't mean it like that, but I just wish they weren't standing so far behind me."

He glanced over at Oliver. "Can I tell you something?"

"Yeah, man, sure." I could feel Oliver's posture stiffen, though, his spine suddenly straight.

"Sometimes I get so jealous of you." Drew stabbed at the ground with the toe of his shoe. "Your parents both wanted you so much. I know that's not fair and I'm sorry it sounds bad, but that's how I feel."

Oliver nodded slowly, taking it in. "I feel like I should apologize or something," he said, and we all giggled nervously. I looped my arm around his, holding him close. "Wanting someone isn't the same as loving them, though," he said. "You know? It doesn't mean the same thing."

"No, I know, I know," Drew said, wiping at his face again. "Sorry, that sounds so awful. I hate that I think that."

"It's okay," Oliver said. "I get it. I do." He put his hand on Drew's shoulder, anchoring him.

"I just don't want Kevin to think that, like, I'm ashamed to be seen with him or something," Drew sighed. "Or that I don't want him around my family. Well, actually, now I kind of *don't* want him around them, but—"

"Drew?"

A dark figure was walking toward us in the parking lot, a little unsure. It was Kevin.

"I texted him," Caro said. "I thought you might want to see him."

Kevin looked at the four of us. I guess we were a little formidable, gathered around Drew like a small army. "Hi," he said. "Um, Caro texted me? She said you were out here."

"Hi," Drew said. "God, I'm a disaster right now. Sorry."

"Hey." Kevin's face grew concerned and he seemed to close the distance between them into two steps. "What's wrong?"

Drew took a long, shaky breath, then hugged Kevin. They were talking, their voices muffled against each other's shoulders, and I was about to gesture to Caro and Oliver that we should probably leave when I heard my mother's voice cut across the parking lot.

"Emily!"

My head jerked up. My parents rarely, if ever, used my actual first name. No one else ever used it. The only time I really heard the name *Emily* was on the first day of school when teachers took roll for the first time. Then I'd say, "I actually prefer being called Emmy," and that'd be it until the following year.

My parents were standing near the school entrance, across the parking lot from us. Even from that distance, I could see that they were furious. My mom looked like she could send herself into the air and fly over to us like she was Iron Man, that's how angry she was.

Even Caro noticed. "Whoa," she said softly.

"Yeah," I said. "Whoa." My knees started to feel wobbly and I glanced over at Drew and Kevin, who were still hugging but both looking in my parents' direction.

"I think I have to go," I said.

"Emmy, *now*!" I heard my mom yell again.

"Uh, yeah, you do," Drew said. "Are they going to lock you in a tower or something? What'd you do?"

"Nothing that they should know about," I said, and then I realized with a sobering rush that I had done a lot of things my parents shouldn't know about, and maybe that wasn't the case anymore.

"I'll go with you," Oliver said, untangling my arm from his so he could hold my hand instead. "You might need a witness."

"Are you going to be okay?" I asked Drew, who just nodded and then buried his face back into Kevin's shoulder. Kevin, for his part, just closed his eyes and hugged him back, and I knew that they'd be fine. Kevin wasn't going to break up with Drew. They'd be okay.

It was suddenly me that I was worried about.

Oliver and I hustled across the parking lot toward my parents. My mom's arms were crossed now and my dad had the deep wrinkle between his eyes that he always gets whenever he frowns a lot. "What's wrong?" I asked as soon as we were close enough. I thought it was a good idea to sound like we were all on the same side, like I wasn't the person who may or may not be responsible for all of the fury that seemed to be coming off them in waves.

"Oliver, your mom's inside," my dad said. "Go inside and find her, okay? We need to talk to Emmy."

"Oh. Um, okay. Yeah, I just—" Oliver let go of my hand reluctantly and I felt our fingertips slip apart. "You're okay?"

"She's fine," my mom said, and the way she said it didn't leave me feeling exactly reassured. It sounded like I was about to be the opposite of fine, like I would be one of those bodies that always seem to turn up in the first five minutes of those *Law & Order* episodes that Caro always watched. They're never fine.

"Oliver," my dad said, and Oliver shot one quick glance back at me before hurrying off. I was glad he didn't try to kiss me.

"In the car," my mom said, and I followed them, trying to think of something that would set them off. No one would tell them about my surfing. I hadn't mentioned UCSD to anyone except Caro and Drew and Oliver and none of them would spill my secret. All of my teachers liked me and I was doing fine in school. I had used my phone in calculus last week to text Caro—was that what this was about? I didn't think the teacher had even seen me do that.

As soon as we got in the car and my dad started the engine, I finally leaned forward between the seats. "Um, can you please tell me what's going on?"

"Isn't that an interesting question," my mom said. "That's my question, too, Emily. Just what is going on?"

"I—I have no idea," I said. "Dad?"

He just drove, though. My dad always did the silent "we are so *disappointed*" routine, while my mom was the one who did the shouting and the "what were you *thinking?*" histrionics. They worked well as a team, except when they were teamed up against me. Then it was a problem.

We drove home in a quiet cloud of anger (them) and confusion (me) and fear (me again). By the time we pulled into the driveway, I couldn't get out of the car fast enough. I even took a few deep breaths of the cool night air, suddenly aware of how suffocating the car had been.

"Inside," my mom said, pointing toward the garage door, and I followed her through the door, the laundry room, and into the kitchen, where she threw her purse down onto the table and then turned to look at me.

"We saw your guidance counselor today," she finally said once my dad was in the room. "And do you know what she said?"

"I don't even know the guidance counselor's name," I said.

"Don't try to be funny," my dad told me. "That's not going to help you."

"I'm not!" I cried. "I genuinely don't know who she is! I've never met with her in my life."

"Well, she knows who you are," my mom said. She was banging around the kitchen now, pulling a wineglass out of the cabinet and a half-full bottle of Chardonnay out of the refrigerator. "Apparently, Oliver pointed you out to her one day."

I paused. "I'm in trouble because Oliver told the guidance counselor about me?" I asked.

"No, Emily!" my mom yelled.

"Then what?" I yelled back. "Will someone just tell me what I did already?"

"Don't use that tone," my dad said.

My mom, though, had enough "tone" for both of us. "Your guidance counselor," she said as she poured the wine, "congratulated us on your acceptance to the University of California, San Diego." She took a sip of wine and looked at me over the rim of the glass.

I suddenly felt nervous all over. "I—I was going to tell you."

"Oh, were you?" my mom said. My dad was standing next to her now, not saying a word. He didn't have to. The frustration was evident on his face. "When, exactly?"

"Wait," I said. "How did the counselor even *know*?"

"The school is notified of admissions," my dad said quietly. Oh, he was *really* disappointed in me. This was worse than my mom yelling. "Your name was on that list. Did you really apply?"

I nodded hesitantly, like there was still some confusion in the matter and the acceptance letter that I had printed out wasn't shoved between the pages of my old copy of *Rebecca of Sunnybrook Farm* on my bookshelf. "I did?" I said. "I mean, I did. And I got in. And I was going to tell you, I swear, but I didn't know if I—"

"We had a plan, Emmy!" my mom cried. "You were going to go to community college for two years and work and live here and save some money and then go to school somewhere—"

Hearing "live here" made me snap. "No, you decided that!" I yelled, and both of my parents looked temporarily shocked. "You decided that, not me! That was your plan for me and you never asked me what I wanted to do or what I wanted! That's what you want, it's not what I want! I want to go to San Diego!"

There it was. The decision. I had been on the fence up until that moment, but having college dangled in front of me and then taken away was more than I could handle. Suddenly, I wanted to go more than anything in the world, even if it meant leaving Oliver behind. "Oh, *why*, Emmy?" my mom cried, her sarcasm heavy. "Why? Is your life so horrible here? You don't pay for a thing except gas for your car—which, by the way, we bought for you and is no longer yours—"

"What?!" I was furious. "That's not fair! You're taking away my car because I applied to college? Who does that?"

"You lied to us," my mom shot back. "Lying is not allowed in this household. Not to mention that we were humiliated tonight. Absolutely humiliated!"

The fury that was building inside my chest was starting to scare me a little. No car meant no surfing. I could handle being grounded, whatever, but after nearly a year of having the freedom to go to the beach whenever I could, I couldn't stand not having it anymore.

"You want to know why I applied to UCSD?" I asked, and now my voice was low and cold.

"Enlighten me," my mom said, taking another sip of her wine.

I turned, grabbed my car keys out of my backpack before anyone could stop me, then ran out to my car. I came back a minute later, my sandy wet suit in my hand.

"Here!" I said, throwing it on the floor. "This is why! Guess what, there's something else you don't know! I've been surfing for the past three years!"

The shock from both my parents rendered them temporarily mute. Even my mom didn't say anything at first. Luckily, I had a lot of words to fill the silence. "Drew's brother, Kane, taught me when we were fourteen! We were at the beach and I was good and I loved it. I loved it more than any of those stupid ballet or gym or karate classes, all those things you made me do! So I kept going and I got better and now I'm really, really good! They think I can try out for the surf team at UCSD, that's how good."

My dad was the first to recover.

"Where did you get that?" he asked.

"Craigslist," I told him. "And it doesn't fit well at all and it lets in a ton of water and it's freezing every time I wear it but I don't care because I still love it. It's mine!" Somewhere in between my words, I had started crying. My heart felt so broken, so shattered. I had gotten so close to so many things and now they were being pulled away so, so fast.

"You could have drowned!" my mom cried. "You could have hit your head! You could have gotten caught in a riptide, oh my God!"

"But I didn't!" I yelled back. "Just stop, okay, Mom? Just stop! Stop pretending like all of this is for me, because really? It's all for *you*."

It was like I had pulled the pin out of a grenade. No one in the room moved for a few seconds. "Right?" I said, because once the pin is pulled, you can't exactly put it back in. "That's what it is, isn't it? You don't want me to leave because you saw the bad thing happen ten years ago to Maureen and you freaked out."

"Don't you dare—" my mom started to say, but her eyes were filling with tears.

"It's like when Oliver came home!" I yelled. "Maureen was expecting him to somehow be the same seven-year-old kid that he was when he left, but actually, you've been expecting me to be that way the whole time! And that's not fair!" I wiped at my eyes fast, too upset to stop talking, and I remembered Oliver's words so clearly from the week before. "I'm tired of paying the price for something I didn't even do!"

Both of my parents stood, shell-shocked, and I stared right back at them, my chest heaving with sobs. "So you can take away surfing," I said. "Or college. Or my car. Whatever you want, but you cannot stop me from growing up and moving out and *finally moving on*!"

"She's right," my dad murmured.

"What?" I asked.

"What?" my mom said. "We—"

"We panicked," my dad said. He sounded tired all of a sudden, and the crease between his eyebrows now seemed borne out of exhaustion, rather than anger. "We've been panicking for ten years."

"*We* were protecting you!" my mom protested, looking at my dad like he had just crossed into enemy territory.

"But you can't do that all the time!" I said.

"When we saw Maureen . . ." my mom started to say, but her tears spilled over, one falling down past her jaw before she could catch it. "When we saw her after," she started again once she got control of her voice, "that pain, how she was so . . ." The words failed her again.

"We love you more than you can imagine," my dad said, and even he sounded a little croaky now. "And watching Maureen spend ten years wondering what had happened to her son terrified us."

"I get it," I said. "I do. You were scared. Scary things happened. But I'm tired of lying to you, okay? It sucks. It's not fun. But I have to because you won't let me do *anything*! Do you know how many times I could have joined the surf team at school? But I couldn't, actually, because I needed a parent's permission."

"You never even asked!" my mom cried.

"Would you have said yes?" I shot back, and her silence was all I needed. "Look," I said. "You can keep being scared. Both of you, that's fine. But I'm done."

"You're done, all right," my mom said. "You're grounded. No car, no Oliver, absolutely *no* surfing, obviously, no phone, computer only for schoolwork."

"I'm seriously the only kid who gets grounded for applying to college," I muttered.

"You're grounded for lying," my mom said.

"We'll talk about college later," my dad added, and he sounded as tired as I felt. "Just go upstairs, get ready for bed."

"It's eight thirty!"

"Emily."

"Fine. But who's picking me up from school tomorrow?"

My parents looked blank.

"No car," I reminded them, knowing that I was seriously pushing my luck. "If I can't drive myself to school, I can't bring myself home, either. Plus, Oliver needs a ride now, too, since I've been driving him every morning."

"You take the car *only* to school." My mom quickly amended her earlier rule. "And you come straight home afterward."

"Fine," I said. "So nothing I said made any impact on you, I take it."

My mom pointed at the stairs. "Go."

"We'll discuss it," my dad said.

My mom threw him a look that very clearly said she was done discussing things, but I didn't see or hear his response as I stormed up the stairs. I was tempted to slam my bedroom door behind me, but if I did, I was pretty sure my mom would start a bonfire in the backyard and use my surfboard as kindling, so I just shut it and then threw my history textbook onto my bed instead. It helped a little, but nothing is as satisfying as slamming a door.

I lay there in the dark for a long time, alternating between seething and panicking. Spending the next however many weeks being landlocked felt like a death sentence, and then I imagined spending two more years that way, my parents still huddled over my every move, and my chest felt tight. I'd be eighteen in a few months, though. I could move out on my own, maybe get an apartment with Caro after all, but I knew that wasn't a real solution. It'd be like putting a Band-Aid on an arterial wound. It wouldn't solve the bigger problem.

Around nine thirty, right when I was starting to fall asleep in my clothes, a light suddenly flashed on and flashed off. I sat up, wiping the hair out of my face, and went over to the window. I could see Oliver's silhouette outlined against the light in his bedroom, his hair hanging in his face as he leaned against the sill.

I did the same, crossing my arms over my waist and wishing they were his arms instead, that he was there instead of a house away. It felt odd to be missing him even though I was looking right at him, when I had spent the past ten years missing him and never knowing where he was. I guess the more you start to love someone, the more you ache when they're gone, and maybe it's that middle ground that hurts the most, when you can see them and still not feel like you're near enough. So close and yet so far.

He turned his light on and off again, our signal. I didn't dare call out to him lest my parents hear me yelling out the second-floor window (wouldn't that just be a stellar way to end the day?) so I flicked my own lamp on, then off again. It blinded me for a minute, but when I blinked again, he was still there. My phone was downstairs so I couldn't send him one last text before it got confiscated, so we just sat in the darkness, all the sadness and loss and fresh starts binding us together until I got confused about where Oliver's life stopped and where mine started.

CHAPTER THIRTY-TWO

The next day at lunch, Caro was sitting in the quad by herself, holding a bag from Del Taco and sucking on a huge straw. I thought about avoiding her entirely since I wasn't exactly sure if we were friends again, but then she saw me and I walked over. "Can I sit?" I asked.

She moved her backpack over in response and I plopped down next to her. "So your parents didn't kill you," she said.

"No," I said. "But honestly, I wish they had." I tossed my backpack on the ground and groaned. "I'm so tired."

Caro passed me her soda. "Oh, thanks," I said, taking it from her.

"Friends share caffeine," she replied, her voice quiet. It was the first conversation we had had since our fight last week and I knew a peace offering when I saw one. (Plus, any peace offering that involved a carbonated, caffeinated beverage was definitely going to be accepted by me.)

"So what the hell happened?" she asked. "And where's Oliver?"

I nodded toward the main school building and took a sip of Caro's drink. "He had a meeting," I said. I didn't mention that it was with the school counselor, that he was talking to her twice a week, still adjusting to normal school life. "He'll be out in a few minutes. He already heard the story this morning, though. I drove him to school, which is pretty much all I'm allowed to do anymore."

"You're grounded?" Caro guessed.

"I'm, like, *beyond* grounded," I said. "My parents found out last night that I got into UCSD."

Caro let out a short, sharp laugh. "You're the only kid who gets grounded for getting into college, I swear."

"I know, right?" I cried. "That's what I said! But yeah, they're mad not because I got it, but because I lied. And then they wanted to know why I did it—"

"Oh no," Caro said.

"Oh yeah," I said.

"Wait, what—oh no." Caro covered her mouth with her hand. "Did you—?"

"Oh, I did." I sighed. "I actually got my wet suit out of my car and threw it on the floor in front of them."

Caro giggled a little. "I kind of wish I had seen your mom's face when you did that."

"No, you don't, because she would have melted you with her

eyes." I sighed and shook the soda, the ice rattling. "It was really bad. And then we started yelling about Oliver and how I'm not him and just because he was kidnapped doesn't mean that I'm just going to disappear into thin air, too."

"Whoa." Caro took the soda from me and took a sip. "It sounds like *Real Housewives*. So . . . what now?"

"Well, I'm grounded until I die, I guess. No surfing, no phone, no computer, no Oliver. And possibly no college, I don't know. My dad thinks I should go, though."

Caro was twirling a lock of hair around her finger, letting it unravel, then twirling it up again. "I think you should go, too," she said quietly.

"What?"

She took a deep breath. "I was upset because you didn't tell me about it. I'm your best friend, you're supposed to tell me these things. But," she hurried on before I could interrupt her, "I think you should go. And maybe I'll find it in my heart to forgive you." A smile tugged at the corner of her mouth, the way it always did whenever she was joking about something. Caro has a terrible poker face. Drew has already said that when we go to Vegas for our twenty-first birthdays, Caro is not invited.

"Oh, Caro," I sighed, then wrapped my arms around her and hugged her tight. "I'm sorry I didn't tell you. I didn't mean to make you feel left out of anything."

Caro hugged me back. "I know," she said. "I'm sorry I freaked out. I was just mad."

"I'll tell you everything from now on, okay? Promise."

"You better," she said back, then squeezed me tight and let go. "Can we eat? I'm starving."

"And here we are, the final suits in our house of cards!" Drew cried, and I glanced over Caro's shoulder to see Oliver and him walking toward us.

"Oh yeah?" Oliver said, dropping his bag next to me and then sitting down with a sigh. "Which one am I?"

"Spade," Drew said.

"No, he's the heart," I said, giving him a kiss on the cheek before any of the lunchtime attendants could spot us. "Oliver's the heart."

"Barf," Drew said.

Caro didn't say anything, only because she was too busy making gagging noises.

"You're cheesy," Oliver laughed at me, but he put his arm around my shoulders, anyway.

"Here, I brought lunch," Caro said, passing all of us burritos. They were as heavy as paperweights and the packets of red sauce were sticky and I was suddenly starving. "Only the finest two-dollar burritos for my friends."

"Did you tell them?" Oliver asked me, unwrapping his burrito.

"Caro's caught up," I said, then turned to Drew. "I'm grounded because I got into college, they'll probably never let me surf again, my parents might kill me, et cetera."

Drew tried to respond, but he had already bitten into his

burrito. "The 'et cetera' part is worrying," he said when he was finally able to speak again. "And no surfing? Are you serious?"

I patted his arm. "I'll have to live vicariously through you."

Oliver reached for Caro's drink and took a sip. I could see why she had gotten the jumbo-sized one. "What about you, Drew? What happened after last night?"

"Oh, shit!" I said. "Drew, I'm so sorry! I didn't even ask about you and Kevin."

Drew shrugged. "Oh, you know. It's okay. He understands. Kane's really pissed at my parents, though. Like, he's *mad*." Drew widened his eyes a little and I could understand why. Kane was over six feet tall and built of solid muscle. I had never seen Kane get upset, which made the prospect all the more intimidating. "He says that I should bring Kevin, anyway, and if anyone has a problem with it, he'll take care of it. And I don't want my brother to hulk out at my grandma's birthday party, *soooo* yeah." Drew squirted some red sauce onto his burrito. "Parents, man."

Oliver cleared his throat a little. "Well, *my* mom wants me to do an interview for *Crime Watch* so they can find my dad," he said. "So I get to be on TV *and* help get my dad arrested."

Caro's eyes flicked back down to her lunch and I knew what she was thinking. *Oliver's dad deserves to be arrested.* But she just said, "That sucks, dude. I'm sorry."

"Thanks," Oliver said. "Should be fun. Can't wait."

"To summarize!" Drew said, sitting up straight. "Emmy's parents have grounded her and are possibly plotting her death as we speak because she got into a four-year university and became an excellent surfer behind their backs."

"Accurate," I said.

"And Oliver's dad kidnapped him for ten years, scaring everyone to pieces, before he finally came home and now his mom is using him to arrest his dad, which will now add tens of thousands of dollars to the therapy bills he's already going to accrue."

Oliver laughed, low and sharp and genuine. "Pretty much, yeah."

"And *my* parents don't want me to tell my grandmother— who, let's be honest, is already in the bottom of the ninth inning, age-wise—that I'm gay and dating the most beautiful man in the free world—no offense, Oliver—"

"None taken," he said. "Kevin's a handsome guy."

"—because if I do, she'll cut us off and my parents would rather I live a lie than have to move themselves into a two-bedroom condo and drive a Ford Focus. And Caro's parents . . ."

"Caro's parents should have stopped at five kids," Caro said, reaching for the soda again. "Because they have no idea what she does all day and don't really care, either."

"Can we please have a moment of silence for Caro's decrepit family life, especially her sister Heather?" Drew said, solemnly placing his hand over his heart.

"*Especially* Heather," Caro said darkly, but let Drew give her a one-armed hug, anyway.

"Well, that's that," Drew said brightly. "The four of us are fucked."

Oliver raised his burrito into the air. "To us!" he said dramatically, sounding like one of the newscasters that had reported on him time and time again. "And to the future!"

We all cracked up at that, clinking our half-eaten burritos in the air as we laughed. "To us and our terrible futures!" Caro echoed. "Now who's hogging all the red sauce? Seriously, you guys, stop doing that."

I grinned up at Oliver, who kissed my forehead and then tossed Caro one of his own packets. *This is perfect,* I thought to myself.

And that afternoon, for one glorious hour, it was.

CHAPTER THIRTY-THREE

I drove Oliver home as slowly as possible, trying to spend as much time with him as I could before I had to go back to the makeshift cell that was my bedroom. At the red light, we kissed until the car behind us started honking, and even then it took a few extra seconds before we were able to untangle ourselves from each other. "How much longer is this going to go on?" Oliver asked as we sailed through the intersection, still holding hands over the front console. "Did your parents say how long you'd be grounded?"

"Nope," I said. "That's part of the fun, the wondering without asking."

"And you're not going to ask." Oliver sounded dubious.

"No way!" I said. "What if that makes them ground me for even longer?" I pulled into our driveway and put the van into PARK very, *very* slowly. "Want to get the mail together?"

Oliver started to laugh as he gathered up his backpack. "I do, actually," he said. "We are so pathetic."

"The worst," I agreed. I wanted to keep holding his hand as we walked, but I knew my mom was home and I wasn't willing to risk her seeing us. It hadn't even been twenty-four hours and I was already missing the ocean like crazy. Any more time added to my sentence and I'd probably start to go into shock from lack of salt water.

The mail was boring, like it always was: bills for my parents, flyers from grocery stores, a couple of envelopes addressed to CURRENT RESIDENT. "I wish people still wrote letters," I said to Oliver as we both emptied the boxes. "Wouldn't that be cool? Like, you'd go to the mailbox and there'd be a letter just waiting for you?"

"I'll write you a letter," he said.

"That might be the only way you'll be allowed to talk to me," I said, and he smiled as he pulled a large envelope out of the box. "What the—oh, wow."

"What is it?" I asked.

"It's from Columbia," he said. "University. In New York."

"Let the college wooing begin!" I cried. "Did you write for info?"

"No, but it's actually my favorite school. My dad and I used to go up to the campus when we lived in New York." He was looking at it almost reverently, and I tried to imagine what he was picturing: wrought-iron gates, brick buildings, cool fall air and the crunch of his dad's shoes walking through leaves as Oliver did the same.

"Columbia'd be cool," I said, trying not to drop anything as I balanced my backpack, the mail, and my keys. "You could go back to New York."

"Are you kidding? If your parents won't let you go to San Diego, there's no way mine's letting me go back to New York. She'd probably try to move into my dorm with me."

"She'd be your roomie!" I said. "You could take classes together, be study buddies . . ."

"Oh my God, stop," Oliver said, but he was laughing, too. "Just stop talking. I don't even want to think about rooming with my mom."

"I'd watch that reality show for sure," I told him. "Like, number one priority on the DVR, no question."

"Emmy!" My mom's voice rang out from the front door. "Time to come in." She sounded unamused, to say the least.

"The warden calls," I whispered to Oliver, who kept his face serious even though his mouth twitched. "Okay!" I yelled back at her, then "accidentally" dropped one of the envelopes. "See you tomorrow?" I said to Oliver as I stooped to pick it up.

"Nice move," he said, smirking at me. "And yeah. Hope you get out on good behavior."

"Emmy! Now!"

"Yeah, don't hold your breath," I said, then blew a kiss in his direction before turning around and trudging up the driveway and into the house.

"You know you're not allowed to spend time with Oliver right now," my mom said the second the front door shut behind me.

"My day was fine, thanks," I replied. "And yours?"

"Emily."

I sighed. "Mom, I drove him home and we got the mail, and now I'm here. Inside. You always overreact."

She just held out her hand for the mail and I gave it to her before going upstairs. "Your dad's working late tonight," she called after me, and I paused on the stairs' landing. "And I have to cater a benefit over in Irvine, so you'll be on your own. I put dinner in the refrigerator for you."

Wait for it, I thought. *Wait for it . . .*

"And you know no one is allowed over tonight while we're gone."

There it is.

"I know, Mom," I said. "The details are pretty clear."

"Well, seeing as how you've been lying to us about so many other things."

She was flipping through the mail, not really paying attention to me, so I gave her one good eye roll before going up to my room. Again, the urge to slam the door was overwhelming. *Maybe that's what I'll do while I'm home alone,* I thought. *Slam my bedroom door a few times. Another wild and crazy night at Chez Emmy.*

Instead, I changed clothes and did my homework sans music or the internet. It turns out that being grounded makes you really productive, and I cranked through two chapters of my civics textbook and diagrammed the Krebs Cycle for bio by the time I realized it was dark outside and my mom was knocking on my bedroom door. "Okay, I'm going," she said. "Food is downstairs for you. Bed by ten."

"'Kay," I said. I must have looked like the model child, sitting at my desk with no distractions, surrounded by textbooks and notepads and highlighters.

"I'll be home by eleven, Dad should be here by ten thirty."

"'Kay."

"Emmy, don't sulk."

"I'm not sulking!" I said. "I just said okay, that's it! What else do you want me to say?"

She ignored my question. "Are you doing your homework?"

"No, I'm plotting a government takeover." I held up a highlighter. "Can't do it without the pink one, though. That's just foolish."

My mom narrowed her eyes at me, but ignored that comment, too. "Bed by ten," she said again. "You stay up too late."

I bit back a comment about how ten p.m. is practially late afternoon, and instead just said okay again.

"Call me if you need anything."

"Mom." I closed my eyes, then opened them. "Okay."

She looked at me one last time, like she didn't know who I was, like I was some stranger who had moved into her daughter's room and was organizing her school supplies. "Bye," she finally said, then went downstairs. I waited until I heard the garage door close behind her, then the sound of her car disappearing down the street, before I closed my textbooks and went downstairs to eat dinner.

It was turkey meat loaf with a mustard glaze and red smashed potatoes, one of my top three favorite meals, and I wondered if it was a concession while I ate and watched an episode of the *Kardashians*. None of the Kardashians were ever grounded. One of them even made a sex tape! My mom would probably sacrifice me to the gods if I had a leaked sex tape. (Which, just to clear up any confusion, is not something that I will ever, ever have. Leaked or not.)

I left the TV on as I loaded my plate into the dishwasher, then turned it off and put on music while I showered and changed into sweats and an old T-shirt that said SAVE THE HEDGEHOG on it (for the record, I don't know why the hedgehog needs saving; it's just a comfortable shirt). I was reading a book that Caro had loaned me that she had gotten from her oldest sister, Jessica, and I was about to start reading it when I saw Oliver's light flick off, then back on.

"Can I come over?" he said as soon as I poked my head out the open window. His voice was different, low and serious and shaky. "I need to come over."

"No one's here," I called back. "I can't—"

"I need to come over."

There was an urgency to him that scared me. I wondered if he and Maureen had had a fight, if that was just the latest trend on our street.

"Okay, okay," I said. "The back door's open. Come on up."

He must have run because he made it up to my bedroom in record time. "Wow, that was—" I started to say, but the words died on my lips once I saw him. His hair was disheveled, his eyes frantic, and he was shaking.

"What is it?" I asked, crossing the room to his side as he shut the bedroom door behind him.

"Pull the blinds," he said to me.

"What?"

"Just do it, Emmy. Please." He sounded like he was choking and I realized that he had the envelope from Columbia in his hands, which were trembling as much as the rest of him.

"Okay, okay," I said, then closed them. When I turned around, Oliver was still standing there, still holding the envelope. His face was something I hadn't seen, scared and lost and hopeful and sick, all at the same time.

"It's not from Columbia," he said.

"What?"

"This. It's not really from Columbia."

"Who's it from, then?"

"Emmy. It's from my dad."

He shook out the contents onto my bed. A shiny, colorful letter-sized pamphlet spilled out, and Oliver picked it up, flipped it open, and pulled out a handwritten letter. "It's from my dad," he said again. "He sent it to me. He knew Columbia was my favorite and he . . . he sent it. It's from him."

Was this shock? It was hard to tell now that I was shaking as bad as Oliver.

"What . . . what does it say?" I said, sinking down onto the bed next to the papers. Oliver sat next to me, hanging on to the letter the way Caro used to hang on to her rag doll, Alice.

"It's, um, I don't." Oliver cleared his throat and I could see his eyes were starting to redden. "I just want to keep it for me, if that's okay."

"Okay, yeah, of course." I put my hand on his back, feeling him shudder under his hoodie. "But what does it say? Does it say where he is?"

Oliver shook his head. "No. But he, um, he wants to see me. Tomorrow. At lunch. I guess he doesn't realize I'm in school right now." Oliver named a restaurant that was about ten minutes away. I had been there with my parents once, but my mom hated their French fries so we never went back.

"What?" If I hadn't been sitting down, I would have needed to sit down. "He's *here*? He's here in our city right *now*?"

"I don't know! I don't . . ." Oliver took a deep breath and let it out slowly. "I don't know," he said again. "But he wants to meet me at this diner tomorrow afternoon. He said he wants to talk."

"Oliver," I said. "Ollie, you have to tell your mom. You have to call the police. This is an actual serious crime!"

"Yeah, I know, Emmy," he said, and he jerked away from my hand and got up from the bed. "I'm actually really aware of that, but thanks."

"You can't go meet him!" I cried. "You know that, right? What if he tries to take you again? What if he, I don't know, what if he has a gun?"

"My dad? With a *gun*? Seriously?" Oliver scoffed at me, but he also wouldn't make eye contact. "Look, you don't know him like I do, okay? He probably just—"

"No!" I said, standing up alongside him. "You keep trying to defend him, Oliver! And I get it, I understand, he's your dad, but people—active police officers—are looking for him. They've been looking for him for ten years! You have to tell someone!"

"You don't understand!" he yelled back, and now we were face-to-face. I had never seen him look so shattered before, so completely lost. "I just need to see him, all right! But I can't drive—"

"Oh no!" I said. "I'm not driving you to meet your dad! Are you serious right now, Oliver?"

"I know when I left that it was hard on everyone but—!"

"Stop saying that!" I screamed and he took a step back, surprised into silence. "Stop saying that you *left*. You didn't just leave, Oliver! He *took* you away from us! He fucking kidnapped you!" I yanked open my closet door with such force that the doorknob slammed into the wall, climbing up onto the step stool and grabbing the dusty shoe box. "Here!" I said. "Look!"

"Emmy—" he started to say, but I just yanked the lid off the box and threw my college application on the floor. There was nothing in that box, I suddenly realized, that was a secret anymore.

The note was still lying at the bottom of the box, still
yellowed and soft, and I pulled it out and let the box fall on the
floor. "Look!" I said again, shoving the note at him. "This is all I
had for ten years, okay? The last time your dad was here, this was
all I had left of you." I was trying not to cry and failing miserably
at it. "And I don't want it to be all that's left, either."

Oliver's face was stricken, and the note seemed so small
between his hands. I could see his jaw tighten, his eyes filling with
tears as he read the words. "Emmy," he said, his voice strained.
"I'm not going to leave you."

"Stop saying that!" I screamed. "You keep making it sound
like it was your fault when it was all *his* fault!"

"That's what you don't understand!" Now he was yelling, too.
"All of this *is* my fault!"

"What are you talking about?" I cried. "You were seven!
That's ridiculous!"

"Not then! Now! All of *this*"—he waved an arm toward his
house, toward the daily struggle of trying to return home after ten
years somewhere else—"*this* is all my fault."

"How?" I yelled, throwing my hands into the air. "Because
you let them take your fingerprint? Enlighten me, Oliver, please!
How exactly is all of this *your* fault?"

"Because I made sure my dad wasn't in the apartment that day!
That's how it's my fault! He wasn't arrested because of me. I made
sure of it."

It was like all the air got sucked out of the room. We were

both breathing hard by now and for a few seconds, that and the blood pounding in my head were the only things I could hear. "What?" I finally said when I was able to speak again. "What are you . . . ?"

"I *told* him," Oliver said, and his eyes were rapidly filling with tears, so fast that as soon as he wiped them away, fresh ones took their place. "That next morning at breakfast, I told him about how they had fingerprinted me at the police station. He didn't really say anything. He just said he had to go out for the day. And then he left."

He sank down onto my desk chair, the tears starting to come fast and furious, but I didn't move from the bed. Oliver was full-on crying now, but I didn't want to stop him from talking. "Did you—tell him that you knew?"

Oliver shook his head. "No, it just happened that way. But I didn't think I wouldn't get to say goodbye to him, you know? I thought I could tell him or at least hug him once more or something. And now he's here and I just want to see him again, Emmy. That's all I want. I just miss him so bad and I fucked up everything and I ruined my mom's new family and the twins and Rick and I thought it would be okay but it's not and I'm sorry, Em, I'm sorry, I'm *so* sorry. . . ."

Oliver was about to say something else, but when he took a breath, the tears finally got the best of him and he pressed his palms to his eyes as his shoulders started to shake. He cried silently, in so much pain that there was no sound to equal it, and in that moment, he reminded me of his mom, of those nights when she would sob at our dining room table, aching for something she couldn't have.

I got up from the bed and walked over to him, sitting down on his lap and gathering him in my arms. He hung on to me tightly, so tight that I thought my ribs might crack, but it was okay. I could take it. I could do it for him. I stroked my hand over his tangled hair, protecting him from anything and everything that had happened, from everything that was about to happen, and I held Oliver while he sobbed.

We sat there for long minutes, until he was gasping and shuddering against my shoulder. My sweatshirt was wet and cold with his tears, soaked straight through to my heart, but I didn't care. I didn't care about anything except the fact that Oliver had been carrying way too big of a burden for way too long. I tucked his hair behind his ear, smoothing it off his forehead the way my mom would do to me whenever I woke in the night with a nightmare about Oliver.

"Fuck," was the first thing he said, and we both laughed a little. "Sorry. Wow. Sorry."

"Stop saying you're sorry," I murmured. "Better?"

He nodded, and I started to get up to get some tissues for him, but he just wrapped his arms around my waist and held on to me. I sat back down, resting my cheek against the top of his hair. "I just don't want the next time I see my dad to be in a courtroom." Oliver sighed. "Or through a plate-glass window while he's wearing an orange jumpsuit."

I just hugged him and didn't say anything. There wasn't anything to say. Sometimes there just aren't enough words to fill the cracks in your heart.

Oliver sighed again, still sounding shaky. His breath brushed against my collarbone as he spoke. "You think I'm crazy."

"No, I don't," I said. "I think you're a kid who got put into a shitty situation that can't be solved. But I don't think this will end with everyone getting what they want, Ollie."

Oliver nodded and then sat up a little. His eyes were swollen and I pressed my thumbs against his cheeks to mop up the tears, just like he had done for me that night on the swing set, when he told me that coming home was like being kidnapped all over again. He looked up at me, his face tired, and I kissed his eyes, the leftover salt water stinging my lips. "I'm sorry," I whispered.

"For what?" he whispered back.

"Just that you have to go through this. That I can't help you."

"You help every day," he murmured, then found my hands with his and twined our fingers together, holding them between us.

"Do you want to lie down for a minute?" I asked, and he nodded.

We lay on my bed in the dark for a long time that night, Oliver's head on my shoulder and my legs tangled with his. Once the lights were out, I raised the blinds again so we could see out the window. It was a full moon that night and its light cast through the room, throwing blue shadows against my desk, my clothes, my bed.

Oliver was quiet next to me, his fingertips stroking up and down my arm. "Can I tell you something?"

"It's a little late to start asking that question," I teased him, but I kept my arms tight around him. "You can tell me anything, you know that."

"Remember last night when we were outside with Drew and he was saying that he was jealous of me?" Oliver paused for a few seconds. "The truth is that I was jealous of him, too."

"Why?" I asked him.

"That night at the party. He had this huge house and the fact that his parents are married and he has this cool older brother that's, like, always there for him. I thought he had it so easy. And plus, he's known you all these years and I haven't. He got to spend all that time with you." Oliver shifted a little against me and I could feel his chest tighten. "You don't think I should go see my dad, do you?"

"No," I whispered back. "But that's just because I'm scared."

"Why are you scared?"

I looked at him, trying to be brave. "Because I'm scared you'll leave with your dad and I won't know where you are again."

"I wouldn't do that," he said, and he kissed me as if to ground himself, to prove that he would stay. "I would *never* do that."

"And I'm scared that your dad is on the run from the police and you might get hurt."

"He would never hurt me, Em."

I turned so we were facing each other, sharing my pillow. "He hurt you enough the first time."

He didn't say anything after that, and I ran my hand under his shirt, stroking his stomach, then rested my arm in the curve of his hip. "Are you going to tell your mom?" he asked.

"No," I whispered. "Are you going to tell yours?"

Oliver hesitated too long for my comfort. "You should," I said. "You should tell someone besides me. Like, an actual adult who can make things happen."

"I know. But I keep picturing him sitting all alone in the restaurant, waiting for me and . . ." Oliver's voice caught a little and I wrapped my leg around his, curling closer to him. "I just can't do that," he said when he could talk again. "I can't have that image in my head."

"Okay," I whispered, even though nothing felt okay, not at all.

Oliver closed his eyes and was about to say something else when his phone started to buzz. "Shit," he muttered, and then he was up and trying to find it. I snuggled into the warm spot he had left behind, smelling his shampoo on my pillow, trying to slow my brain down from its breakneck pace.

"It's my mom," he said. His voice was raw after crying so hard. "She wants me to come home."

"Okay," I said, sitting up a little. "Do you think she's going to tell my mom that you came over?"

"I'll make it sound like we were just studying if she asks about it," he said. "Can I?" He gestured toward the bathroom and I waved him in. I watched as he splashed water on his face, then used my towel to dry it off. I had to look away when he looked in the mirror. It hurt too much, watching him look for answers in his own reflection and not finding anything there.

I got up and walked him downstairs. My hair was probably a disaster and my shirt was still damp, but I didn't care. It was funny, I never cared about those things with Oliver. I didn't worry about how I looked. All that mattered was how I felt.

"See you at school?" he said.

"You better," I replied, then stood on my tiptoes to kiss him goodbye. "I mean it. I'm driving you there and back tomorrow."

"Noted," he said, then kissed me one last time before pulling his hoodie up over his head and going out the door. I watched until he had disappeared into the dark, then locked the door, turned off all the lights downstairs, and went back upstairs. Usually, it freaked me out to be home alone in the dark at night, but I was too exhausted to care that night.

Even so, I lay awake for most of the night, blinking at the man in the moon as he stared back at me. I heard both of my parents come home separately, and I also heard both of them open my bedroom door to check on me. I pretended to be asleep then, but part of me wished they could tell I was faking it, that they could figure out the truth without me having to tell them.

But they just closed the door and walked away, their footsteps fading down the hall, and that night when I finally fell asleep, I dreamed I was chasing Oliver down the same hallway, his hooded figure getting smaller and smaller until I couldn't see him anymore, until he was gone once again.

CHAPTER THIRTY-FOUR

School was a joke the next day. Between insomnia and nightmares, I was sort of a disaster and managed to forget my math homework, my lunch, and my house keys. "Trifecta," I muttered to myself once I realized that they were all missing.

When I wasn't busy forgetting things, I was keeping an eye out for Oliver. I normally didn't see him until lunchtime, but I caught a glimpse of him ducking into the counselor's office at the start of lunch, which made me relax a little. Maybe he was telling her about the letter? Maybe they were calling the police right now?

I spent most of lunch in the library, redoing my calculus homework that was due next period. I kept glancing up, waiting to see Oliver standing in front of me, but he never appeared. I dashed through the problems, not even checking to see if they were right, and as soon as I was done, I went to where Oliver, Caro, Drew, and I had all eaten lunch the day before. (Had that really just been the day before? It seemed like a lifetime ago.) "Sorry!" Caro yelled when she saw me, and I froze. "The burrito queen is out of stock today! You've exhausted her benevolence!"

Drew just rolled his eyes. "Today is DIY day, apparently," he said to me. "Hope you brought something. Because otherwise, it's a giant bag of Funyuns for you. Which, despite the clever name, are never fun." He looked pleased with himself for realizing this.

"Where's Oliver?" I asked, and there must have been something in my voice because Caro and Drew seemed to sober up fast.

"Um, I don't . . ." Caro looked around like he was hiding behind her, ready to pop out and yell, "Surprise!" "I haven't really seen him, but I don't see that much, anyway."

"Yeah, same," Drew said. "You okay? You look a little . . ." He grimaced, which was apparently the universal facial symbol for "stressed and terrified."

"Yeah, I. I, um, I have to find him," I said, backing away from their lunch. The bell suddenly rang, shrill and impatient, and I jumped. "I have to go."

"Wait, Emmy," Caro said. "You have class, Em, you can't—"

But for the first time in my life, I didn't care if I got caught ditching. Oliver wasn't on campus. I knew it. I just knew it. I knew it the same way I knew he was gone when he didn't show up that Tuesday for school ten years ago. Even back then, something hadn't been right and that rock in my stomach was settling back into its old, familiar spot once again.

I did a quick loop of the campus, then went past his locker

and scanned the library, just in case I had missed him. But he wasn't anywhere and it felt like my dream from the night before was suddenly becoming a horrible reality. Oliver was gone and I couldn't find him.

But this time was different. This time, I knew where he was.

I ran to my car, my hands shaking so hard that my keys jingled together. The parking lot was packed with people returning from lunch, so no one noticed when I pulled out and sped down the street. I wanted to call my mom, but I was scared that she would freak out. I wanted to call Maureen, but I didn't have her number. And I wanted to call the police, but I was scared that Oliver would somehow be in trouble, that he'd be charged with helping his dad. I didn't know what the rules were, or if his dad was even waiting for him.

So I got into my car and went to find Oliver.

CHAPTER THIRTY-FIVE

The restaurant was half empty when I drove past it. Apparently, my mom wasn't the only person who hadn't liked their fries. At first, I had been afraid that I wouldn't remember how to get there, but then familiar markers—the gas station on the corner, the dollar store, the psychic who only charges twenty-five dollars to lie to you—started to pop up, and when I pulled into the parking lot, I saw Oliver and his dad sitting across from each other in a booth.

The rock in my stomach shifted again and I thought I might throw up. I couldn't really see his dad but I could see Oliver, who was fiddling with a coffee mug. I had never seen him drink coffee before.

I parked, then got out and walked to the restaurant on wobbly legs. I had no idea what I was doing, but now that I had seen Oliver, I wasn't going to leave. I wondered if, somehow, that's how Maureen had felt when he came home, that once he was back in your sight, it was such sweet relief that you'd do anything to keep him there.

I walked past the hostess and went toward the booth. Now all of me felt wobbly and when I got close, I realized that the man he was sitting with was, in fact, Oliver's dad. He just looked so much older than I remembered him. My memories were of a tall man with thick, dark hair and sharp eyes, just like Oliver's. But this man was gray, with a thinning hairline, and when he glanced at me, his eyes were just tired and sad.

Oliver turned to see what his dad was looking at, and I stood there dumbly, staring at both of them. "Emmy," Oliver said, but he didn't say anything else. He didn't have to.

The realization quickly dawned on Oliver's dad—on *Keith*—that I was the little girl from next door. "Oh my God," he exhaled. "*Emmy*. Oh my goodness, you're so . . . grown up." He smiled nervously and glanced at Oliver. "The two of you are so grown up."

"It's okay," Oliver said to me. "Come sit down, it's all right. It's fine." He patted the booth seat and I slid in warily next to him, then reached for his hand and grabbed on so tight that he winced.

"You've grown up to be so beautiful," Keith said, and I just stared at him. For ten years, he had been the bad guy, the literal monster that takes children away from their homes, and now sitting across from him, he looked so normal, so average, like any older guy wearing khakis and a polo shirt with a wrinkled, slightly frayed collar.

"Thanks," I said, my mother's politeness training apparently still in place. My voice was flat, though.

"I was just telling my dad about you," Oliver said.

"Yes, um, Oliver said that you and he have become close friends again. I'm so happy to hear that." Now Keith was the one fiddling with his coffee mug. His hands were shaking just like Oliver's had the night before. Oliver was watching him and I pressed my leg against his, feeling the tension in both of us.

"In fact," Keith continued, "I was just telling Oliver how glad I am that he and his mom are able to be together again."

"Oh, are you *fucking* kidding me?" The words slipped out before I could stop them. So much for Mom's politeness training, after all.

"Em," Oliver started to say, but Keith held up his hand.

"No, no, Colin—*Oliver*, it's fine. Oliver, sorry." Keith waved him off. "It's all right. Emmy's right. I, um, I did some things that were pretty terrible."

"Yes, you did," Oliver said softly, and I knew him well enough to hear the anger that laced his words. It was the quiet kind, the most dangerous kind of all.

Keith just nodded, glancing out the window and then back down at his coffee. "That's why I wanted to see you today. I wanted to apologize, say I'm sorry. I know we didn't get a chance to talk about it."

Oliver sat back against the booth, then ran a hand over his

face before hunching back over himself. "Why?" he said. "Why? Just tell me why you did this. Because I swear I'm trying to understand, Dad. I'm trying so hard to make sense of this and I can't figure it out."

Keith's mouth wobbled a little and his eyes got even more watery. "I can't explain it." He shrugged. "When your mom and I, when we were divorcing, I was drinking a lot—"

"That's what Mom said," Oliver murmured.

"Yeah, well, your mom is right. And I knew she was trying to get sole custody because of that. Which she was right to do, by the way. I wasn't a very suitable dad back then."

"You were a good dad," Oliver said.

"Well, not at that point. But that weekend . . ." Keith's mouth trembled again and I felt cold just thinking about it, Oliver being spirited away to Chicago, lost and confused, while the rest of us searched for him in vain. "That weekend, you were sleeping at my house and you looked so little in my bed. You were a small fry. Remember how I used to call you that? 'Small-fry guy'?"

Oliver nodded, his jaw tightening.

"You just looked so small and I just couldn't imagine not being able to see you anymore. I didn't think I would survive it. You had these little teeth and tiny hands and you would wear that Little League uniform from your T-ball team, remember? You would wear it everywhere."

"Mom still has it," Oliver whispered. "She saved it. She saved everything."

Keith's eyes spilled over at that. "Good. I'm glad she does." He sniffled loudly and wiped his palm across his cheeks, trying to pull it together. "But I just kept thinking that I couldn't bear to not see you grow up. And I panicked. That's all. I made a decision and by the time I realized what I had done, I realized that it was too late. If I took you back, I'd never see you again."

"But you told me that Mom didn't want us," Oliver said, and I had never heard such quiet fury before. His hands were clenched together under the table like he was holding himself back, and I sat very still and didn't say a word. I had this feeling that I had stumbled onto the stage of a play and didn't know who I was or what I was supposed to say. I wished I had stayed in the car, that I had just watched from the window or waited outside the restaurant instead. This was a private conversation and I was sitting right in the middle of it.

"I know," Keith said. "I know I said that about Mom. And I'm so sorry, Oliver. I didn't . . . I made many terrible choices and I tried to give you the best life I could, but I couldn't undo some of those things. I'm sorry. That's all I can say." He wiped at his eyes again. "I was selfish. I'm sorry. I tried to make it up to you."

Oliver's eyes were overflowing now, and I carefully reached under the table and took one of his hands in mine, unknotting his fist before running my fingers over his palm. His pulse was pure staccato, tripping over itself. "All those nights, though, when I kept asking for Mom, though? When I would wake up crying for her?" Oliver shook his head and laughed through the tears. "I can't believe you would just let me hurt like that."

"I can't believe I would, either," Keith murmured. "I just loved you so much."

"Love isn't something you say," Oliver snapped. "It's something you do. God, I hate you so much for doing this. And it's, like, at the same time, I'm so glad to see you. This is so fucked up, I can't . . ." He trailed off, wiping his eyes before looking back out the window.

Keith was quiet for a minute. "Oliver," he finally said. "I'm sorry I left you in the apartment that day."

Oliver's head whipped back around, his eyes wide.

"It's okay," Keith continued. "You knew what you were doing that day on the field trip. I know. And I'm not upset or mad or anything like that. I understand. I couldn't keep this from you forever. And it's all right. I just panicked, that's all." Keith chuckled to himself, but it sounded more sad than funny. "Your old man's kind of a screwup."

Oliver looked like he had been caught stealing candy out of a store. "I . . . I just . . . you wouldn't talk to me, and Mom's name was blocked and I—I saw articles at the library and I hadn't seen her in so long and when I saw that *she* was looking for *me* . . . ?" A tear ran down Oliver's cheek and he hastily wiped it away. "You let me hate her for ten years and the whole time, I should have been hating *you*."

"I know—" Keith started to say.

"But the real problem," Oliver continued like he hadn't said anything, "is that I can't hate either one of you, not really. I hate that you put me in this position. But I don't hate you."

Keith nodded sadly. "I can't say enough how sorry I am."

"You're right, you can't." Oliver rested his elbows on the table and covered his eyes with his hands. "Oh God, I just want this to be over," he sighed. "I just want to feel normal again."

Keith started to stand up from the table and Oliver's head shot up. "Where are you going?"

"Just the bathroom," Keith said. He attempted a smile but Oliver and I just looked at him. "Be right back."

As soon as he was gone, Oliver let out a long, low breath and looked at me. "You doing okay?" he asked. "Sorry you got caught up in all of this."

"I don't care how *I'm* doing right now," I replied, which was the truth. "How are *you*? Are you all right?"

"I kind of lost it when I first saw him," Oliver admitted. "I don't think I let go of him for, like, five minutes." He smiled a little in embarrassment. "Manly shit, you know."

Then he wrapped one hand around my wrist, rubbing my arm with the other. "I'm glad you're here," he whispered, kissing my temple.

"I am so, so sorry that I was sitting here during all of that," I admitted. "Seriously, that was a discussion for you and your dad, it wasn't for—"

"Hey," Oliver interrupted me. "I told you I'm glad you were here. Don't apologize."

"Okay," I said, but I still felt terrible.

We pulled apart when Keith came back, and the waitress poured more coffee for him and Oliver. "Emmy, I'm so sorry," Keith said. "I didn't ask you if you wanted anything. Pie or a pop, maybe?"

"I'm fine," I said. The idea of food made me want to throw up.

"How are your mom and dad? Is your mom still cooking a lot?" Keith smiled at me and I could tell that he was uncomfortable. It's one thing to apologize to Oliver, but he hadn't realized how many people were owed apologies.

"Fine," I said again. "They're fine. She owns a catering business now."

"She always made the best rigatoni, I remember," Keith said. "I used to try and make it for Oliver, but it never came out right."

"No, it didn't," Oliver said with a laugh. "But your spaghetti's good. And I like that chicken casserole thing, too."

"And I made that cake for your tenth birthday, too." Keith grinned. "Double-decker."

Oliver was fiddling with his napkin, even as his smile grew wider. "That was a good day," he said. "And you got me that bike."

"Taught you how to ride it, too," Keith said. "Even got the helmet and the knee pads. Made sure you were safe." He looked at Oliver dead-on this time, his eyes suddenly serious. "I know I didn't do a lot of it right, but I tried. And I'm trying now, too."

Keith reached across the table and took Oliver's hand. "Oliver, I'm taking responsibility for what I did because I don't want you to have to do that for me anymore."

Oliver just stared at him. "But I—"

"I know you feel bad that you turned me in," Keith said, and he sounded so calm, so mollifying. "And I've done enough to hurt you. We had seventeen really good years together. I got to see you grow up, but your mom didn't, and I have to pay the price for that. You've paid enough. It's my turn."

That's when I heard the first siren. It was far away still, but the restaurant was quiet enough to hear it. Keith glanced out the window and I realized that he was putting his jacket back on.

Oliver heard it then, too. "Wait, what's—" He looked out the window, then back at me. "Did you call the police, Emmy?"

I just shook my head, as confused as him. The sirens (there were more than one now) were getting closer, screaming toward us, and Keith started to get out of the booth.

"Wait," Oliver said. "Did you—*Why?* Dad, why would you do that?" He seemed as panicked as Keith was calm. "Why would you call them? You have to go, you have to . . ."

But Keith just stood next to the table as two police officers started to get out of their cars. I climbed out of the booth, Oliver scrambling after me, and he grabbed his dad's arm, tears streaming down his face. "Why?" he asked again, but his voice was broken.

"Come on," Keith said, holding his arms open. "One last hug."

Oliver hesitated for the briefest of seconds, then threw his arms around his dad. They were both crying together, and Keith rested his hand on the back of Oliver's head and held him tight.

"I'm so sorry," I heard Keith whisper. "I love you."

Oliver couldn't talk, but I saw him nod.

Keith broke the hug when the first officer stepped into the restaurant, one hand on his gun. "Keith Sawyer?" he said. "Put your hands where I can see them."

Keith did just that, lacing his fingers behind his head as Oliver reluctantly let go of his dad. "It's okay," Keith said to him, but then the officers descended and got him on the ground. I don't know why, but I was standing on the booth's plastic-lined seat by that point, and I put my arms around Oliver's shoulders and hung on to him. He cupped his hands around my wrists in response, as we watched his father be arrested for kidnapping.

"Son?" one of the officers said, and both Oliver and I looked at him. "You all right?"

"Fine," Oliver said, wiping at his eyes. "I'm fine. Is he—you're not going to hurt him, right?"

"No, son," the officer said. "Why don't you both come outside with me?"

They took Keith out first, handcuffed with his head down, his thin jacket flapping in the wind. Oliver and I and the officer followed, and that's when I saw Maureen jumping out of another police car.

I waited to see if she would throw herself at Keith, tear him apart for putting her through ten years of torturous days and nights, but she never even glanced in his direction. She was only looking for one person.

"Oliver!" she cried, and when he heard his mom's voice, Oliver looked up at her.

"Mom!" he said, and then she was grabbing him in her arms, holding on tight and not letting go. He was taller than her by at least a few inches, but it didn't matter. Right then, she was the strong one, and he sagged against her and buried his face against her shoulder.

"Emmy!" someone else called, and when I turned around, I saw my own mom coming toward me.

"What are you doing here?" I asked, but she didn't answer. Instead, she just pulled me into a hug and held on, and that's when I finally started to cry.

CHAPTER THIRTY-SIX

After.

After Keith was booked at the local police station and taken into custody. After Oliver threw up in the bushes outside the restaurant, then rode with his mom to the police station to give a statement on what had happened. After my mom drove me home and we sat in the kitchen with my dad and I told them everything that had happened. After they didn't yell or get upset, after they just listened to me.

After all of that, it was just me in my bed at night, watching for Oliver's light.

"Emmy?" There was a knock at my door, then my mom's head poking through. "You asleep, sweetie?"

"No," I said. "What's wrong?"

"Oh, nothing, it's all right. Just wanted to talk for a minute." She slipped into the room, then crawled up on the bed next to me and lay down. We both stared at the ceiling for a minute, then she started to talk.

"Are you all right?" she asked.

"Yeah, I think so," I said. "I wish I could talk to Oliver, but I know he probably can't."

"Maureen texted and said that they're still at the station, so, yeah." My mom reached down and took my hand. "Sweetie, I wanted to talk to you."

I didn't say anything. The lump in my throat was too big.

"Do you know," my mom said, "when you were little that every time I used to try and use the bathroom, you would stick your fingers under the door?" She laughed at the memory. "I'd be peeing and look down and see these tiny fingers!"

"What?" Now I started to laugh. "Gross! Sorry about that."

"No, don't be sorry. That's what kids do. They want to spend all this time with you. You take them to school and they cling to your legs and they don't want to go in the door." She took a shaky breath. "But the funny thing is, you blink and the next thing you know, they're trying to leave and *you're* the one clinging to *them*."

"Mom . . ." I started to say.

"No, let me finish," she said, squeezing my hand. "You know how we reacted after Oliver was kidnapped. I don't need to tell you that, you were there. You lived it. Love makes you do the most insane things for your children, crazy stuff that you never thought you'd be capable of, and your dad was right the other night. We panicked. But the idea of losing you was just too much."

"It's okay," I said. "Mom, it's okay."

"No, it's not," she said. "And I'm really sorry that I've never seen you surf."

Now she was crying, blinking the tears away as she stared up at the ceiling. "You're so much stronger than me," she said. "You lost Oliver, too, and when he came back, you just went with the flow. You became friends again. You've always rolled with the punches and I love that about you, and you deserve more than just being our safety net. I'm sorry I didn't see that."

It hurt too much to talk, so I just nodded.

"Okay?" my mom said, rolling over to face me. "I just wanted to say that to you. I know we don't usually talk like this, but I wanted you to hear it."

"Okay," I managed to squeak out, and then I hugged her hard.

"Good," she said. "I love you."

"I love you, too."

After she let go of me, she grabbed the box of tissues on my desk and handed one to me before taking one for herself. "I don't think I've cried this much in my life," I admitted as I blew my nose.

"Same here," she said, dabbing at her eyes. Even in the dark, I could see her smeared eyeliner and mascara.

"Hey, Mom?"

"Hmm?"

I fidgeted with the edge of my comforter. "It's supposed to be a really good swell on Sunday, if you want to come watch me surf."

"A good swell," she repeated softly. "I'd like that. Can I just bring a first aid kit, though?"

"Mom!" I laughed. "No! Oh my God!"

"What about eighty SPF?" she continued, and that's how I knew she was teasing. "Nosecoat? One of those sun hats that also hold beer cans?"

"You can bring a hat that doesn't involve alcohol," I said. "And you can bring Dad. But that's *it*."

"Fine," she said, but she was smiling, and I smiled back.

And across the lawn, one lamplight flickered on, then back off.

Oliver and I were home.

EPILOGUE

"Emmy!"

"I'm coming!" I yelled back, but my voice was muffled over a pile of sheets and towels. "I need a box!"

"Here!" Oliver called, and came into the room with a box that was way too big. "It's the last one," he said. "I paid twenty dollars for it on the black market."

I eyed him. "There's a black market for cardboard boxes?"

"That's what your dad said. I didn't think it was a good idea to argue."

"Wise choice." I shoved the last of my extra-long twin sheets and blankets into the box, then taped it up with a tape gun. "Okay, I think that's it."

Oliver looked around my half-empty bedroom. The bed was stripped, the dresser cleared of lotion and perfume bottles, the desk empty. "It looks like someone looted in here."

"It was me," I said as he took the box from me. "Oh, thanks. How chivalrous."

"Just tell me if I'm about to trip over a label maker or anything."

"Ha," I said as I started to follow him down the stairs. "Like my mom would ever set that thing down. Even the label maker is labeled 'LABEL MAKER.' She loves it."

"Emmy!" my mom yelled again. "Caroline and Drew are here!"

"Double-time," I said to Oliver, then skipped the last two steps and went into the foyer, where Caro and Drew were standing. Drew's hair was wet, and I envied his morning of surfing while I packed up every last possession I had, ready to move it into my dorm room at UCSD.

"This is so weird," Drew said as he hugged me. "I can't believe you're leaving."

"*You're* leaving in, like, three days," I pointed out. "Berkeley is calling you."

"They just want me for my hot soccer body," he replied.

"Drew," my mom groaned.

"We're going to finish packing up the car," my dad said, ushering my mom and Oliver outside. "You kids take your time, San Diego isn't going anywhere."

"For now," Caro said ominously.

"Thanks, Caro, I feel much better," I said as I hugged her.

"So are you nervous?" she asked.

"Kind of," I admitted. "I'm more excited. I'm only going

two hours away, though. It's not like I'm moving to London or something."

"My turn again," Drew said, and this time he hugged both Caro and me.

"Our little triangle is breaking up," Caro sighed, and I held on to both of their waists.

"Nothing breaks us," I murmured. "We're just traveling for a bit, that's all. We'll always come back together."

"Emmy's right," Drew said. "Oh! Speaking of traveling!" He pulled our hug apart but still hung on to Caro's and my arm. "Did you tell her?"

"Oh! Oh!" Caro was jumping up and down. "Guess what, guess what!"

"What, what?" Now I was jumping up and down, too.

"Heather got a job!"

"No!"

"Yes! In Fresno!"

"Aahhh!" We were all screaming and jumping now.

"I'm going to have a room all to myself!" Caro cried. "For the first time in my life!"

"That is such amazing news," I told her. "You deserve it after all that you put up with from Heather."

"The first thing I'm doing is steam cleaning the carpets," Caro sighed dreamily. "And then I'm going to shut the door and take a nap."

"Wow, sorry we're going to miss that party," Drew said.

"I need you and Kevin to help me load the steam cleaner into my car, though," Caro teased him.

"Kevin and I are very busy that day."

"Doing what?"

"None of your business." Drew tapped her on the nose as she laughed. "He says bye, by the way," he said to me. "He had to fill in for someone at the Bucky."

"The Bucky?" Caro and I both said.

Drew just shook his head. "Don't ask. That's what they all call Starbucks, apparently. I know, it sounds ridiculous. The things you do for love."

I glanced past them, where I saw Oliver shutting the trunk of the car. "Indeed," I said, then instinctively gathered my friends back up in one last hug. "I love you guys."

"We love you, too," Caro sighed.

"Right back atcha," Drew murmured.

After they left (and after Drew promised my dad that Kevin would definitely hook him up with some free Frappuccinos), my mom and I loaded my suitcase into the backseat, next to another box filled with more clothes. "I never knew you had so much stuff," she said, huffing and puffing a little.

"I know," I said. "I guess this is what happens when you finally clean out your closet."

"Imagine if you had done it every year like I had asked you . . ." She widened her eyes innocently when I looked at her. "I'm just saying."

"You can help me organize the one at school, how's that?" I

said. "Matching hangers and everything."

She just nodded toward where Oliver and my dad were standing and talking, Oliver's hands shoved deep into his pockets. "You might want to go say goodbye," she said softly. "We have to get going."

"Okay," I said, and she graciously went to gather my dad and give us some privacy.

"So," Oliver said as soon as we were alone. He had gotten tanner since spending most of the summer surfing with me at the beach, and the freckles that had bloomed across his nose and cheeks made me want to kiss each one.

"Soooo," I replied. "I guess we have to get going."

"Yeah, I figured," he said, motioning to where my parents were buckling themselves into the car. "You nervous?"

"No, not really. Just, you know, a little sad."

"Hey, no sad allowed," he said, chucking my chin with his thumb. "No sad. Just happy."

"Weren't you telling me last week how important it is to acknowledge your emotions?" I teased him.

"Well, that's for me." He grinned, his smile warmer and wider than ever. "You're different. Get your own therapist."

He had been seeing someone three times a week, a man named Dr. Hilbert, who listened and seemed to say things that Oliver needed to hear. Oliver didn't tell me very much about those sessions, but he didn't have to. I knew they were working. He was happier, calmer, and his relationship with Maureen was a lot better. They even had a standing coffee date every week where they talked about Oliver and his time spent with his dad.

As for his dad, there wasn't a trial. He pled guilty to all the charges and was sentenced to fifteen years in California state prison. Oliver hadn't seen him yet, but they wrote letters back and forth. "It's so weird," Oliver had laughed one night as he was looking for a stamp. "All this technology and I have to use a pen and paper to talk to my dad."

And now that things were better, it was my turn to go.

"I'll Skype you tonight," I told him. "After I get unpacked and everything."

"Great," he said. "The twins will probably want to say hi."

"I miss them already."

"Do you want to take them?" Oliver took a step back toward his house. "Because there's probably room on the roof next to the surfboard if—"

"Stop!" I laughed. "No, the twins like you better now, anyway." And it was true. They were crazy about their older brother. (I still hadn't heard the Angelina Ballerina voice, though. Oliver absolutely refused to do it for me.)

"Yeah, they're not so terrible," he said. "Not if you bribe them."

"I'm really going to miss you," I said to him. "Who's going to turn their light on and off?"

"I will," he murmured, brushing my hair off my face. "You just won't see it."

"But what if—?" I started to say, but he leaned down and silenced me with a kiss.

"Emmy," he whispered. "It's your turn to leave and it's my turn to stay. So leave already."

"I love you," I whispered. "I love you so much."

"I love you, too." He kissed me again, deeper and longer than the one before, and I didn't care that my parents were probably watching in the rearview mirror. "And it's just two hours away, like you keep saying."

"We found each other once," I said. "Shouldn't be too hard to do again."

He smiled against my mouth, then kissed me again. "Not goodbye. Just see you later."

I nodded, trying not to cry. "Okay?" he said again.

"Okay," I said, clearing my throat, then looking up at him. "See you later."

We shared one last kiss before I climbed into the car. He stood at the end of our driveway and waved goodbye, and I waved back, trying not to cry.

"You okay?" my mom asked gently from the front seat.

"Yes," I said, because I was. I was okay and so was Oliver. We were going to be fine.

I looked out the back window as we drove away. Oliver stood in the driveway, waving goodbye, and I waved back.

I watched as we drove farther away, as Oliver got smaller and smaller on the horizon.

I watched until he was gone.

THE WAVE

The first time Emmy and Oliver see each other is when they are one day old. People will tell you that babies cannot see very far at that age, maybe just a few inches in front of their faces, but no one ever tells the babies that. And in any case, no one ever told Emmy and Oliver.

Oliver is a whole pound heavier than Emmy, but she's a few hours older, which makes them pretty much even. Emmy's also bald and has to wear a little hat, the sort of hat that would look ridiculous on anyone more than two days old. She wonders if anyone else has to wear a hat in the hospital nursery, so she turns her head to the left just as Oliver turns his head to the right.

They look at each other for a minute. Their dads are standing in the window, taking pictures and wearing goofy smiles and congratulating each other. Oliver sort of waves his hand, and Emmy tries to wave back but she's all swaddled up and can't move, so she blinks instead. She notes that Oliver isn't wearing a hat. How nice for him.

She really wants to wave, but before she can figure out how exactly to do that, a nurse comes over and starts to wheel Oliver's bassinet away.

Emmy's seen a few other babies leave the hospital, so she understands what's happening. It still makes her sad, though. She'll miss her new friend.

But it's time for Oliver to go home.

ACKNOWLEDGMENTS

All my love and thanks to my family, especially my mom and brother. They are some of the best people I know, and I consider it my good fortune to be related to them. Thanks for always saying nice things to me, especially when I'm on deadline.

I've been with my agent, Lisa Grubka, for over eight years now, and I can't begin to describe how grateful I continue to be for her unwavering guidance and honesty throughout my career. Thank you for always having my back and reading my first drafts. Thanks also to the wonderful team at Fletcher & Co., including Sylvie Greenberg, Jennifer Herrera, Melissa Chinchillo, and Rachel Crawford; and to Stephen Moore at Paul Kohner.

Thank you to the amazing team at HarperTeen, including my editor, Kristen Pettit, who bought my very first book in 2007 and has continued to be a wonderful friend ever since then. I'm so grateful we got the band back together! Her assistant, Elizabeth Lynch, is not only excellent at her job, but also sends me funny emails and lets me talk to her about my favorite Taylor Swift songs. Thanks, Elizabeth!

My gratitude also to Jen Klonsky; Kathryn Silsand; David Klimowicz; Sarah Kaufman, Alison Klapthor, and Matthew Allen; Christina Colangelo, Elizabeth Ward, and Kara Brammer; Gina Rizzo; Susan Jeffers Casel; and Liz Byer. Thank you so much for all the hard work you've put into my book. It means the world to me.

To the wonderful community of YA authors, who are hilarious and giving and brilliant, I'm so grateful and proud to be one of you. Extra special thanks to Amy Spalding, Aaron Hartzler, Morgan Matson, Jordanna Fraiberg, and Stephanie Perkins, all of whom read *Emmy & Oliver* in its various drafts and offered up their support and critiques. Coffee's on me next time, my friends.

Thank you, as always, to the librarians, teachers, parents, readers, and bloggers who have made my career such a joy. I would not have this job if it wasn't for you, and I promise to try and continue to be the author that you deserve.

An extra special thank-you to Jenna Sabin and Meg Roh, both of whom took the time to talk with me about what it's like to be a teenage girl who surfs. I hope Emmy makes you proud!

My dog, Hudson, continues to be an absolute delight, and has taught me the most important part of the writing process: treats.

At its heart, I wanted *Emmy & Oliver* to be about friendship, and I am full of gratitude toward my friends, all of whom make my life so fun and funny and wonderful, including Johanna Clark, Adriana Fusaro, and Maret Orliss. Thank you for all of your love, support, and generosity.

It takes a village to write a book. I am so grateful for mine.

#HASHTAGREADS

books worth talking about

Want to hear more from
your favourite **YA authors**?

Keen to **review** their latest titles
before anyone else?

Eager to read **exclusive extracts** and
enter **fantastic competitions**?

Join us at **HashtagReads**, home to
Simon & Schuster's best-loved
YA authors

Follow us on Twitter
@HashtagReads

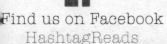
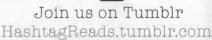